FORSAKEN

A Kaley Presley Thriller

TERRY TOLER

Forsaken
Published by: BeHoldings, LLC

Book Cover: BeHoldings Publishing
Contributing Editor: Donna Toler

For information email: terry@terrytoler.com.

Our books can be purchased in bulk for promotional, educational, and business use. Please contact your bookseller or the BeHoldings Publishing Sales department at: sales@terrytoler.com

For booking information email: booking@terrytoler.com.

First U.S. Edition: July, 2024
Printed in the United States of America
ISBN 978-1-954710-25-2

OTHER BOOKS BY TERRY TOLER

Fiction

Save The Girls
The Ingenue
Saving Sara
Save The Queen
No Girl Left Behind
The Launch
Body Count
Save Me Twice
Powerful Enemies
Deadly Games
Don't Be Careful
Wintervention
Saving Alex
Cliff Hangers: Anna
Cliff Hangers: Mr. & Mrs. Platt
Cliff Hangers: The Quarterback
Cliff Hangers: Macy
Cliff Hangers: Not, Not Guilty
The Blue Rose
Triggers
Seven Year Rich
Noel
The Book Club
The Book Club Murder
The Book Club Rescue
The Longest Day
The Reformation of Mars
The Late, Great Planet Jupiter
The Great Wall of Ven-Us

Saturn: The Eden Experiment
The Mercury Protocols
The Heart of Pluto

Non-Fiction

How to Make More Than a Million Dollars
The Heart Attacked
Seven Years of Promise
Mission Possible
Marriage Made in Heaven
21 Days to Physical Healing
21 Days to Spiritual Fitness
21 Days to Divine Health
21 Days to a Great Marriage
21 Days to Financial Freedom
21 Days to Sharing Your Faith
21 Days to Mission Possible
7 Days to Emotional Freedom
Uncommon Finances
Uncommon Health
Uncommon Marriage
The Jesus Diet
Suddenly Free
Feeling Free

For more information on these books and other resources visit terrytoler.com.

Thank you for purchasing this novel from best-selling author, Terry Toler. As an additional thank you, Terry wants to give you a free gift.

Sign up for:

Updates
New Releases
Announcements

At terrytoler.com

We'll send you an eBook, *The Book Club*, a Cliff Hangers novella, free of charge.

For Elijah

1

Somewhere off the coast of Norway

Brad answered on the first ring.

"Do you want the good news or the really bad news?" I asked my CIA handler.

"Give me the good news first, Penny," he responded, "then I'll tell you if I even want to hear the bad news."

Kaley Presley was my real name. We never used our real names on a mission.

"Lucky and I found the submarine and rescued seven girls."

Lucky was actually A-Rad, my partner on this mission and someone I had been dating for less than a month. We had worked together for several years and A-Rad was a nickname given to him years ago because of his willingness to take risks and do radical things that no one else would dare to do.

We may have made a mistake in the names in this case. Lucky Penny. We thought we were being clever. I felt anything but lucky at the moment.

"We detained the person behind the kidnappings and we're holding him on the submarine," I said. "We also captured three of his twisted, depraved rich friends."

"That's good news. So what's the bad news?"

"Five of his guards are dead."

"How is that bad news?"

I took a deep breath. It took a moment before I could bring myself to answer. "They were members of the Royal Guard."

Dead silence on the other end. He didn't say anything for what seemed like a minute as he processed that disturbing information.

"And who were they protecting? I'm afraid to ask."

"Cai Belling," I said, reluctantly.

"The Crown Prince of Norway?" Brad's voice rose with shock.

"Yep," I answered grimly.

"The heir to the throne?"

It sounded like a question, but Brad already knew the answer.

"Now you see the problem."

He let out a loud and frustrating groan matching my mood.

"We didn't know until it was too late," I said, defensively.

"Get out of there!" Brad shouted with urgency. "Take the girls with you and leave the men behind. And whatever you do, don't harm the prince."

"We can't leave."

"Why not?"

"The Norwegian Naval Forces have us surrounded."

The phone line fell silent. The deafening void lasted for at least a minute.

"Then give yourselves up," he finally said.

"We could use the prince as a hostage and get back to the yacht."

"I told you to surrender! Put down your weapons. You'll only make things worse. If that's even possible."

"Then what?"

"I don't know."

"I'm not giving in without some guarantees from you."

"I can't make any promises," Brad said, with resignation in his voice.

"You sent us on this mission. You can't let us take the fall."

"This wasn't a CIA mission. This was an AJAX mission. You know the drill. If things go south, we never knew you."

"So that's it? You're washing your hands of us?"

"We'll use every resource available to help you. Within reason."

"We're going to jail. They'll arrest us for murder. They'll cover up the kidnappings. We're talking about the King of Norway's son."

"I know. The best thing you can do is keep your mouth shut. Don't tell them anything."

"They might not arrest us. They might simply make us disappear."

"There's nothing I can do. I'm sorry."

The line went dead.

2

"What did Brad say?" A-Rad asked me.

I had just hung up with him when A-Rad walked into the control room of the submarine. I hadn't even had time to process all the ramifications of Brad's admonitions.

Even though this wasn't technically a CIA mission, Brad's fingerprints were all over it. I suspected he was frantically covering his tail at that very moment.

"He said to give ourselves up."

A-Rad's eyebrows shot up higher on his forehead than I'd ever seen before.

"That's ridiculous. Surrender is always the last resort."

"I don't see any other option."

"Why not? We have the prince in our custody. He's secure in one of the rooms along with the bodyguard we didn't kill. We take the prince and the girls back to the yacht until we decide what to do with him. I say we kill him and dump his body in the ocean."

"Brad specifically told me not to harm him."

"So we don't tell him. We deny it. What's he going to do?"

I pulled up a camera feed from outside of the sub and did a 360 scan around the perimeter of the vessel. Two heavily armed Royal Navy boats were clearly visible on each side of us. I counted at least a half dozen men on each boat carrying machine guns. Another two men sat on each boat behind a gatling gun with a swivel base. I estimated the automatic weapons could each fire close to a thousand rounds per minute.

A-Rad stood upright in shock, his mouth gaped open.

"How did this happen?" he exclaimed.

"The COB sent out a distress call before I could stop him."

The COB, captain of the boat, was now tied up and locked in another room out of earshot of the conversation. A-Rad began to pace around the control room, his usual response to a crisis. He said it helped him to think better.

I blamed myself. I should've gone right to the control room when we boarded the sub. Instead, I did what I almost always did. Secured the girls first.

Once we made sure the girls were safe and the prince and his cohorts were no longer a threat, I went to the control room to deal with the person operating the sub. At the barrel of my gun, the man spilled it all. Told me everything.

He was a young admiral in the Norwegian Navy. When approached with this job, he gladly accepted and was paid handsomely. All he had to do was keep the sub hidden, the girls alive, and the vessel ready for a rendezvous with the prince at a moment's notice. He never ventured out into deeper waters and generally kept the sub slightly below the surface in one of Norway's many bays.

But then he said something that sent shivers down my spine.

"You won't get away with this," he warned.

"I believe we already have," I retorted smugly.

"The Royal Navy is coming."

I scoffed.

"That's right," he said defiantly. "I called them as soon as I heard the gunshots."

I looked deep into his eyes for any deception. He was telling the truth. When planning the mission, I figured that was a possibility. But I calculated that we could get in and out of the sub before they arrived.

"How long do we have until they get here?"

"They're already here."

"What? How is that possible?"

"The prince always has protection with him. They were only a mile away from our location."

"I don't believe you."

He turned on the cameras and showed me. That's when I saw the two gunships.

A-Rad finally stopped pacing and broke the silence.

"The Royal Navy is a problem," he said.

"That's an understatement."

"But we've been in worse predicaments."

While that might be true, I didn't remember one as dire as this one. If I thought about it, I could probably think of some, but I didn't want to waste any mental energy on it at the moment.

"This was a misstep," A-Rad admitted. "But we can fix it."

"You are the king of understatements today," I joked, half seriously. "Kidnapping the Crown Prince of Norway and killing his bodyguards is much more than a misstep. It borders on a catastrophe."

"The prince is trafficking girls. Holding them in this floating dungeon. Making them do unspeakable things. I say we use him as a hostage and get off this submarine. Force him to tell them to stand down. Then we kill him once we get back to our yacht. He deserves what's coming to him."

I didn't disagree.

Nothing disgusted me more than human trafficking. That's why I had devoted my life to fighting it. I was willing to die for these girls.

Was I willing to voluntarily give up my life without a fight to protect my country?

It seemed like we had no other option. Brad was right. We couldn't risk harming the prince. Even though this was an AJAX mission, the whole thing had been with Brad's blessing and assistance. As Assistant

Director of the CIA, if the details of this mission ever got out, he'd be thrown in jail. Perhaps even charged in an international war crimes court. We'd be right there with him.

It didn't matter that our cause was noble. The seven girls would be an afterthought compared to the international incident this would cause.

"Norway is part of NATO," I said, giving voice to what I was thinking. "They're our allies. We can't kill the next in line to the throne."

"He deserves it."

"Regardless, Brad said to turn ourselves in and not kill him. He said he'd help us any way he can."

"He might've said that, but he won't. We're on our own. The CIA will say they have no idea who we are. You know the rules. If something goes bad, they disavow even knowing us."

"Brad can't abandon us."

"He can and he will, but Jamie won't."

Jamie Austen was the owner of AJAX. Once the foremost CIA operative in the world and the deadliest assassin. A-Rad and I had been on more missions with her than we could count. She was like family. I would do anything for her.

It suddenly dawned on me. Jamie couldn't help us. Not in that way. At one point in time, Jamie would've given her life for both of us. Not anymore.

"Jamie's got two babies on the way," I said. "She'd never put herself in harm's way. Not even to help us."

She had retired from her dangerous missions to get herself out of harm's way. I was supposed to take up her mantra. This was my first mission since she turned the reins over to me. She helped plan the mission, but we all knew that's the extent of it. Her days of being shot at were over.

It was my turn to lead these missions.

I grimaced on the inside. It didn't take long for me to screw up the trust she had placed in me.

"I know Jamie and Alex," A-Rad insisted. "They'll help us."

Alex was Jamie's husband. The other half of AJAX. Named after the two of them. AJAX was an art distribution company. In reality, a cover for our covert operations.

A-Rad was right. Alex would move heaven and earth to help us. Even if it meant getting shot at.

But how did that help us now?

"What is Alex going to do about our current predicament?" I voiced the argument rattling around in my head. "He's thousands of miles from here."

A-Rad stopped pacing and looked at the cameras again. Studying every angle.

"We could fight our way out," he said.

Another problem entered my mind causing my heart to jump.

"Maybe," I agreed, "but how do we get the girls safely off the boat? We can't risk leading them into the line of fire. If we surrender, the prince might keep them in their underwater prison, but at least they'll still be alive."

"I hadn't thought of that," he admitted.

"Besides, the only way out of this thing is the hatch. The moment we stick our heads out the hatch, they'll blow them off at the first sign of trouble."

"I'll go first. I'll draw the fire and you get the girls off the sub."

His words warmed my heart and sent cold chills to the tips of my toes at the same time. Four weeks ago, A-Rad asked me to marry him. I turned him down but agreed to date.

Now I couldn't stand the thought of our relationship ending before it really began. His proposal this time was basically a suicide mission. Watching him die while I escaped wasn't an option. Living without him would break my heart.

"No," I said firmly, fighting back the tears that had unexpectedly formed in my eyes. "You can't take on both boats by yourself. We have to give ourselves up and live to fight another day. They'll take us to Norway. Once we're on dry land, we can look for an opportunity to escape. Like you said, Alex will find a way to help us."

"That's assuming they don't kill us and dump our bodies in the ocean on the way there."

"That's a possibility. If they try, then we fight back to the death."

At least we'll die together.

"Do you know how to drive this thing?" A-Rad asked, referring to the submarine. I knew what he was thinking. The thought had already crossed my mind to make a run for it. We both knew how to fly a plane and captain a boat, but a submarine was a different beast. We might be able to figure it out, but we also might end up stranded at the bottom of the ocean.

"The COB does. But where are we going to go? They'll follow us. This is a shallow bay. They could even block us from getting to deeper water. Then what?"

"I don't know."

"I've made a decision. We're going to give ourselves up and hope for the best."

"That's probably what we should do."

"It is. This way, the girls will be safe. We'll escape. The mission isn't over. We found the sub once and we can find it again."

"Sounds like a plan. They'll question us. I doubt they'll torture us. This is Norway. They don't even have the death penalty. And there isn't a jail made that can keep me in it."

"We won't say anything. We'll keep silent. That'll freak them out."

"Agreed."

"They'll know we're Americans, but they won't be able to tie us to the CIA."

A-Rad knew the drill as well as anyone. American interests had to be protected above all else. Us dying was a much better alternative for Brad than having the mission exposed. The CIA simply could not be seen kidnapping or killing the future head of a sovereign country. Especially an ally.

"My lips are sealed tighter than a submarine's hatch," I joked awkwardly.

A-Rad twisted his lips to the side.

"Maybe not the best analogy," I said. "It sounded better in my head."

A-Rad still had his weapon in his hand. He placed it on the floor. Pulled his spare handgun out of the holster hidden under his shirt and sat it on the floor next to it. He took out two knives and discarded them as well.

"If I don't get rid of my weapons now, I'll be tempted to use them later," he explained.

I pulled mine out of their hiding places and placed them beside his.

"Let's do this thing before I change my mind," he said, as he headed for the door.

I looked at him with admiration. It might even be love. For the first time, I could see myself falling in love with him.

I hope we live long enough for that to happen.

3

"I should've listened to you, Kaley," A-Rad said as we descended towards the living quarters where the prince and his bodyguard were being held.

"That's all I'm saying," I said, jokingly. "Something good may come of this after all, if it makes you realize you should always listen to me."

He playfully glared at me.

"No. I mean it," he said, his tone turning serious again. "You had a bad feeling about this whole situation. I rushed us to make a move when we weren't ready."

"We made the decision together. Technically, it's my fault. I'm in charge of the mission."

"I was the one who wanted to act immediately. You said we should wait."

"You didn't know the Crown Prince was behind the kidnappings."

"No, I didn't. But you were right. We should've taken the time to figure it out."

"Is that what Jamie would've done?"

"I don't know. Doesn't matter. Jamie isn't here. Like you said, it's your call not hers."

Jamie was the one who discovered the sex trafficking ring in Norway where college girls had been disappearing at an alarming rate. She tracked a missing girl's cell phone signal to a boat and used satellite images and sonar to locate it in a bay in the Norway Sea.

She watched as the girl was loaded into a submarine. She sent A-Rad and me to Norway in search of the sub to rescue multiple girls she believed were on board.

We focused our search in the same general area where Jamie had stumbled upon the sub. Norway had 2456 kilometers of shorelines, 246 islands, and too many fjords to count. Expanding our search would've been like looking for a needle in a haystack.

We spotted a boat on sonar and followed it on a hunch. Hoping it might be the same boat. To our shock, the boat rendezvoused with the sub. We could hardly believe our luck. Or as it were, our misfortune. We didn't know the boat and sub were owned by the prince.

"It looks like a fancy yacht owned by some rich dude," A-Rad had commented at the time.

"We should call Alex and have him find out who owns it," I suggested.

Alex was the premier computer hacker in the world. If information was available on the net, he could find it.

"That'll take too long," A-Rad argued. "We have a small window of opportunity before they close the hatch, and we lose our chance. I say we go for it."

So we acted.

When we boarded the submarine, the guards confronted us. We shot first and asked questions later. Obviously, a big mistake. It didn't take long to discover the owner's identity, even though he tried to hide it at first. I recognized him from a picture in the CIA mission file.

"Anyway, it's all water under the bridge," I said.

"More like water over the bow," A-Rad quipped.

I chuckled nervously.

Without warning, Jamie's voice echoed in my ears.

Missions never go perfectly.

Expect complications.

Don't second guess yourself until the mission is over.

"I don't think we should be talking about it," I stated. "Jamie drilled that into us. Don't dwell on things you can't control. What's done is done. We can analyze our actions after the mission is over. She'd be yelling at us right now if she heard this conversation."

"You're right. Jamie was adamant about that rule. We need to keep our minds in the present. We'll dissect our decisions when we get back home."

"Assuming we get out of this alive and make it back home."

"That's another Jamie rule—always assume you will."

"Okay, let's focus on the present. Are we doing the right thing by surrendering?"

"I think so. We have to get off this submarine, then regroup. It's our only chance to get out of this alive."

"Why do I feel like giving up is letting Jamie down?"

"Because she's in your head. She's a part of you. You're an extension of her."

A-Rad stopped walking and grabbed my arm, turning me to face him. He looked deep into my eyes.

"Do you think Jamie ever got herself in a tough situation?"

"I'm sure she did." I laughed then finished a compelling thought. "I know she did. I've been in plenty of scrapes with her. Some I thought we'd never get out of."

"Did you ever see her make a mistake?"

"Not many."

"I have. I can't count how many times we made the wrong decision and barely escaped a tough situation by the skin of our teeth. It happens. This isn't the first time and won't be the last. Sometimes you don't realize it's the wrong decision until after you've made it. Like this one."

I groaned. "I'm sure Jamie knows about my mistake by now. She's going to be disappointed in me."

"Why do you keep bringing her up? Jamie chose you for this mission because she believes in you. I know her. She won't second guess your decisions until she knows all the facts. Even then, she knows what it's like in the field. She hated it when the suits questioned her judgment. I think she'll understand why we did what we did."

"I suppose."

"Kaley, listen to me. You have to stop thinking this way. Self-doubt will get you killed. Jamie chose you to take her place, because she knows you can do the job better than anyone alive."

"Except for her."

"No! Those days are gone. You have to get out of her shadow."

"Would Jamie turn herself in?"

He let out a sigh of exasperation but answered the question anyway. "Yes. That's what she would do given these circumstances. She'd say to keep ourselves alive. Live to fight another day. That's what we're going to do."

We started walking again. I was amazed how long it took us to get from one end of the sub to the other.

"I need to talk to the girls," I blurted out suddenly, as the thought popped into my mind.

He stopped walking again. "How much time do we have before the folks outside with the big guns get impatient and force the issue? They could storm the sub at any time."

"I don't think they will. They'll assume the prince is alive and being held hostage. They'll wait for us to make contact. We have time. I have to explain to the girls why I can't help them right now."

"I'll go with you."

When we got to the door to their living quarters, I knocked, which seemed like a strange thing to do after I'd already done it.

"I don't want to startle them," I explained to A-Rad although he didn't question it.

I opened the door slowly.

"Don't be afraid," I said before entering. "It's me."

The seven young women were huddled together in the corner of the room. Shivering.

As soon as I saw them a shooting pain pierced my heart.

How could I tell them I was abandoning them?

When they saw it was me, their faces lit up like a sunrise.

Earlier, after we took out the guards and cleared the area of threats, I searched for the girls' room. They were overjoyed when I told them that I was there to rescue them.

I warned them to stay in the room while I went to secure the control room. I promised I'd come back for them. That I was going to get them out of there.

They would mistakenly think I was returning to keep my promise.

It looked like they wanted to run towards me but didn't because of the massive man standing next to me. He was muscular and his lower body built like a tree trunk, strong and solid. A-Rad could be intimidating—he was as fierce as a bulldog when dealing with bad guys and as gentle as a lamb the rest of the time.

"This is Lucky," I introduced him. "He's one of the good guys."

They came running towards me, overflowing with excitement. I couldn't hold back the tears as I prepared to tell them the painful truth.

"Are we safe now?" one of them asked anxiously.

"We killed the men who were guarding you," A-Rad said. "You're safe for now."

"Did you kill the prince, too?" one of them asked incredulously.

"No," I admitted sadly. "The prince is still alive. He's tied up in the other room."

Their expressions turned to anger. Their body language became tense and hostile. Collectively, they balled their hands into fists and their brows furrowed in frustration. Their anger quickly turned into bitterness, and they began to speak out against him. Talking over each other.

"It's all his fault! He's the one who kidnapped us."

"He's holding us against our will."

"They won't let us leave."

"He makes us have sex with him."

"And his friends."

"They're disgusting."

"He said he'd kill us if we didn't cooperate."

"He said he'd kill our families too."

If I were to give them five minutes alone with the prince, they might tear him apart limb by limb without hesitation. I was certainly tempted to let them. Even help.

"I know," I replied calmly instead." That's why I came here to rescue you."

As I looked around the room, it was clear this wasn't a typical prison. It resembled a luxurious suite in a five-star hotel. The older Ula-class submarine had been renovated. The prince spent a fortune turning it into his depraved pleasure boat. Under different circumstances, it might even be considered opulent.

I was disgusted. The putrid scent of fear and despair hung heavy in the room staining the walls.

"So we can go home?" one of them said, hope filling her voice.

My heart sank as I had to tell them the truth.

"Not yet," I said painfully. "I'm sorry, but I have to go. And I can't take you with me."

"You're leaving us here?" they cried out in disbelief.

"I have no choice," I replied, feeling helpless myself.

"But you promised to help us," they screamed.

"If I could, I would," I said, trying to keep my own emotions in check. Nothing I could say would make them understand.

They started to shout all at once.

"You have to help us! We've been here for months."

"I know."

"Why did you lie to us? Are you working for the prince?"

My heartache turned to rage. It'd take all of my self-control not to extract vengeance on the prince. I had to hold back, or we'd all die.

"Listen closely," I said. "I can't do anything about your situation right now. You're going to have to stay here a little while longer."

"No, we can't take it anymore!" they said, their voices shrill and filled with fear. "We want to go home."

"I'm sorry," I said, my heart breaking with guilt. "There's nothing I can do."

A collective cry of despair filled the room.

"I'll find a way to come back for you," I promised. But even as the words left my mouth, I knew they held no weight. How could they believe me when I didn't even believe it myself?

So many obstacles stood in the way: if the prince didn't kill us, if we managed to escape from prison, and if we somehow were able to find the submarine again. Even then, the prince would surely have tighter security around it. It would be like breaking into an underwater Fort Knox.

"We're never getting out of here," someone cried, collapsing to the ground in heavy sobs.

With tears silently streaming down my face, I knew I had to leave before I broke down completely. I abruptly turned and walked to the door. Several of the girls followed, pulling on my arm. Begging me not to leave.

My heart was shattered into a thousand pieces.

A-Rad followed me out, locking the door behind us. I knew why he did it. We couldn't risk the girls trying to escape on their own.

"You shouldn't have made that promise," A-Rad said sternly, but with a hint of compassion behind the words.

"I know. But they need some hope. I wanted to give it to them."

I wiped away my tears and felt resolve swell up within me.

"Let's go see the prince," I declared, walking with a purpose towards the main bedroom of the submarine—an even more lavish suite, paid for by a depraved madman.

He may be a prince, but in my eyes, he was anything but. He was nothing more than the lowest form of human excrement I'd ever encountered. He could have thousands of willing women. Instead, he had to force himself on the unwilling. Rob them of their life, dignity, and free will.

What a coward!

I was determined to make him pay for his cruel actions. Maybe not today, but soon. I might die trying, but I was resolved to do everything in my power to rescue these poor girls.

Another of Jamie's rules jumped to the forefront of my mind.

It's not over, until I say it's over.

4

Kaley was learning a valuable lesson. Something A-Rad had learned years before.

You can't save everyone.

It took Jamie years to learn this lesson. When she first joined the CIA, she wasn't assigned to the sex trafficking division. During a mission to South America, she infiltrated a drug lord's house and killed him. While she cleared the house of other threats, she found a young woman being held captive by the drug lord.

At great peril to herself, she refused to leave the girl behind. Somehow, she managed to escape with the girl but was slightly wounded by an enemy bullet. The incident emboldened her. She found her purpose in life and demanded her handler transfer her to the sex trafficking division.

The higher-ups saw her as too valuable an asset for such an unimportant division of the CIA. They thought her many talents would be wasted there. She persisted and eventually they relented. It turned out to be a good move for her and for the CIA.

In this role, Jamie successfully rescued a record number of victims and also brought down terrorist groups, arms dealers, corrupt governments, and even prevented several nuclear attacks. By the time she retired, Jamie was revered as one of the foremost CIA operatives in history.

At the beginning of her career, her motto was *No Girl Left Behind*. After many wars waged against some of the most ruthless organizations in the world, she realized the impossibility of fulfilling that mantra every single time.

Too many variables went into a successful rescue mission.

Sometimes, the girls didn't want to leave. On one mission, Jamie went to the Arctic Circle and uncovered a cult leader who was kidnapping girls and holding them captive in a large underground facility. Although she successfully rescued a number of young girls, the wives of the cult leader refused to leave the compound and died when the leader blew up the facility burying them alive.

In another instance, Jamie was on a private plane being used by a sex trafficker to carry young women to the Winter Olympics forcing them into prostitution. She discovered the man behind the scheme was on the ten most wanted list.

She had his name and location. A shootout caused the plane to be in distress and in danger of crashing. It left her with a difficult choice: jump from the plane and get the information to the authorities or stay on the plane with the girls and risk dying in the crash.

She chose to parachute out of the plane even though it meant leaving the girls behind. She watched in horror as the plane crashed into the side of a mountain and the girls perished.

Her decision ended up saving countless lives. The trafficker was arrested, and his organization dismantled. She rescued hundreds of other girls he had forced into slavery.

CIA operatives like Jamie faced life and death situations all the time. It became painfully clear to her that she could never get every decision right and even if she made the right decision, it could have tragic consequences.

Jamie tearfully said to the mission team, "I'm not Jesus. I'm not the savior of the world. All I can do is all I can do."

Something Kaley was learning now.

In this situation, leaving the girls behind was the only option. A-Rad had no doubt about it either. They walked together in silence from the girls' room to the prince's quarters. When they arrived, they didn't enter right away. A-Rad sensed that Kaley had something to say to him.

She leaned in close and whispered so the prince couldn't hear, "We need a plan."

"Yes, we do. What are you thinking?"

"I say we give ourselves up outside the sub. We let the prince exit first with instructions to tell his people to stand down. We'll tell him we won't kill him if he cooperates, and he guarantees he won't harm us if we let him live."

"Not that his word means anything," A-Rad muttered.

"I know, but it's all we have. We need to make him fear us, so he knows what will happen to him if he betrays us."

"We killed five of his guards. I think he already knows what we're capable of."

"Let's talk about what happens once we're off this sub. If the prince turns on us, we'll jump into the water, and swim to deeper water. Then circle back around the island and hide in the dense forest. We'll meet up when the coast is clear."

"Let's hope we don't have to do that. I don't like those chances."

"I don't think we'll have to. I'm guessing the prince will want to keep us alive. He'll take us to some undisclosed location and interrogate us. He'll want to know who's behind this."

"I agree. The question is will he keep us together or separate us? There are two boats. He might put us on different ones. Even if they put us on the same boat, we could be taken to different locations."

"When we escape—" Kaley began.

"When," A-Rad said. "I like your optimism."

She nodded.

"When we escape, we need a meeting place. In Oslo, there's a tiger statue outside the train station. Let's meet there at four a.m."

"Why not six p.m.?" A-Rad asked. "You're the morning person. What if I want to sleep in?"

He smiled broadly so she'd know he was kidding. Having a meeting point was a good idea and the early morning hours made sense with fewer people around.

A-Rad noticed tears shining in her eyes.

"If I escape first," Kaley said, "I promise I'll be there every morning until you can get there. I'll wait for you."

A-Rad took her in his arms and pulled her close.

"I'll do everything I can to come to you," he whispered in her ear. "I'll even drag myself out of bed every morning to see if you made it."

He felt her chest rise and fall against his own as she laughed or cried. He didn't know which.

Slowly he released his embrace, but she didn't pull away. Unexpectedly, Kaley pushed him roughly against the wall and began to kiss him passionately, almost ravaging his lips.

At first, A-Rad was unsure how to respond, but he quickly began to match her intensity. Years of unspoken feelings were being expressed and it felt good. He'd been in love with Kaley almost since the day he met her.

The kisses turned softer and were bathed in tears. Hers and his.

A wave of desire washed over him. Not sexual. Rather a deep desire to be with her. To protect her. To give his life for her.

Now he understood the bond between Alex and Jamie. He used to kid them about their frequent public displays of affection. It made sense now. They had an unshakable resolve to get through every challenge and survive it. To cherish every moment not knowing when it might be their last.

They couldn't die now.

He refused to let the prince take away their future moments like this. From the way Kaley kissed him back, he could tell she shared the same resolve. It felt like a declaration that they belonged to each other, in this mission and beyond.

With one final embrace, she backed away and wiped away the tears on her cheeks and in her eyes. His shirt felt wet against his skin.

"Let's do this thing," she said.

A-Rad unlocked the door and they entered the room.

Kaley laughed out loud when she saw the prince and his bodyguard were hogtied.

A-Rad's handiwork. He had bound their wrists with rope, then their ankles, and tied their wrists and ankles together in the most uncomfortable, even painful position. Something he learned from Alex. While it might appear to be vindictive and was to some extent, it was the most effective way to secure a combatant. The whole purpose of tying someone up.

If the prince walked with a painful limp for a couple of weeks, then all the better.

A-Rad untied the prince first. Once he was freed, he scooted away from them before standing.

"Release me immediately," he demanded in a nobility voice, although unable to hide the fear behind the words.

"I already did release you, you fool," A-Rad said. "You should be glad I didn't kill you."

"Do you know who I am?" he said, gaining confidence. "I'm the Prince of Norway! I demand that you let me go right now or you *will* regret it."

"I already regret it," A-Rad said. "Nothing you can say to me will make me regret the whole nightmare more."

"Who do you work for?" he demanded.

Kaley was busy untying the guard.

"You have no right to enter this royal vessel and kill my soldiers," he continued, belligerently considering A-Rad was the one in control. "This is an act of war."

Something the prince said triggered Kaley's anger. She stopped untying the guard and flashed across the room toward him. She pushed him up against the wall and got right in his face.

"Do you think being a prince gives you the right to kidnap girls and force yourself on them?" she said with as much venom as A-Rad had ever heard come out of her mouth.

"Those women are here on their own volitation," the prince argued, although not convincingly.

"You're lying!" Kaley shouted.

The prince trembled in fear.

"You can't get a woman on your own?" Kaley asked, her hostility rising to a fevered pitch. "Why? You must have a really small—"

Before Kaley could finish, A-Rad cut her off. He pulled her away from him. She didn't go easily.

"If I were you, I'd keep your mouth shut," A-Rad warned, once the prince was safe again. "She can kill you with her bare hands in a hundred different ways."

Kaley went back to the task of untying the guard with swift movements. When she finished, she couldn't resist kicking him in the ribs. The guard cried out in pain.

As quick as he could, he bolted to his feet. Though still wobbly, he managed to keep his balance. He rubbed his wrists and breathed heavily.

A-Rad watched as the prince and the guard made eye contact.

Don't even think about it.

The prince had given the guard a signal. Kaley had turned her back to him. A-Rad knew why. She was giving the guard her back, baiting him to attack her. He'd seen Jamie do the same thing on more than one occasion.

Kaley probably hadn't seen Jamie do it, but they were cut from the same cloth. It wasn't enough to kill a man, it had to be done with flare.

The idiot guard took the bait.

He lunged for her.

Stupid move.

Kaley was ready for him. She shifted her weight from her right foot to her left. The guard's rage caused him to lead with his head with his arms outstretched. Like he was going to wrap them around her.

Kaley pivoted and rotated her body toward him, using his momentum against him.

His face met her elbow.

A maneuver Kaley executed so fast the man didn't see it coming. The sound of shattering bones bounced off the walls of the sub and made a gruesome noise.

The prince shrieked like a little girl.

The guard managed a moan that joined his final exhalation of air.

He fell to the floor in a heap. Unconscious. He'd be dead soon if he wasn't already.

The prince stood frozen against the wall.

A-Rad turned to him and said, "I told you she could kill a man with her bare hands a hundred different ways. She just showed you one of those ways. So are you going to cooperate, or should we just go ahead and kill you now?"

5

The guard was dead. To me, there wasn't much difference between five dead guards or six. We were in a world of trouble either way.

Having the power to kill a man was a heavy burden to bear and came with great responsibility. Jamie not only taught me how to kill, but she also taught me the moral code behind it.

When and why I could.

"Righteous kills" as she called them.

As I discussed the terms of our surrender with the prince, a philosophical argument on that topic erupted between us for some unknown reason.

"You're turning yourself in?" he asked with a sneer and puzzled expression. "Why would I believe your word on anything? You're a murderer."

"I am not a murderer!" I exclaimed.

For some reason, his accusation had sent me into a tirade.

"You murdered six of my guards," he scoffed.

"I did not! I *killed* six of your guards."

"What's the difference? Thou shalt not kill."

Quoting the Bible sent my disdain for him into an out-of-control emotional tornado. Growing up in a religious orphanage, I knew the Bible better than most people.

"The Hebrew word for 'kill' is actually murder," I said with as much vitriol as I could muster behind the words. "Your men tried to kill us. We simply acted in self-defense."

"They were bravely serving their country."

"They were complicit in the commission of a crime."

"Who made you the judge and jury?"

"I did."

"The laws of Norway and the laws of the Almighty God will decide who is the criminal here."

"Martin Luther would roll over in his grave if he heard you using the Bible to justify your actions."

I'd read in my research of Norway that the royals were required in the constitution to be Lutherans. The prince would've received significant religious training as a child. I'd read that his father had a Master of Divinity degree.

"Don't invoke the name of the great Martin Luther around me," he said roughly.

"Luther was a pious man who would find your actions deplorable."

"Luther said trying to keep the laws was folly."

"So you think you can break them at will with no consequences? Which one of the laws of Norway or the laws of the Almighty God were you breaking when you kidnapped these girls and forced yourself on them? People like you were stoned under the Old Testament law."

"He who is without sin cast the first stone."

I glared at him. I wanted to slap the smugness off his face.

"Do we really have to discuss this now?" A-Rad said, interjecting himself in the argument for the first time.

He was right. It didn't seem like the right time. We had bigger worries.

That didn't mean I wasn't still peeved. I had the moral high ground and resented the prince questioning my motives.

In order to keep the moral high ground, I lived with limitations. The rules of engagement were clear. Jamie had drilled them into us. We could kill for one of two reasons: self-defense or to prevent a current or future crime.

Regardless of the prince's fake moral piety, he fit into both of those categories. He was the mastermind behind the kidnappings and owned the sub. Killing him was within my purview even if he was no longer a threat to us. If I could, I'd send him to Almighty God right now and let the prince make that same argument before God that he had made to me.

His guards were also complicit in his crimes and helped him to execute them. As soon as they became a threat to us, we eliminated them. I wouldn't lose a minute's sleep over it.

Those were the type of judgment calls I had to make in the field. I was the judge and jury and executioner. If someone deserved to die, then I was tasked with carrying it out myself.

This wasn't America with its constitutional rights. The prince wouldn't be granted due process, read his Miranda rights, or considered innocent until proven guilty. In my mind, he was already guilty and needed to be stopped to prevent future girls from enduring his indignities.

I didn't care that he was a prince and could quote the Bible like a theologian. He was as much scum as a sex trafficker in Thailand. He had even more culpability in my mind. Using his wealth and power to perpetrate crimes against his own people was beyond depraved. Using his position to cover it up was despicable.

Quoting the Bible only made him look more arrogant and hypocritical than he already was.

I despised the man.

What we did there was righteous. We followed the code.

The prince abruptly changed the subject. "If you're going to turn yourself in, what do you want from me?"

"Here's how it's going to go down," I said. "You'll exit the sub first. I'll be right behind you. You will command your men to stand down. If you don't, trust me when I say this, I can easily kill you with one blow. And I will. Before you even know what hit you."

"If you kill me, my men will kill you."

"Maybe. But you'll be dead as well. I'm trying to find a way for all of us to make it out of this alive."

"Turn yourself in without a fight and I give you my word that I won't kill you."

He had just lied. I was trained to spot deception. A skill that had saved my life on more than one occasion. He did intend to kill us at some point.

I wanted to make sure we were on land first to give us a fighting chance.

"That's good to know that you don't intend to kill us," I said, playing along. "We're willing to go back to Norway and stand trial."

"Who do you work for?" he asked for the second or third time. I had lost count.

"I'll tell you when we get on land."

This time I lied. He wouldn't know it. I was also trained to lie without getting caught. He could give A-Rad and me a dozen lie detector tests and we'd pass every one of them.

"Okay, we have a deal," the prince said. "No funny business?"

"You have my word."

While it pained me to make this deal, I didn't have a choice. Our days as CIA operatives were probably numbered, and definitely over if we killed the prince. If we wanted to somehow salvage our future, we had to figure out how to get out of this mess without digging ourselves a deeper hole.

As Jamie said on more than one occasion, "When you're digging yourself into a hole, stop shoveling."

"Let's go," I said. I motioned for him to lead the way toward the hatch. I stayed close behind him, within striking distance.

"I hope your deal with the devil works," A-Rad said as we were walking.

The prince was in front, me right behind him. Ready to end his life if he double crossed us. If it got to the point where we were going to die anyway, at least I'd make sure he never harmed another girl again.

"I think it will," I said with more confidence than I felt.

My mind raced thinking of all the possible scenarios once we were outside the sub. Jamie taught me to anticipate the enemy's actions. I'd gotten pretty good at it watching her over the years.

Outside the hatch was a flat surface to walk on. I anticipated several armed men positioned there ready to defend their prince at all cost. With me in close proximity to the prince, they wouldn't dare open fire for fear of hitting him. They'd wait for his instructions.

I was counting on the prince being terrified of me. That's one reason I killed the guard in front of him, so he'd know what I was capable of.

If things didn't go as planned, we could dive off the edge of the sub into the water, but A-Rad was right. Those odds weren't great either. The Royal Navy gunners would fill the water with bullets. If we somehow managed to avoid them, we'd have to swim a great distance underwater to get away from them. Even if we did, we'd be trapped on the island.

Too many unknowns to predict an outcome.

The promise I made to reveal who was behind this once we reached land would hopefully be enough incentive to let us live for a while anyway. If he killed us here and dumped our bodies in the ocean, he'd never know our identities or who sent us. He'd be looking over his shoulder for months or years.

We both knew my demand that he put us on trial in Norway was never going to happen. He couldn't risk us exposing his operation. They'd take us to a secure location, interrogate us, and then dispose of us. At least I presumed that was his plan. That's what I'd do if I were him.

I hoped that was his plan. I liked our odds better in that situation. It bought us time.

We'd take the first opportunity to escape and would leave the country.

What happened after that was unclear. Would the CIA welcome us back in the fold? I doubted it. Could we still work for AJAX? Not likely. Even if Alex and Jamie were sympathetic, we'd be too hot. Every mission would be a huge risk for them.

In the best-case scenario, the CIA would terminate our relationship. In the worst-case scenario, they'd try to terminate our lives. Cover this up forever.

I forced myself to put the negative thoughts out of my mind and focus on the task at hand. Worrying about the future was a distraction that could get us killed.

When we arrived at the door of the hatch, I grabbed the prince's arm. "Don't forget. I'm right here behind you."

His arm was shaking in fear. He was clearly scared out of his mind.

I was surprisingly calm. A-Rad let out a deep breath. He might be nervous, but he had a steely resolve about him and didn't show it. The breath was meant to steady his heartbeat and reminded me to do the same.

The prince's voice trembled as he asked, "Can I open the door?"

Fear and uncertainty filled me, but I forced myself to remain calm and in control.

"Yes," I answered.

The hatch opened to a blinding burst of sunlight, causing me to squint and shield my eyes. As we stepped into the open, I could feel the weight of multiple guns trained on us even if I couldn't see them clearly as I struggled to bring my eyes into focus.

"Don't shoot," the prince yelled, his hands raised in a gesture of surrender.

My hands were kept in close proximity to his body. Read to strike his neck, kidney, temple, or simply reach out and break his neck in one motion.

Despite my best efforts to control it, my heart pounded in my chest, anticipating the storm of bullets that could rain down on us at any moment. Especially if I let the prince get too far away from me.

But there was no turning back now.

We had crossed the line and were fully committed to whatever fate awaited us.

6

Everyone was frozen in place. It's as if time stood still and we were all trapped in some kind of time warp. At any time, a director would yell cut and we would all go our own way.

I've had recurring nightmares about this type of thing. In my dreams, I'm often in a gunfight and my body won't move, I can't raise my gun fast enough to shoot, or I'm trying to run away from a threat and it's like I'm standing in quicksand.

The soldiers surrounding us were confused as well, unsure whether to aim their guns at us and toward the direction of their own prince or keep them pointed towards the ground as gun safety dictated.

Were A-Rad and I friend or foe?

I preferred they keep the guns down. Some nervous trigger finger could ruin my carefully planned scheme.

Now would've been a good time to use the confusion against them. The boat we used to travel from our yacht to the sub was still tied to the back of the sub, less than twenty yards away from us. I could envision simply walking to it, untying it, and driving off into the sunset.

If it were only that easy.

Rather than giving everyone time to decide what to do, I impulsively chose to act and stepped out from behind the prince.

Here goes nothing.

Jamie always said, "Whatever you do, act like you intended to do it."

People responded with respect to confidence and authority.

So I stepped out from behind the prince and brazenly walked toward the soldiers, making sure to keep my hands visible. I didn't sense A-Rad behind me, so I figured he was still standing near the prince, within striking distance in case I got into trouble.

My actions were met with confused looks, no aggressive response at all. Even the guns remained pointed down. The obvious leader of the group stood from a crouched position when I approached closer. Ignoring him, I walked past and headed towards his boat tied at the other end of the submarine. With a careful grip, I climbed onto the boat and sat down in the back. Like that's what I was expected to do.

No one followed me onto the boat. The thought crossed my mind that I could start the engines and speed away. The keys were still in the ignition. It's something Jamie would probably do and get away with it, but I had a plan in motion that seemed to be working so far.

The prince remained in place like the proverbial deer caught in headlights. A-Rad nudged him to break the stupor. A-Rad's lips moved, and they started walking towards the soldiers who immediately tensed up and put their guns on ready although still pointed down.

A-Rad and the prince were met halfway by the man in charge. The prince said something to him. The leader took A-Rad by the arm and led him over to the boat that I was on. Once aboard, A-Rad sat down next to me.

Now would've been a good time to commandeer the boat now that A-Rad was with me. I calculated the odds at sixty percent that we could get away. The main obstacle was that the boat was still tied to the sub. A-Rad would have to somehow make it to the front and untie us without being noticed.

The opportunity passed quickly, and the commander of the boat began yelling instructions in Norwegian. A-Rad and I both knew enough to understand what he had said. Two of the burlier Royal Navy soldiers immediately entered our boat with guns waving in our direction for effect.

The commander didn't know that two soldiers weren't enough to guard us, even with weapons. We didn't have guns, but we possessed several weapons.

Jamie said more times than I could count to remember that I always had a weapon on me. My knees, elbows, head, feet, and hands could all be as lethal as a gun. Around the boat were any number of weapons. A well struck blow to the head with a fire extinguisher could kill a man in an instant. The cord from the radio wrapped around a man's neck could choke him out in less than a minute.

For that matter, A-Rad and I could disarm the two guards and relieve them of their weapons before they even knew what hit them. With the element of surprise, we could kill the rest of the soldiers and the prince before they could get a shot off at us. They were in the open. We were protected by any number of places to hide in the boat.

But our moral code held us back. The kills wouldn't be righteous. We knew nothing about these soldiers except that they were part of the Royal Navy protecting the prince.

Did they know about the women in the submarine? I didn't know for sure but doubted it. The prince would keep his inner circle small.

So we couldn't just kill them. They had families and loved ones, maybe even wives and kids. Protecting the prince wasn't a crime. As the prince argued on the sub, it was their patriotic duty. Unlike the soldiers on the sub who knew what the prince was doing, they didn't fall into the category of needing to be killed for self-defense nor were they complicit in the prince's crimes. At least there was no evidence to suggest otherwise.

If I initiated the action and began firing at them and they fired back, killing them wasn't justifiable self-defense on my part. They were simply protecting themselves and the prince.

These were gray areas we spent many hours discussing. Our targets were the bad guys, not innocent soldiers, law enforcement officers, or civilians. That didn't mean that innocents didn't sometimes get caught in the line of fire, but it meant that we go to extraordinary lengths to try to keep that from happening.

One of the soldiers approached me with zip ties in hand. I held out my wrists in a position of surrender. I didn't see any way around it without creating a confrontation. The prince seemed to be keeping his end of the bargain, so I intended to keep mine.

I intentionally flayed my wrists when he tightened the ties, making them more comfortable. I'd spent nearly a week of training with Jamie on how to escape restraints. Tighter was easier to get out of, but all I had to do was lift my hands in the air and bring my arms violently down and hit them against my stomach and my elbows against my hips and these particular zip ties would break apart.

The soldier secured A-Rad's wrists next which caused me to chuckle under my breath. As soon as he was done, I'd joke with A-Rad that the soldier found me to be a bigger threat. That's why he bound me first.

Before I could make the snide remark, the prince disappeared into the submarine drawing my attention. He emerged about five minutes later. Alone. He immediately got into the second boat which sped away. We didn't follow, which confused me. The gunmen in our boat were stoic and disinterested as we idled in the water.

The captain eyed us closely but didn't seem tense or hostile.

"What are we waiting for?" I asked him.

He didn't answer.

I looked over at A-Rad who shrugged with his eyes, confused as well.

The gentle breeze was soothing and felt relaxing to me. The air was thick with the smell of saltwater and the beach. Overhead, seagulls circled, their cries echoing in the vast expanse of sky. Behind us was an island with lush greenery. To our north I could see a mountain range.

Under any other circumstances, this would've been a beautiful place to visit.

A-Rad and I took turns closing our eyes to get some rest.

"Sleep and eat when you can," Jamie used to say. "You never know when you might get another chance."

When the captain offered us water, we both took it. My stomach growled, making me wish I had access to our boat which had several energy bars in it.

About an hour later a tugboat arrived and the captain began connecting a tow line to the sub. After considerable effort, he returned to his command post and began slowly dragging the sub out of the bay and into the open sea.

We followed behind, although I wasn't sure why.

Without warning, the tugboat stopped, and its captain went to disconnect the line from the sub.

"What's he doing?" I asked A-Rad.

"I guess they're going to fire up the sub."

"That must be why the prince went back inside. To find the Admiral."

"I suppose."

He would've been easy to find. I tied him up in a room off of the control room.

"The hatch is still open," I said with some sense of urgency once I realized it.

"Surely the Admiral knows that."

The tug suddenly revved its engines, emitting a strong smell of burning diesel, and filling the sky with thick black smoke. The waters churned from the powerful engines. The efforts caused the sub to list back and forth from the waves.

I let out a scream when I realized what he was trying to do.

The captain of our boat looked at me in confusion, unsure why I had reacted so strongly.

"The hatch is open! The submarine is going to sink."

As if on cue, the sub rocked violently to the left, met a wave and jerked to the right, tipping over completely, the hatch no longer visible, now under the water. Within seconds it had turned completely upside down. Water would fill the sub. It was only a matter of time until it would sink to the bottom of the ocean.

I stood to my feet.

One of the soldiers pushed me back down.

"Stop!" I shouted to the tugboat captain at the top of my lungs, even though he was too far away to hear me.

The tugboat circled the sub creating more waves until it disappeared completely under the surface of the water.

"No! No! No!" I cried out. "There are people on that sub. You have to help them."

"There's nobody on the sub," the captain coldly said.

I began to sob.

A wave of hopelessness engulfed me.

I could no longer see the sub. It was too late to do anything about it anyway. My heart sank with it. Grief overwhelmed me.

It became crystal clear what had happened. The prince ordered the submarine sunk. To cover up his crimes even if it meant sacrificing his own Admiral's life in the process.

I had no idea he was this evil.

Our boat sped away. I kept looking back even though I knew it was gone. The horror of seven innocent college girls trapped inside the watery grave sent my emotions into a spiral. A-Rad reached over and squeezed my hand.

I looked into his eyes and saw the same pain I felt. I saw resolve as well. His jaw was clenched in anger. The reality of the prince's cruelty weighed heavily on us both, fueling a fire within me that threatened to consume my emotions.

Ordering the sub to be sunk was a despicable act. Leaving the girls left to die a slow death trapped in the underwater tomb was beyond any depravity I'd ever witnessed.

Amidst the despair, a plan began to form in my mind, and I exchanged a determined glance with A-Rad, silently communicating our shared resolve to seek justice for the lost girls. We had to escape from the clutches of the Royal Navy and expose the prince's heinous actions to the world.

As our boat carried us away from the carnage, I let myself feel all the intense emotions from utter rage to a sense of guilt and sorrow. Regardless of the political ramifications, and regardless of what it'd do to our careers, one thing was clear: the prince had to die.

Right now, we were helpless. It wouldn't always be that way.

7

CIA Headquarters
Langley, VA

Brad stared at the highly classified information brief sitting on his desk. The events in Norway were rapidly unfolding, and he opened the file to read its contents for a second time.

This was bad—very bad.

He'd faced tough situations before. It came with the territory. His career had begun as an analyst and eventually progressed to handler even though analyzing data was his first love. He was considered an expert at dissecting intel briefs and coming up with solutions to problems.

Not so much this time.

This day was destined to happen as soon as he was assigned to oversee Alex Halee and Jamie Austen. Two of the most prolific CIA operatives in the history of the Agency, but also two of the most difficult to handle.

Jamie and Alex were constantly getting themselves into jams that seemed impossible to get out of. Jamie in particular had cost him many a night's sleep. When she became pregnant and retired, he had hoped for quieter days with Kaley.

He should've known better.

In some ways, Kaley was a looser cannon than Jamie, if that were possible. She was younger and brasher and even more unpredictable and reckless than Jamie.

Over the years, Jamie had learned to be more cautious and calculate her actions as she gained experience. She still took risks, but knew the lines better, and only crossed them when necessary and made sure to fix any problems before they got back to him.

When Brad received the call from Kaley that she and A-Rad had killed five Royal Guards and that the perpetrator of the sex trafficking operation was the Crown Prince of Norway, he about fell out of his chair. He was beyond stunned. As much as it pained him to do it, he hung up on Kaley. He had no choice.

American law was clear, foreign leaders could not be targeted for assassination. While the CIA had done it many times over the years, they always managed to cover it up. He didn't think he could cover it up if Kaley killed the prince and he didn't know for sure that she'd follow his admonitions not to do so.

Kaley was like Jamie in the sense that the only good sex trafficker was a dead one. Jamie wouldn't care if the trafficker was the President of the United States. He'd deserve to die, and she'd use every ounce of her significant abilities to make it happen.

Brad half expected to get a call at any moment that the Crown Prince was dead. He was shocked that Kaley did what she was told and didn't kill him.

That didn't change the gravity of the report on his desk.

He turned to page three of the report and began reading again a transcript summary of news reports coming out of Norway in real time.

He grimaced.

His biggest fear had become a reality.

The whole mess with Kaley and A-Rad had hit the news. Somehow the incident had been leaked to the press. Brad had a team of people monitoring the various Norwegian news channels for updates and compiling a report for him minute by minute as the events unfolded.

4:25 p.m.

Regularly scheduled programming was interrupted on NRK1. The largest news channel in Norway with the highest viewership.

The headlines blared in bold red letters.

CROWN PRINCE TARGET OF TERRORIST ATTACK

"We have breaking news. Crown Prince, Cai Bolling, was the target of a terrorist attack this afternoon," the news anchor said. "No further details are available at this moment although we believe the prince has survived the attack. It wasn't clear if he was injured."

4:31 p.m.

Details started emerging. NRK1 news reported that the Crown Prince was on a sightseeing excursion to an island near Rakvag. The small and secluded village of roughly 305 people was located in the inner part of the Stjornfjorden in what used to be the old municipality of Rissa.

"We're told that the prince is unharmed and is on his way back to the Royal Palace. A spokesman for the Royal House of Norway says that the king has spoken to his son. The prince is shaken but unharmed."

4:50 p.m.

The Prime Minister of England, Edward Charles McCloud, expressed outrage over the attack and is urging all Britons to stay indoors until more information is available.

He said, "British nationals are advised to exercise extreme caution, monitor the news reports, and follow the advice of the local authorities."

Over 17,000 Britons lived in Norway, and more than 300,000 visited each year.

The one thing Brad asked of his operatives was not to create an international incident. To not do anything that would bring scrutiny to their actions. This incident was spreading around the world like wildfire in a field.

4:51 p.m.

The Norwegian Prime Minister, Padrig Sayer, said he's shocked at the attack and has pledged that Norway "will not rest" until we find out who was behind the attack and bring them to justice.

Let's hope that never happens.

Sayer also mentioned that he'd been to the Indre Fosen region on many occasions as a boy and had many fond memories of the area. Every July, boat owners from across Norway gather in the small village for an event called Rakvag-dagene, which was something Sayer's grandfather used to take him to before he passed away.

5:05 p.m.

Justice Minister, Derog Nist, stated that Norway had not changed its threat level after the attack, but they were closely monitoring the situation. He said the king and queen were at their royal holiday retreat in Magaro when the attack occurred but have been moved to an undisclosed location for their safety.

"The debate on the threat level is ongoing," he said.

5:07 p.m.

The Norwegian police have released more details about the attack. Deputy Police Chief, Dillon Connog, was on the scene and described what he believes happened. According to reports, two assailants carrying automatic weapons attacked the prince's boat shortly after nine a.m. that morning. Members of the Royal Guard on board returned fire. There was currently no available information on casualties or how the prince escaped unharmed.

5:15 p.m.

King Edgar IV of England expressed shock and sadness in a statement released moments ago by Buckingham Palace. His Majesty sent thoughts and prayers to those affected by this tragedy and their families.

Out of an abundance of caution, he urged all British residents of Norway to remain indoors until further notice.

Here were his words:

"In light of the tragic events of the day, we are deeply saddened. The Queen joins me in expressing our sincere sympathies to Your Majesty and to the people of Norway who have been affected and are suffering from this unspeakable tragedy."

The flags at the Norwegian embassy in London were seen flying at half-staff.

5:16 p.m.

Unconfirmed reports that five of the prince's royal guards were killed in the gunfight.

5:20 p.m.

Norwegian newspaper VG was reporting that the prince escaped the gunmen by diving off the boat and swimming to a nearby island where he was later rescued by a patrol boat that arrived at the scene shortly after the attack happened.

5:47 p.m.

Reports were sketchy and information conflicting. Another unconfirmed report stated that six guards were on board the prince's boat when the attack occurred. According to the same source, the prince's boat was struck several hundred times by gunfire and sank.

5:55 p.m.

The Deputy Chief of Police confirmed that six guards perished. Previous reports put the death toll at five.

"We now believe that all six members of the Royal Guard are unaccounted for and presumed dead," he said. "A search and rescue operation is underway in the area. At some point, we expect it to become a recovery operation."

5:59 p.m.

An anonymous source within the Royal Palace said that the prince witnessed the boat sinking. He confirmed that six guards were on board.

"He said, and I quote, 'It's unlikely that any of the guards survived or that the boat will ever be recovered.'"

6:01 p.m.

Norway Labor Party spokesman, Taleisin Maddy, said that the water was still being searched for more victims.

6:10 p.m.

Norway's Justice Minister stated that the gunmen were not Norwegian.

6:23 p.m.

According to reports, the king and queen had been reunited with their son. His Majesty appeared visibly shaken as he embraced his son. Her Majesty was seen wiping away tears.

7:14 p.m.

The Norwegian Prime Minister praised the bravery and heroism of the fallen guards.

"Their actions likely saved the prince's life."

7:45 p.m.

The king briefly addressed the nation and expressed gratitude for the outpouring of support received from all over the world. He shared that many heads of state reached out to him personally by phone and sent messages.

The President of the United States called the king to express his condolences and to offer his support from the American intelligence agencies.

The president said, "I've instructed the CIA to assist in the efforts to discover who was behind the attack and to determine if there were any international connections."

Not going to happen.

Brad would spend the rest of his life in jail if anyone ever found out he had anything to do with this mission.

9:01 p.m.

Norwegian Foreign Minister, Dewydd Bithel, said he was outraged by the brazen attack.

"Norway is one of the most peaceful and safest places on earth."

He expressed his shock and called the attack incomprehensible.

9:04 p.m.

The search for the missing guards had been suspended for tonight. An anonymous source stated that it's unlikely that any of the guards could survive the night in the frigid waters.

9:15 p.m.

Unverified reports were coming in that the two suspects who carried out the attack are dead.

9:20 p.m.

They were learning more about what the prince told the authorities.

"I heard someone shout, 'kill them all,'" the prince said. "I'm not sure why, but I jumped into the water when the shooting started. I swallowed a lot of water but managed to stay under the surface long enough to get away. I had on my clothes and shoes, and they were heavy making it harder to swim away. Somehow, I made it to dry land, and I ran and hid in the trees until the reinforcements arrived. I didn't get a good look at the assailants. It all happened too fast."

10:02 p.m.

More details were emerging about the two patrol boats who came to the prince's rescue. They were in the vicinity when they received a distress call from the prince's boat. They sped toward the scene when they encountered the suspects fleeing in a boat. One of the boats followed the assailants while the other went to check on the prince. The patrol boat engaged in gunfire with the assailants.

One of their bullets hit the gas tank and caused an explosion disabling the vessel. When they got closer, the suspects opened fire again. They returned fire and the two assailants were killed. The suspect's boat sank before the bodies of the gunmen could be recovered.

The boat will likely not be recovered.

10:03 p.m.

The Foreign Minister expressed belief that the threat has passed and that this was an isolated incident. The king ordered flags to be flown at half-staff.

The army patrolled the streets of Oslo creating an eerie sight in that normally peaceful and tranquil country.

10:15 p.m.

In Oslo, people streamed out of their homes to gather at various cathedrals around the city to lay flowers and light candles. Mourners were creating makeshift altars around the city for the victims who had now been identified.

The king and queen returned to the Royal Palace and were meeting with family members of the victims.

The final paragraph of the report was chilling. Here's a summary of today's events:

6 members of the Royal Guard are dead.

The Crown Prince survived.

The two suspects are presumed dead.

The investigation is still ongoing.

Brad had seen enough.

He closed the report and sat back in his chair contemplating the ramifications. As the Assistant Director of the CIA, his job was to advise the director and potentially brief the president. He hadn't been summoned to that meeting yet but would be soon.

The gravity of this situation could not be overstated. Before he could formulate the words he'd use with the president, his phone rang interrupting his thoughts.

It could only be one person.

Jamie Austen.

"I guess you heard," he said solemnly when he answered.

"Tell me what you know," she said.

He had dreaded this conversation almost if not more than his meeting with the president.

8

"Kaley isn't dead," Brad said to Jamie Austen without bothering with a greeting.

Brad answered Jamie's call on a phone not connected with the CIA. All communications inside the CIA were monitored and this was not one they wanted recorded.

"I didn't believe the news reports," Jamie told him. "They didn't ring true to me."

"The official reports are rarely accurate these days," he said with a sense of defeat behind his words. "Not that they've ever been."

As the Assistant Director of the Central Intelligence Agency with years of experience, he was as responsible for the spread of disinformation as anyone. His tenure went all the way back years to when subterfuge was an art form. Now, more often than not, he was the one spreading the lies. Putting his own spin on things which may or may not have any basis in fact.

He knew he'd have to be honest with Jamie. She'd see through any attempted ruses on his part. Not that he wanted to lie to her, but she wasn't going to like what he had to say.

Jamie spoke calmly and without emotion. He figured the emotions would rear their ugly heads soon enough.

"The news from Norway claimed that Kaley and A-Rad fired several hundred shots at the guard boats," she said. "No way. Not to kill five guards. I trained them. I'm guessing it took ten rounds at the most. Two for each dead guard. I doubt they even had hundreds of rounds with them. I'll disown them if it took more than a couple dozen shots to kill five men."

Brad groaned on the inside. That's exactly what was about to happen. Jamie would have to disown them, just like he had been forced to do.

He kept his tone calm and steady matching her tone even though his stomach was churning with emotions. "The guards were killed on the sub. Kaley called me right after it happened."

"She called you?"

"Yes."

Jamie let out an audible sigh. "I wonder why she didn't call me?"

"No time. The Royal Navy had them surrounded. No way off the sub without a major shootout."

"The captain must've got off a mayday call," Jamie said, as her voice trailed off in the distance. "They should've secured the control room first."

"I think they did. Only too little, too late."

"We discussed this. It's almost impossible to reach the control room before the captain can radio for help. I specifically told them to block all outgoing signals from inside the sub. Did they do it?"

"I don't know, and Kaley didn't say. Doesn't matter now."

"What did you tell her to do?"

"I told her to turn herself in. I didn't see any other choice."

A moment of silence ensued as Jamie was clearly processing that information. He could imagine her mind spinning like a computer looking for a solution no one had thought of.

Not that it mattered. What's done is done. Jamie would know that as well as anyone. He'd at least give her the opportunity to vent, even second guess, if she wanted to take it.

She didn't.

"Is that what they did? Turned themselves in?" she finally asked.

"Yes. They were taken to Mostad. Probably for questioning."

As soon as Kaley's call came in, Brad had activated satellites based on the location of her signal. He watched as they were unloaded off the submarine and onto a boat. He followed the boat all the way to Mostad.

"They took them to Mostad to kill them," Jamie said, resolutely. "After they interrogate them. Torture if necessary."

"I suppose so."

"Mostad is in the middle of nowhere," Jamie said. "It's an abandoned village. It's not even accessible by roads."

Brad was constantly amazed by Jamie's vast knowledge of the world and ability to retain information. She had helped plan this mission behind the scenes, although Kaley had been given full authority to plan and execute it.

"It's a good place to make them disappear," Brad said.

"That's why they fabricated the story about their deaths during the attack and claimed their bodies were lost at sea," she said. "That's where they intend to take them once they are through interrogating them."

"That's right."

"Do you believe they're still alive?" Jamie asked.

"Don't even think about it!" Brad's voice was firm as he warned Jamie. He had been expecting this from her and was ready to react as strongly as possible.

"What?" she asked innocently.

"You know what."

"I asked a simple question."

"I know you better than you know yourself," Brad said.

"All I asked is if they're still alive."

"I'm ordering you to stand down! Do not try to rescue them. This situation is too hot."

"Ordering?"

"Strongly suggesting."

Jamie didn't respond, but he could hear the wheels turning in her mind. She was already considering rescue operations. He wouldn't be surprised if Alex, Bond, and Colonel were already on a plane to Norway. They made up the core team for AJAX, along with A-Rad and Kaley. Probably the most effective mission team ever assembled.

He couldn't help but wonder if this was the end of that partnership.

"I'm serious, Jamie. If you trained them well enough, they'll be able to escape on their own."

"And then what?" Jamie countered. "They can't come back here, and their careers are ruined."

"There's nothing we can do about that now."

"They'll have to live in hiding for the rest of their lives."

"They knew the risks when they signed up for the mission."

"I have to help them!"

"No! Look at the reports. The world sees this as a terrorist attack on the royal family. We're the ones responsible. Imagine if that information ever got out. We're lucky that Norway has declared them dead. It's the best situation for everyone."

"Not for Kaley and A-Rad."

"If you try to help them, you could make things worse. Right now, it can't be traced back to you."

"Where's our yacht?"

"The yacht was taken to Mostad as well."

Brad understood how much that yacht meant to Jamie. Not for personal reasons, but also for their operations. She had rescued thousands of girls with that yacht.

She also wouldn't be worried about it being traced back to them. Alex was a marvel at covering their tracks. He didn't doubt Alex's ability to make it untraceable, but they couldn't stop it from being searched by the Norwegian authorities.

Jamie had stolen the yacht from an Arab sheik during a legitimate AJAX art trip to Abu Dhabi. She went there to buy a piece of art that the sheik owned. The meeting took place at his art shop in downtown Abu Dhabi. After their business was complete, she excused herself to use the restroom. On the bathroom mirror were the words "Help Me" written in red lipstick.

The sheik had been accompanied by several beautiful women and Jamie assumed one of them wrote the message. In typical Jamie fashion, she didn't leave without finding the source of the cryptic message. The trip turned into a full-blown mission, and she discovered that the sheik was indeed trafficking the women. He lured the girls to Abu Dhabi under the guise of modeling for his agencies. Once there, he wouldn't let them leave.

She rescued the girls, after making sure the sheik was dead. In the harbor of his massive estate was the yacht. Jamie used it to get the girls out of the Middle East and Alex worked his computer hacking handiwork and transferred the title to AJAX.

This success fueled a new aspect of their organization. A Robin Hood philosophy of worldwide CIA missions. Jamie and Alex acquired billions of dollars worth of assets from arms dealers, drug lords, and sex traffickers. With Jamie and her team leading the way, they infiltrated some of the most ruthless criminal organizations in the world and stole their planes, yachts, and art collections, among other things. Alex emptied their bank accounts. There wasn't a financial institution in the world he couldn't hack into.

AJAX used those funds to finance their operations including using yachts to discreetly transport rescued girls from their precarious situations. A brilliant plan. Who'd ever think to look in a luxury yacht for rescued girls?

The Norwegian authorities would be just as baffled that a yacht would be used in this attack. They'd search it but wouldn't find any answers. The yacht was filled with hidden compartments. Even if they did somehow discover them, they might find a weapons stash, but Alex and Jamie were meticulous. Even the weapons had the serial numbers removed and couldn't be traced back to them.

While Jamie would hate to lose that yacht, she had several more at her disposal and could get another one in a moment's notice if she wanted it.

The emotional toll of losing valuable team members like A-Rad and Kaley was what was hard to bear. Ability aside, A-Rad and Kaley were like family. Taking ability into consideration, they were simply the best resources Brad had now that Jamie was retired. The thought of losing both Jamie and Kaley in a matter of months was a significant blow to his operations.

"What's your next move?" Jamie asked.

"I have no moves left. I'm completely out of the game. I suggest you follow my lead."

"What happened to the girls?" Jamie asked, as if she hadn't even heard the admonition.

"I don't know," he lied. If he told her that the girls had drowned in the submarine and the prince had killed them, she'd go ballistic. Nothing would stop her from extracting revenge.

"I know what happened," she stated. "I saw the satellite images in your file. The sub and the girls are at the bottom of the ocean."

"Jamie! Those files are highly classified. Alex shouldn't be hacking into my files without my permission."

"Easier to ask for forgiveness than permission."

"You're not forgiven."

"I didn't ask to be."

"I don't like where this conversation is going."

"I can't believe you're forsaking A-Rad and Kaley."

"This is higher up than me. You know what that means."

Meaning the directive was coming from the president himself. It hadn't yet but would soon enough. She wouldn't know either way.

"Promise me you'll stand down," Brad said.

"I don't know if I can promise that," Jamie said. "Colonel, Bond, and Alex are ready to go to Norway at a moment's notice."

Brad was relieved to learn that they hadn't left for Norway yet.

"Don't do it," he said with resignation in his voice. Knowing he couldn't stop them even if he wanted to. "You'll only make things worse. I don't want to lose them too."

His voice cracked as he said it.

"It could've just as easily been me," Jamie said. "You know our code. We aren't going to sit back and do nothing."

"There's nothing you can do."

"No one knew that the prince was behind the kidnapping of the girls. If anything, I blame us. We sent them there with bad intel. I feel responsible. That's why we have to help them. I can't because I'm pregnant. But our team can."

"It's nobody's fault. But that doesn't change anything. They really screwed up this time."

Neither of them said anything for a good minute. Jamie hung up first. There was nothing more to say.

9

Mostad, Norway

Hefina Rosser had been working on damage control for the prince for more than twenty-five years. She began her career as an intelligence officer for the NIS, the Norwegian Intelligence Service or Etterretningstjenesten as it was formally known.

She started out in the Ministry of Defense as a highly trained soldier in the Norwegian special forces and rose through the ranks fairly quickly. She was proficient in martial arts and could shoot a worm out of a bird's mouth from a hundred yards away. More than that, she was loyal to a fault and as tough as a sled dog in Lapland.

Her career took an unexpected turn when she was pulled out of special forces and reassigned to the Royalty Protection Unit responsible for providing security to His Majesty and the other members of the royal family under the jurisdiction of the Norwegian Police Security Service, the PST.

Her life immediately became boring. Things only got worse when the prince was born, and she was assigned to his detail. In essence, she was nothing more than a glorified babysitter.

The prince had a proficiency at getting into trouble before he could barely walk. The biggest security threat to the prince was the prince himself. She continually found herself covering up for his childish behaviors and indiscretions and had to constantly worry about him accidentally killing himself or someone else. Notably, the half a dozen times he almost burned down the royal palace.

Her exceptional skills on the job were not lost on the royal family. She attributed her diplomacy skills to her college degree in public relations. By the time the prince was six, her role had changed to "fixer," a mafia term usually used to describe someone who cleaned up the evidence of a crime. The person who knew where all the bodies were buried. So to speak.

There had not been any buried bodies until now.

"What happened?" Rosser had asked the prince.

"You heard what I told the investigator," he answered aloofly.

She arrived on the scene shortly after the prince's boat arrived on land but not before the investigator had taken a statement. She was livid that he had given the investigator a version of events without talking to her first.

His arrogance made him believe he could get away with anything. He could but only with her help.

"I heard what you told him!" Rosser said. "Now I want the truth."

The prince scoffed and tried to deflect. She got right in his face. She's one of the few people alive who could get away with such a thing.

"That story is complete rubbish and we both know it," she practically screamed. "I can't help you if you don't tell me the truth."

He opened his mouth but looked away, preparing to lie again. Rosser wasn't sure she even wanted to know everything but needed him to be more truthful than he was now.

"Me and my buddies took some college girls on a submarine."

"What submarine?"

"My own."

"Where did you get it?"

"It was headed for the scrap heap. I renovated it and use it with my friends to have some fun."

"What kind of fun?"

"We party. You know. We get some girls. There's a little drinking. We have a good time."

"Who are the girls? What are their names?"

"I'm not sure."

"I don't believe you."

"Please don't tell my parents."

The prince's demeanor made it clear to her that this situation was more serious than those from the past. He seemed genuinely afraid. Like he had really screwed up. She had to find out why.

So she pressed in until he began to confess to the whole sordid affair. She stopped him before he could go into all the gruesome details, but she ascertained that the girls had been kidnapped against their wills and the assailants had come to rescue them.

She couldn't believe he had been so stupid, but her job wasn't to sit in judgment of the prince but figure out how to protect him.

Not him. The monarchy. She couldn't stand him.

"I panicked," he admitted. "They killed all six of my guards and I thought they were going to kill me. For whatever reason, they surrendered. That's when I ordered the submarine sunk, so no one would know about the girls."

That's when Rosser came up with the cover story that the two assailants were dead and their bodies would likely never be recovered. The girls were at the bottom of the ocean and were missing anyway. Their cases would never be solved.

The only problem with her story was that the two assailants were still alive. She thought about killing them immediately but needed information.

Who were they? Was the prince their target all along? If so, why didn't they kill him when they had the chance?

She devised a plan to make them talk. The male assailant was currently being questioned at a nearby location. The interrogation had probably turned to torture by now since the early reports were that he was uncooperative.

She believed she'd have better luck with the young woman, so she took it upon herself to try and get her to talk.

She waited until a thorough search of the yacht was completed. They found nothing. Even that was suspicious. Why would anyone plan a terrorist attack using an expensive yacht? Who funded the operation? Why did the yacht have no ownership trail to follow?

All she had to go on was that they were probably American. Which raised even more questions. Were they acting alone? Highly unlikely considering the value of the yacht.

But where did the two learn such skills? Killing six royal guards even with the element of surprise was no easy task.

Were they CIA? US Special Forces?

Why would they be running an operation in Norway? Surely the Americans wouldn't sanction such an operation.

For years, Rosser had heard whispers about a supremely skilled larger than life CIA operative who ran sex trafficking rescue operations for the Americans. A woman. Up until now, she had dismissed the stories as nothing more than rumors. Myths. Tales of fiction. No one was that good.

Now, a young woman sat in the next room with similar skills. Who had pulled off an incredible operation in Norwegian waters. But the girl in the other room was too young. The CIA mystery woman had been running operations for years and was supposed to be blonde. The girl in the other room was a redhead.

Rosser had to figure out how to make her talk. Maybe this girl was trained by the phantom Wonder Woman.

A plan had formulated in her mind.

Rosser opened the door where the young woman was being held and entered the room, with a friendly smile on her face. The female captive sat in a chair, shackled to a table, looking bored.

Rosser entered without caution even though every fiber of her being was on alert. She'd been told by the prince that the woman was dangerous and that he saw her kill one of his guards with her bare hands.

Rosser sat down in the chair across from her. "My name is Dwynwyn Binnion," she said.

She fought back a smile. She always used fake names that were hard to pronounce, spell, or remember.

"Is there anything I can get you?" she asked, sincerely. She'd give the girl whatever she wanted within reason. The first tactic was to earn her trust.

The girl remained stoic, briefly making eye contact only to look her up and down, probably to assess the threat.

Rosser repeated her offer. "I'm your friend. Can I get you anything?"

The girl didn't respond.

"I'm here to help you," Rosser said. "I'm the lawyer who has been assigned to your case. I'm here to advocate on your behalf."

The young girl changed positions in the chair. Rosser tensed slightly at the sudden movement but tried not to let it show on her face.

The sounds of chains rattling eerily echoed through the room which was nothing more than an abandoned run-down building that hadn't been used in years and wasn't that nice even when it was new.

Rosser did her own assessment of the young woman.

Five foot seven. Muscular.

Not in a weightlifting or masculine kind of way. More like a cross-country runner with highly defined muscles.

Body fat, less than fourteen percent.

Impressive.

She maintained her own BMI of ten in her unhealthier and obsessive days. It was somewhere around thirteen now and harder to maintain as she got older.

The girl had cute features. Not like a model, but more like a pretty girl next-door. She wondered if the two assailants were married or dating. If so, the girl in front of her didn't seem too concerned about her companion. She didn't even ask about him or blink when Rosser mentioned him.

"The government of Norway is charging you and your friend with murder," Rosser said in a more professional voice. "Six counts. These are very serious crimes. You can be sent away to prison for life."

The young woman remained unresponsive, her expression giving nothing away. It made Rosser think that this woman had CIA training.

"What's your name?" Rosser inquired.

"Dwynwyn Binnion," the girl said sarcastically, speaking for the first time. "But you can call me Dwyn."

"Very funny. I'm trying to help you here. What's your name?"

"Personen som skal drepe prinsen," the girl said. Rosser sat back. The girl had just answered in perfect Norwegian, "The person who's going to kill the prince."

Then she added, "Og du hvis du kommer i veien for meg," meaning, "And you, if you get in my way."

Rosser decided to ignore the threats and intensify the interrogation.

"Are you American?" she asked, searching the girl's eyes for any hint of confirmation.

But the woman gave nothing away. Rosser was trained to spot deception. This girl didn't give her a response of recognition or deception.

This might be tougher than she thought.

"Here's what's going to happen. You're going to court in a few days before a judge and the prosecution is going to present the preliminary charges. I'll plead 'not guilty' on your behalf, but in the meantime, you need to help me come up with a defense strategy."

The girl then said something that made Rosser laugh out loud. "Har du royka sokka dine?" she said. The girl had just literally asked her, "Have you smoked your socks?" Meaning, "Are you crazy?"

It made her wonder if the girl was Norwegian after all. Maybe she had American parents but grew up in Norway.

"Where did you get the yacht?" Rosser asked.

For the first time, the girl looked up and their eyes met. Mentioning the yacht must've struck a nerve.

"Jeg stjal den." *I stole it.*

Rosser had considered that possibility and looked into it. No yachts had been reported stolen recently. If it was stolen, how could this girl change the paperwork title?

The girl suddenly leaned forward in her chair.

"Vet du om jentene på ubåten?" she said sternly. *Do you know about the girls on the submarine?*

"What girls?" Rosser asked, trying not to let her own facial expression give anything away.

The girl leaned back and smiled smugly, nodding her head as if she knew that Rosser did know. Rosser was kicking herself for letting this girl control the conversation. Only someone with CIA training could be this cool under pressure and have the ability to recognize her deception.

Or maybe she was just good at bluffing.

"Why do you ask?" Rosser said. She really wanted to know how much the girl knew.

The girl leaned forward in her chair again.

"Because I'm making a list of everyone I'm going to track down and kill after I kill the prince," she said in English, confirming once and for all the girl was American.

"I have to advise you as your attorney that threats against the royal family in my presence can be used against you."

"You're not my lawyer," she said coolly. "And there won't be a trial. You've been lying to me since you walked through that door. I also know that you're going to kill me. I'm anxious for you to try. So why don't you get on with it."

The girl leaned back in her chair with her arms crossed.

Rosser had heard enough. That's exactly what she intended to do, kill the girl. At first, she was going to let the guard do it. But now, she wanted to do it herself. It'd been a long time since she'd killed anyone. That's what she was trained to do, and in a weird sort of way, she missed it. She'd take great satisfaction in watching the life and the smugness leave this woman's face for the last time.

She left the room and asked the guard for a weapon. He gave her one. Rosser checked the gun to make sure it was in working order and a bullet was chambered.

She put her hand on the door to reenter, then hesitated. She needed to think this through. Was now the right time to kill the girl? Should she torture her first? Once the girl was dead, all her secrets were dead with her.

That's the best thing, she decided. The sooner the girl was dead and her body at the bottom of the ocean, the better it'd be for everyone.

She turned the handle to the door and entered the room. She felt her mouth fly open in horror.

The chains were sitting on the table. The only window in the room was open.

The girl was gone.

10

I barely escaped by the skin of my teeth. *What does that even mean? Teeth don't have skin, do they?*

The weirdest thoughts pop into my head at the most inopportune times. I was in a full out sprint for a forest of trees about fifty yards away. At any moment, I expected a couple of guards to unload their weapons in my direction.

As I was running for my life, the meaning of the phrase was the last thing I should be thinking about. Did I want this to be my last thought on earth? All that mattered was getting to the shelter of the trees as fast as possible.

The adrenaline had sent my body into overload and my mind spinning out of control. Getting away from the gunmen was my first priority, but I was acting on instinct. That gave my mind the opportunity to dwell on less important things.

"What does 'by the skin of one's teeth' even mean?" I had asked Jamie once after she used the metaphor. Was it a euphemism or a metaphor? I couldn't remember.

If I remembered right, the two of us were in Vietnam rescuing girls from a ruthless sex trafficker. We had a gun fight with a dozen or so armed men guarding his compound. We'd already rescued the girls who were kept in Ho Chi Minh city, but Jamie wanted to find the compound and finish him off.

We did but not without considerable risk. I could still hear the sound of the bullets whizzing by my ears. Afterward, when the bullets stopped flying and we were safe, I asked her what the phrase meant.

"It's a Bible reference," she answered. "It comes from Job 19:20."

I was familiar with the biblical story of Job but didn't remember reading that verse.

"Job almost lost everything," she explained. "One day he said to God, 'I am just skin and bones. I escaped with only the skin on my teeth.'"

"Do teeth even have skin?" I asked.

"They must have, if it's in the Bible," she replied.

So I took to using the phrase even though I didn't fully understand it.

My legs were moving quickly as my arms kept perfect rhythm. I felt light and swift like a gazelle, making my way toward the forest of trees nearby.

The fifty yards was thirty. It still felt like I was running in slow motion.

Recalling my conversation with Jamie wasn't necessarily helping me run faster, but it did distract me from the fear of bullets hitting my back.

As long as those thoughts occupied my mind, it meant I was still alive.

Gunshots rang out behind me. Several bullets whizzed by my head and struck the trees in front of me shredding their bark. I let out a shriek.

That was too close for comfort.

A fitting metaphor. Even more fitting, it came within an inch of my life. That I understood. More than by the skin of my teeth.

Skin of my teeth. Inch of my life. What difference did it make?

Either way, the reality remained: I wasn't out of the woods yet.

The thought almost brought a chuckle to my lips. Another metaphor that wasn't relevant. I wasn't in the woods. I'd feel a lot better if I was in the woods under the cover of the trees. If I could reach them now, I wouldn't want to leave anytime soon.

The sounds of shouting behind me spurred me on to move faster. Jamie had taught me not to look back. All that'd do was slow me down. My lungs burned from the cold air and the high altitude and the realization that a bullet could send me sprawling at any moment.

I was so close. Thirty yards. Twenty yards. Ten yards.

More bullets flew past me. Some landed near me as the ground shook from the pepper of bullets against the surface. If I'd been ten yards slower, one of those bullets would've hit me.

As soon as I reached the cover of the trees, the shooting stopped, but I didn't stop running. I slowed slightly as I became aware of the uneven terrain and the possibility of tripping on a rock or root sticking out of the ground.

Every muscle in my body wanted me to slow down, but I couldn't afford to. This was their territory, and they'd follow me into the woods.

My thoughts were still on metaphors.

It was a close call. Or was it a close shave?

Shut up, Kaley!

As I bounded up a nearby rocky cliff, I wondered if I'd have been better off staying in the room and taking my chances there.

No. Definitely not.

When the woman came into my makeshift prison cell pretending to be my attorney, I saw through the ruse immediately. She was fishing for information. While I had to give her credit for creativity, she didn't fool me.

But more than that, the woman had skills. Evident by the way she carried herself. By her toned muscles. I suspected immediately that she was proficient in martial arts.

Jamie had always said that if she trained me right, there wasn't a single person in the world who could beat me in a fight. Besides Jamie, of course. While that might be true, if this woman had walked into the room with a gun, I'd be helpless to do anything about it.

Thankfully, she only wanted to question me at first. Before she entered the room, I freed myself from the handcuffs and chains, but kept them wrapped around my wrist and ankles to give the appearance that I was still bound. The woman didn't notice.

But when I realized she knew about the dead girls I had to get out of there as fast as possible. I had already deduced that they brought us there to question us, then make us disappear.

We were taken to Mostad. I knew that because I saw an old, dilapidated sign when we docked. This was a remote part of Norway. The village had long been abandoned. It wasn't even accessible by roads.

I didn't kill her right away because I wanted to get my own intelligence from her. But when she left the room, I figured she went to get a guard to come back and kill me, so I escaped through a window with the intention of finding A-Rad.

Once I was outside the building, I had no choice but to get as far away from the machine guns as possible. Looking for A-Rad would have to come later.

Now I had a bigger worry. I heard dogs barking. I'd seen them when we first landed and knew them to be Puffin dogs.

I remembered reading about them before we came to Norway. The Norwegian Lunde Hund were a rare dog trained to hunt puffins. What made them remarkably unique was the six toes on their feet.

Under different circumstances, I might've enjoyed playing with them.

What made them scary was their ability to hunt prey. Meaning me. The small, spitz-type dogs were agile and well suited for the treacherous cliffs and rocky terrain I now found myself on.

I estimated that about a dozen guards were now on my trail.

Rather than sticking to a straight path, I took a detour. Climbing up a steep hill, once I reached the top, I scrambled down the other side and circled back in an attempt to lose them. The only thing I accomplished was making my situation worse. When I came upon the shoreline of the Norway Sea, it cut off one direction of escape and the pursuers were able to trap me against the vast sea.

I caught a glimpse in the distance of our yacht which was moored in the bay. I considered making a dash for it and trying to get away, but it didn't seem like a feasible plan. In reality, I was battling the entire Norwegian Armed Forces. They'd have every resource available to them. It wouldn't take them long to track me down on the yacht.

The best course of action was to flee on my own. One person in that vast wilderness would be hard to find. If I played my cards right.

How many metaphors would I be able to work into this one escape plan?

I didn't have time to answer my own thought. Nature was working against me. The temperature had dropped rapidly, and darkness was descending. That was a good and a bad thing. Good in that it'd provide some cover. Bad because it made it harder for me to see and the cooler temperatures could become problematic.

As it got deeper in the night, it would get colder. I'd have to rely on my survival instincts. Unless I could find a cave, I wouldn't be able to make a fire. Smoke from the fire could be seen from a distance. The dogs might be able to smell the burning embers.

At some point, I'd need to eat something to regain my strength. If I found food and cooked it over the fire, which sounded good to my growling stomach, the dogs would definitely find me in no time.

Not only did I have the cold to worry about, but I had various predators to concern myself with. Bears, mountain lions, moose.

The chilly wind coming off the sea sent shivers down my spine as I stood on the shoreline trying to decide what to do next. I wasn't dressed for the weather. I was still wearing my mission clothes. Black leggings and a black long sleeve pullover shirt. Lighter clothing for freedom of movement. Thin for mobility.

The specially designed sneakers with slight heels were great for running and kicking someone, but not ideal for the rocky terrain or wet ground.

The sound of the barking dogs told me they were getting closer. I decided to follow the shoreline north in hopes of finding a stream running into the sea. The smartest thing to do would be to run up that stream.

When I found one, I had to rethink that plan. The cold, frigid mountain water would lower my temperature rapidly. My clothes and shoes would stay cold all night.

I didn't like those chances.

So I kept moving. The dogs were steady and were obviously not going to give up anytime soon. The only thing for sure, if I stopped moving, they'd find me in no time.

I felt like a coon being chased by a bunch of hound dogs.

More like a puffin than a coon. A puffin was a cute bird. How did these dogs track them? Couldn't the puffins just fly away?

Those thoughts were quickly put out of my mind. I simply couldn't waste the mental energy on them.

The soldiers had spread out. The dogs were close to outflanking me and trapping me against the shoreline. I had no choice but to follow the stream inland.

I did everything I could to lose them. Zigzagging back-and-forth, I went up small hills, down the other side, around them, over rocks, and crossed through several streams. This frantic game of cat and mouse went on for hours.

I even considered taking off an article of clothing and leaving it somewhere as a diversion, so they'd get confused, but the thought of the cold against my bare skin made me quickly dismiss the idea.

My energy began to wane. Exhaustion was settling in. The dogs would have boundless energy.

I came to the conclusion that I might have to stand and fight. What other choice did I have? If I could get one of their guns, it might even the odds. Could I isolate a guard and disarm him?

I was back on the shoreline. It didn't seem like the time to stop and face the soldiers, so I headed north. This time with no intention of stopping.

My best laid plans led me to an even worse situation. I came to a cove with steep cliffs surrounding it. The only option was to go back in the direction I came. Back toward the barking dogs and the soldiers with guns.

Several more metaphors popped into my mind.

I was between the devil and the clear blue sea. That seemed applicable as I looked out on the sea to my left.

I looked the other direction at the steep cliffs.

Another metaphor seemed the most appropriate of them all.

I was between a rock and a hard place. Literally.

11

In a difficult situation, Jamie taught me to do the unexpected. It didn't often get more difficult than this. I'd followed the shoreline north to a dead end and now the soldiers and their puffin dogs were closing in on me from the south.

Despite my best efforts, I hadn't done anything to improve my situation in several hours. Darkness had descended on Mostad, bringing with it dropping temperatures. I was hungry, thirsty, and on the verge of exhaustion.

The unexpected action I chose was to run south toward the approaching soldiers hoping to make it back to the yacht unnoticed. Inside the yacht was food, water, and shelter. More importantly, weapons.

Hopefully, the dogs would continue to follow my trail north while I passed by them undetected. If they did pick up my scent, I counted on the guards being confused. They wouldn't expect me to come back toward them and would force the dogs to continue north.

The bright full moon wasn't helping my efforts. It glistened off the Norway Sea and acted like a spotlight on me. Luckily, the guards closest to the shoreline were following the trail I had left a few hundred yards inland.

When I flanked around them the dogs reacted, but the soldiers urged them on in the direction of my original trail. That'd keep them occupied for a while. My northern route led to a stream they'd have to cross before reaching the rocky cliffs that formed the dead end.

The dogs were barking like crazy, and the guards cursed them. I stood motionless, waiting to see what would happen next. When I heard them heading north, I released a huge sigh of relief.

With renewed determination, I followed the shoreline down to Mostad, the abandoned town where we first landed and where I was held captive and interrogated. As I drew nearer, I slowed my pace, figuring there'd be guards watching the boats and the yacht. The map in my head told me I was close. Even though I couldn't see it, I estimated that the yacht was just a couple hundred yards south of my location in the bay on the other side of the trees.

My initial plan was to take refuge in the yacht and regroup with warmth, food and water, and a change of clothes. A more daring idea came to me. Could I commandeer one of the guard's boats and speed away in it?

I dismissed the plan when I got close enough to see the guards loitering around the two boats. They had gathered around a fire, smoking cigarettes and joking among themselves. They weren't paying attention at all, and I'd have the element of surprise, but it wasn't worth the risk.

I could've snuck up on them and taken them out, but if one of them managed to get off a shot, it'd let the other guards and dogs know where I was. Right now, everyone thought I was further north. Deep in the woods. Running into the wilderness.

At that point, I made a strategic decision and waded into the sea immediately regretting it. The cold water almost took my breath away. It turned out to be the right decision as I was able to swim about twenty yards from shore without being seen and boarded the yacht from the back.

Thankfully, no one was guarding the yacht, and the guards on the shore didn't notice me.

Once inside, I made a beeline to my room and changed out of my wet clothes. The yacht had clearly been searched, but they hadn't found any of our secret compartments. Even if they discovered the main one, which would be next to impossible, they wouldn't be able to open it without a serious number of explosives.

I entered the combination and slipped inside finding much needed food and water. I scarfed down three energy bars and two bottles of water, barely stopping for breaths between bites and gulps.

On a shelf was a backpack that I began loading with supplies including more energy bars and water as well as euros, dollars, and two fake passports, one for A-Rad and one for myself. I secured a holster around my waist and selected a handgun out of the more than dozen options from the small arsenal in the weapons compartment. Another handgun went into the backpack along with several magazines. I also packed a set of spare clothes for A-Rad and one for myself in case I got wet again.

I considered putting on a wetsuit but decided against it. It would restrict my movements and if I ended up in the water that meant my plan had gone horribly wrong anyway.

The temptation was strong to lie down in the compartment and sleep. Even with the burst of energy from the bars, I was exhausted. They'd never find me in the hidden compartment. I could stay there for days but now was my chance to escape undetected. If I waited until morning, I'd lose the advantage of the darkness.

At this point, I wanted to get as far away from this place as possible and meet A-Rad at the tiger statue in Oslo. This was my best chance.

Satisfied that the backpack had everything I needed, I threw it over my shoulders and checked the security cameras inside the compartments one last time. The guards were still gathered around the fire. It gave me a full view of everything around the yacht and assured me that the coast was clear. I closed the secret compartment and made my way back to the rear of the yacht.

On the side of the yacht was a small rubber boat with a motor. It was on the other side out of the view of the guards on shore. I lowered the boat into the water, careful not to make a sound that might alert them to my presence.

Once the boat was in the water, I stowed my backpack inside and climbed aboard. The bay was relatively calm, and I was able to push away from the yacht easily enough and paddle away.

I wondered if I'd ever see the yacht again. It really was a shame to leave it behind.

"I'm sorry, Jamie," I whispered under my breath.

My heart skipped when I heard barking dogs in the distance. They must've figured out that I had circled back this way.

How much time did I have?

Could I paddle away fast enough, or would I have to turn on the motor?

The moonlight would give away my location if the guards looked in my direction. If I turned on the motor, they'd hear me.

I paddled furiously but wasn't making progress. The current kept pushing me back towards shore. With no other choice, I started the motor. Thankfully, it started on the first try.

As soon as it roared to life, the guards on the shore reacted almost immediately.

They began shouting. Looking over my shoulder, I saw them run toward my side of the yacht. They pointed in my direction, then raised their guns.

The sound of gunfire ripped through the night. Muzzle flashes illuminated the scene as fear coursed through my veins. I wasn't concerned about them hitting me. They were firing wildly and were too far away to hit me or the boat.

I was more concerned about getting away before they gave up and boarded their boats to chase me. My boat was pushed to the limit, and I was desperate to put distance between them and me. As I feared would happen, the firing stopped, and I heard the sounds of their own boats firing up. That was more problematic. My small vessel would be no match for the speed boats.

The moonlight was my enemy and would betray my location if I ventured out into the open water. Mountains loomed on one side and blocked the moon giving me a temporary sanctuary, but it wasn't the direction I wanted to go.

To my left a town glittered with lights a great distance away across the widening sea.

That's where I desperately wanted to be, but I'd have to go out into open water to get there.

I could feel their search lights inching closer to me. It was only a matter of time before they found me.

At some point, we were going to have to shoot it out.

I gritted my teeth and grabbed the gun from my holster while keeping my other hand on the throttle. The waves tossed the boat violently as I increased my speed and left the calmness of the bay. I tried to will the boat to go faster even though I had trouble keeping it steady with only one hand. Adrenaline coursed through my body as I absorbed the bouncing of the ever-increasing waves.

I'd have an advantage in a shootout because of Jamie's training. I knew how to shoot in the midst of chaos. Jamie made me practice shooting in all kinds of situations and distractions with every gun imaginable. Including one time when she had me shooting for hours while spinning around in a torturous contraption. I couldn't walk straight for days. I hated it at the time but was thankful for the training now.

Handguns were notoriously unreliable except at a close distance even in the best of conditions. Trying to hit men in a wildly bouncing boat would test my skills.

Even with my superior skills, I didn't like the odds. The guards on the boats would have the same problem shooting in those conditions, but they didn't necessarily have to hit me. It'd only take one bullet penetrating my rubber raft to sink it. The raft had a life preserver on it, but I wouldn't survive ten minutes in the frigid waters. It'd take longer than that to swim to shore.

Maybe I should've brought the wetsuit after all.

In my head, I could hear Jamie's voice scolding me for second guessing myself. What difference did it make now?

The boats were closing in on me and I had enough to worry about without doubting my decisions that got me in the situation. Outrunning them wasn't an option so I came to a stop and prepared to fire at them when they got closer.

Movement out of the corner of my eye startled me.

What?

I blinked twice.

Did I see that right?

Was it my imagination or did the yacht actually move?

The water behind it churned and I realized it was definitely backing away from the dock. My mind raced. Were they coming after me in the yacht as well? Before I could process all the possibilities, the guard boats were getting in range, and I had to focus.

I raised my weapon and prepared to fire. But waited. I needed them closer.

Two muzzle flashes pierced the night in the distance. Coming from the yacht.

I winced and braced for the bullets I was certain were headed for me.

I heard two loud bangs. It sounded like bullets hitting metal.

The two guard boats suddenly stalled in the water. An eerie silence ensued as their engines shut down.

What just happened?

It took me a second to figure it out. Two perfectly aimed shots from the yacht took out the motors on the guard boats.

Only two people I knew could execute two shots like that from that distance. One was back in the United States and pregnant. She definitely wouldn't be there.

The other was . . . Bond.

Suddenly everything clicked into place.

Alex and Bond must be on that yacht!

I wanted to let out a cheer at the top of my lungs.

Did they come to save me?

They had indeed saved me. The two guard boats were slowly drifting away. I revved up my motor and put more distance between myself and the threat of their weapons.

"Come pick me up!" I wanted to stand and wave my hands in the air and shout those words to Alex. But I knew it'd be foolish to draw attention to myself now. Bond and Alex obviously knew I was there.

The sleek white yacht drew closer. I slowed my motor to an idle and waited patiently for them to get to me.

As it came within a hundred feet, it didn't slow. It kept going. Its engine was at full throttle as it sped past me out towards the open sea.

Confused and bewildered, I sat back down in the boat.

Was it some kind of cruel joke?

I kept expecting Alex to turn around, come and pick me up, then razz me for pulling one over on me.

It never did. I watched it disappear on the horizon and the sound of its engine fade into the distance.

Why did they leave me here in this desolate place?

I wasn't out of danger yet. An overwhelming feeling of despair came over me.

I felt completely abandoned and alone. Cruelly forsaken.

12

As the yacht carrying Alex and Bond disappeared into the distance, I didn't have time to feel sorry for myself. I was still in danger. The current had drifted the two guard boats closer to me. So close, I could see and hear them frantically trying to radio for help.

It made me smile.

Alex and Bond had obviously installed a signal blocker somewhere in the area. All cell phone and radio communications were interrupted giving me a better opportunity to escape. We were supposed to use a blocker on the submarine, but the device malfunctioned. Had it been working properly, perhaps all of this disaster would've been avoided and the captain on board would not have gotten off the distress call.

Such were the complexities of missions. So many factors at play that could go wrong.

It appeared that Alex's device was working fine, and I had to move fast while I had this window of opportunity. The anger inside wanted to lash out at Alex and Bond for leaving me, but I needed to channel that anger toward the real threats at hand.

They had their reasons and my analysis of why would have to come later.

Heading toward the lights of the town was my best option, even though it was risky. The guards in the boat would surely spot me motoring in that direction, but I was counting on Alex's device giving me a good six-to-twelve-hour head start.

Enough time to get to Oslo I hoped, if everything went according to plan. Not enough time to get to the tiger statue by four a.m. but enough time to meet A-Rad there the next day.

The engine on my boat was still idling and I hit the throttle. The vessel jumped with the same sense of urgency I felt.

I glanced one more time in the direction of the yacht and moaned when it was no longer in sight. The rumble of my boat's engine matched the feeling of unease and angst, and the bouncing of the waves stirred the emotions inside of me like butter churned in a vat.

Wild conspiracy theories swirled through my mind, both realistic and absurd. But amidst all the chaos, one thought rose above everything else. Finding A-Rad.

I feared for him as I'm sure he feared for me. Part of me wanted to turn back and search for him but I knew the prudent thing to do was get to the rendezvous point in Oslo.

What if I went back to Mostad looking for him and he had already escaped? What if I got caught again? I'd have to find a way to escape a second time, and I might not be so lucky. The fear of getting caught again loomed over me like a dark cloud that had suddenly blocked the moon leaving me in total darkness.

The only point of reference was the lights of the town. My hand was steady on the course I had chosen. It was the right thing to do. The negative thoughts still stirred my emotions, but I pushed them down into the deep recesses of my soul.

But my anger refused to be tamed. Tamping down the other emotions allowed it to rise up and fill the void. I had so much pent-up anger with no one to take it out on. Jamie said when I found myself with this much anger, I needed to find a bad guy to kill.

An obvious target for my wrath came to mind.

The prince, first and foremost.

All of this was his fault. My rage burned for revenge.

The logical voice in my head reminded me of the need for caution. The prudent thing to do would be to meet up with A-Rad and get out of the country as fast as possible. But the urge was strong to hunt down the prince like a dog and kill him.

My heart ached for the girls in the submarine. My desire for revenge burned bright. Tears welled up in my eyes just thinking about it. They threatened to spill over and mix with the spray of the waves that also wet my face. I roughly brushed them all away with my free hand.

I now knew why things were so emotionally tough on Jamie. She would often take weeks off from missions to be alone. To get away from the stress of running sex trafficking operations for her own sanity.

She had wanted to have a family, and I wondered if she left the trafficking world just in time. Before it became too much.

I thought about the pain and trauma I had already experienced in such a short time. Only a fraction of the pain Jamie saw and went through, and it already seemed like too much.

Losing those girls on the submarine had hit me hard. How did I live with it? The only way would be if I killed the prince. Even that wouldn't bring the girls back, but at least some good could come out of it.

I reminded myself that it wasn't my fault.

Jamie's voice inside my head kept nagging at me not to blame myself or second guess my decisions. My will was strong and pushed back.

Regardless of what Brad said, I should not have left the girls there. If I had known the prince was going to send them to an unspeakable death at the bottom of the ocean, I never would have turned myself in.

Knowing that, I didn't think I could walk away. A-Rad might insist we leave the country, but I'd push back harder. The thought of that evil prince becoming the king of Norway and continuing his atrocities against innocent women was too much for me to bear.

I could hear A-Rad's arguments raging in my head. "Killing the prince will be next to impossible. Security will be tighter than ever."

My mind was made up. I had to try. With or without him.

"Your career with the CIA will be ruined."

It probably already was.

That was the least of my worries, although it probably should've been foremost in my mind along with escaping. Killing the prince would be the final nail in the coffin of my short-lived stint with the CIA, but it had to be done.

"You'll have to live the rest of your life on the run," I could hear A-Rad arguing.

I would try to convince him to let me go alone. He had so much more goodwill built up with Alex, Jamie, and the CIA that he could withstand the fallback. I had some, but nothing like what he had.

He could even blame me if he wanted. After all, I was the mission leader.

I forced myself to think about something else. My negative thoughts immediately turned to the yacht which wasn't what I wanted.

I had a lot of anger for what Alex and Bond did, what I considered a betrayal, even though I tried to make myself understand it. It angered me to think that they'd come all the way to Norway just to steal the boat. Even if it was worth a half a billion dollars.

It seemed out of character for Alex. He didn't care about money. They had billions and more than one yacht.

Did they come to rescue us?

No!

They didn't stop for me. Why not? They obviously knew I was there. How hard would it have been to stop and pick me up?

I could hear A-Rad in my head defending them.

"The situation is too hot. The guards in the boats would have seen them pick you up and that'd put Bond and Alex in the middle of this mess."

My thoughts went to a darker place.

"If it had been you, A-Rad, they would've stopped."

Bond would advise Alex and tell him to keep going. He was a big picture guy and practical in that way. Above all else, a master strategist who once worked for MI6, the British CIA, and was one of the best spies in the world according to Jamie.

I had witnessed his skills firsthand on countless missions. As far as spycraft was concerned, Bond was the best of us. I learned so much running missions with him. Jamie taught me most of what I knew, but Bond taught me some things I didn't know. He was an expert at surveillance, losing a tail, planning meets.

Jamie had recruited him away from British intelligence when he said he was looking for a change. Ironic that a British agent was named Bond. I didn't know if that was his real name or a nickname. I didn't even know his first name.

I didn't think Colonel was on the yacht. He would never advise Alex to leave me behind.

He was another member of the AJAX team, an Air Force colonel who ran more missions in Afghanistan than any other man alive. His role in AJAX was to plan missions and he was an expert at infiltrating compounds, developing strategic battle plans, and bringing to bear the resources necessary to execute them.

With his experience on the battlefield, I don't think he'd ever leave anyone behind. Sitting around telling war stories, I'd heard him say as much.

Colonel would never leave A-Rad behind for sure. That's why I knew he wasn't on the yacht.

The two of them had worked together for years, flying planes into hurricanes to collect data. That's how Jamie met them. She was on a mission to the Caribbean. Some girls were kidnapped on their senior high trips and Jamie went to rescue them. The girls were being held in Cuba.

The problem for Jamie was that a hurricane was in the Caribbean headed straight for Cuba. Jamie got the not-so-bright idea to parachute into the eye of the hurricane to rescue the girls. She convinced A-Rad and the Colonel to fly her into the hurricane and go along with her crazy but daring plan.

Colonel even parachuted with her. He wouldn't let her go alone. After successfully rescuing the girls, Jamie's legend in the CIA circles grew immensely after that almost unbelievable stunt.

Jamie convinced Colonel and A-Rad to join AJAX and the core of the team was formed. The five of them, Alex, Jamie, Colonel, A-Rad, and Bond had been together for years and had been in more dangerous situations than any of them could count.

They'd never leave each other behind and I had believed that I was part of that circle as well.

But I saw it with my own eyes. They *did* abandon me. For whatever reason.

Or did they? I didn't actually see Bond or Alex on the yacht.

They were there.

Who else would steal the yacht? And I was convinced Bond was the one who took the two shots.

So why didn't they help me?

Fury boiled inside of me as I struggled to keep my thoughts in check. The betrayal and abandonment from the people I thought were my friends gnawed at my mind like a vicious disease.

If I did see Bond again, he'd argue that he did help me. He shot out the motors on the boats so I could get away.

But they didn't stop and rescue me. I couldn't help but think that if it had been A-Rad on the rubber raft, they would've stopped for him. Without question.

My thoughts spiraled out of control. The lights of the town were closer, but I was only about halfway there. If I continued to let my thoughts run rampant, no telling what I could make myself believe by the time I got there.

A sickening realization struck me like a lightning bolt from a storm cloud.

What if they weren't helping me at all?

They needed to put those two guard boats out of commission so they could escape with the yacht. The thought sent an anger raging inside of me with the power of the hurricane in the Caribbean that Jamie dared parachute into.

The worst twisted thought of all popped into my head and sent a pain through my body with the intensity of a heart attack.

What if they had rescued A-Rad and he was on the yacht?

13

By the time I reached the small village across the sea, I was thinking more clearly and had come to the realization that Alex and Bond not stopping to pick me up in their yacht was the best thing. If I'd ended up on that boat, there's no way Alex would have dropped me off in Oslo. He was in a race to get the yacht into international waters and as far away from Norway as possible.

The nearest location he could have dropped me was in England. Even then, I could picture him insisting on sailing all the way to his private island near Aruba before stopping. If that had happened, it would've taken me weeks to make my way back to Norway to meet A-Rad at the tiger statue.

Even if he had made a detour to England, it would've taken days for me to reach Oslo and the trek back would've been filled with peril. The Norwegian authorities were obviously looking for me. Taking a plane was out of the question and all the other entry points would be monitored closely.

Once I was on dry land, I sunk my small boat by the dock where I landed, not willing to leave a trail the authorities could follow. Then I quickly made my way into the shadows. My spirits buoyed when I saw vehicles and reasonably maintained roads providing an escape route to the outside world. Having already determined that the only way to get to Oslo was to steal a car or bum a ride. While I preferred to steal a car, I didn't want to harm an innocent person, so I set out looking for other alternatives.

In the heart of the village was a truck stop advertised as the last stop before the backcountry. There I found a trucker who said he was headed to Oslo and was willing to give me a ride. More than willing. As soon as he saw me and I asked him for a ride, his eyes lit up like a Christmas tree in downtown New York City.

While he looked me up and down in a flirty sort of way, he seemed harmless. I didn't feel threatened by his intentions, since I had my two guns in my backpack and the ability to kill him a hundred different ways with my hands. Had he been there, A-Rod might've knocked the lustfulness off his face in a jealous rage, but I'd put up with about anything to get to Oslo, as long as the man didn't put any actions behind his thoughts.

We boarded his newish and fairly comfortable eighteen-wheeler and left right away. Something I was thankful for. I couldn't wait to get out of there. The playful banter continued, and I participated to a limited extent. Eventually, he must've realized that hitting on me wasn't going to get him anywhere, because he turned the conversation to small talk and started asking personal questions.

I almost preferred the flirting. Probing questions like my name and where I was from made me uncomfortable. All I could do was feed him a bunch of lies and turn the questions back on him.

What I really wanted to do was sleep. Having to keep all my lies straight took a lot of mental energy I didn't have. When he finally exhausted that line of inquiry, he shut up for the first time and I started to relax a little.

My jaw dropped in disbelief when, about an hour into our journey, he blurted out, "Did you hear about the terrorist attack?"

Could he be talking about my confrontation with the prince on the submarine?

My head was racing trying to calculate the ramifications if he was.

That's not possible.

"No." I said with more of a puppy's bark than a reply when I realized I was taking too long to answer.

"Have you been living under a rock?" he asked.

I was fully awake now.

"I've been camping in the backcountry for the last two weeks," I said begrudgingly.

"Where's all your gear?" he sneered in a tone that suggested he didn't believe me.

Fortunately, we were in the middle of nowhere in the dead of night and he couldn't see my angry reaction. The only illumination were the headlights reflecting off the road and into the cab and the dim lights on his dashboard.

"I went with a friend. It's her stuff. It's back at her house," I said defensively.

"Do you think that's a good idea?" he asked.

"Is what a good idea?"

"Two girls out in the wilderness alone? You can get yourself in a lot of trouble out there."

He didn't know the half of it.

Three times over the last twenty-four hours, I had been in grave danger. My pride wanted me to lash out with bravado and tell him I could take care of myself and didn't appreciate the insinuation. Instead, I changed the subject back to the question burning the tip of my tongue.

"What was this terr ... terrorist attack you were talking about?" I struggled to get the word terrorist past my lips.

"It's all anyone is talking about. It's all over the news," he said.

My heart pounded in my chest like a raging drumbeat. So loud, I'm surprised he couldn't hear it. As panic pulsed through my veins, I could picture my face plastered on the television screen by every news station.

Calm down.

The trucker hadn't given me any indication that he recognized me, so I dismissed the feeling that he knew who I was and was plotting to turn me in.

I took a deep breath and exhaled it quietly.

Doing a quick calculation in my head, I deduced that the authorities couldn't have circulated my picture or description that quickly. At least not to the general public. If the trucker was talking about the attack on the prince, he'd have no way of knowing that I was involved.

"Tell me about it," I said through gritted teeth, trying to sound casual so as not to raise any alarm bells.

"Two terrorists tried to assassinate the Crown Prince," he said, sending a surge of adrenaline through my body at the mention of the prince's name.

The jolt turned to white-hot anger.

How dare they label me a terrorist? *I'm the good guy!*

I wish we had killed the prince, was what I really wanted to say, but stopped myself.

"Tell me what happened," I said, more calmly than I felt on the inside.

"The prince was on a sightseeing tour in the Lofoten Archipelago. His boat was attacked and six of his guards were killed. He escaped."

"How did he escape?"

"He jumped off the boat and swam to an island where he hid."

I almost laughed out loud.

"Oh, he did, did he?"

That liar.

Focus.

"What happened to the two terrorists?" I asked.

"They're dead."

My heart sank to the bottom of my chest as questions raged in my head. Was A-Rad dead? Did they think I was dead? Was it all propaganda? Did it mean they wouldn't be looking for us?

I needed more answers. "How did the terrorists die?"

"Another boat arrived on the scene and killed them as they tried to escape in their boat. The boat sank to the bottom of the ocean and hasn't been recovered."

"Ahh."

Propaganda.

The prince's cunning mind concocted a clever cover-up story to hide his heinous crime. With no mention of the submarine or the dead girls who were now entombed at the bottom of the ocean, the public was made to believe whatever he wanted them to think.

Why am I not surprised?

As if I could be any more repulsed by this man.

But in reality, his actions had inadvertently done me a favor. There'd be no all-points bulletin. If a picture of me was being circulated, it'd be discreetly. How could they tell the public that the two supposed "terrorists" were dead, then immediately plaster my face on every television screen urging people to be on the lookout for me? They wouldn't want to give away any information about me until I was in their custody, and they were certain of my identity.

I felt like a pawn in their twisted game, but they didn't know that I was playing chess, and they were playing checkers. For now, the prince was winning, but it wasn't that simple. It wouldn't always be that way. Not if I could do anything about it. They had no idea what I was capable of.

I chuckled under my breath.

The prince was probably shaking in his royal boots. I knew about the dead girls and that he had kidnapped and murdered them. He'd be as anxious as a mouse in a cage with a snake until I was neutralized. I was the definition of a loose end.

They'd definitely be looking for me, but discreetly, constantly fearing that I might find a way to expose their dark secrets. The story released to the news media was more confirmation that I had escaped in the nick of time and that they never intended to let me live.

I said a quick prayer that A-Rad was safe and had escaped as well.

"This is the biggest thing that's happened in Norway in a while," the trucker said, bringing my thoughts back to reality. "The whole city is on high alert."

"I suppose it would be big news."

"The news agencies are on the story like flies on moose poop."

"I saw a lot of that hiking in the backcountry," I said with a nervous chuckle, trying to lighten the mood somewhat.

He nodded. "It's the worst terrorist attack in twenty years," he said, maintaining his serious tone.

"What happened twenty years ago?" I asked, even though I knew the answer. I'd rather have him talking about that incident than what happened yesterday.

"In September of that year ... I believe it was September right after school started."

It was, but whatever.

"A far-right extremist exploded a car bomb in Oslo near the royal palace."

I was well aware of the devastating events of that day. The explosion killed eighteen people and injured a hundred or more, many severely. All this information was detailed in the CIA report given to me for this mission.

"The terrorist was a crazy man," the trucker continued somewhat excitedly. "Two hours later, he showed up at a school in a police uniform and pretended to be there to protect the kids. Instead, he opened fire and killed a bunch of them."

The trucker's words added a layer to the horror that before had only been words on paper to me. I read that the gunman killed nearly a hundred kids and teachers and injured dozens of innocent souls. A horrendous crime. It seemed more real to me now to hear the trucker describe it with emotion.

"Too bad the two terrorists who attacked the prince are dead," he said, referring back to yesterday's incident. "I'd like to get my hands on them."

The words dripped with bitterness. The trucker uttered an expletive directed at the gunmen, not realizing it was directed toward me. How ironic that he was aiding and abetting one of those terrorists by giving me a ride to Oslo. A few minutes ago, he wanted to get his hands on me for different reasons.

While that thought brought a smile to my face, at the same time, it sickened me that I was being compared to such a despicable monster as the gunman who killed children. I wanted to defend my actions against the prince but had to bite my tongue. The trucker could never know my identity or connection to the event for obvious reasons. I wouldn't kill him. He was an innocent person, and seemed like a nice enough guy, but the worst possible scenario was if he somehow began to suspect my involvement.

I didn't know what I'd do. Probably just flee. The thought of leaving the comfort of the truck and facing the elements on the run again made me grimace inside. I'd try to avoid that at all costs.

"Among the dead was a cousin of Norway's crown prince at the time, now the king," he added.

I let out a sound of acknowledgement. That information was in the report. It now made sense why our attack on the prince evoked those memories and caused such nationwide terror.

"An attack on the royal family is an attack on all Norwegians," he said bitterly. "They say there may be more of them out there."

He looked over at me. "You should be careful. Hitching rides with strangers is a dangerous business. You never know who you might be riding with. There's a lot of evil people out there. My country is at war now and if the prince is not safe, who is?"

I reminded myself not to take offense at his patriotism or the reference to evil people unknowingly directed at me. After all, he didn't have all the facts. I wished I could explain to him how corrupt the royal family truly was.

How could I without him being suspicious? And who was I to talk? I was an American. I knew all too well that many influential figures in the American government were just as corrupt. Maybe more so.

A few years before I joined the CIA, the CIA director had gone after Alex and Jamie and almost succeeded in stealing all their assets. He even tried to have them killed and they were arrested. They eventually turned the tables on him, and he was the one in jail, but not before he almost succeeded in destroying their lives.

Jamie and I had often talked about how we wished we were allowed to operate on US soil. We would turn our skills on the bad guys and clean up the corruption.

"Things will never be the same in Norway after yesterday," he said with resignation in his voice.

"It's horrible," I mumbled.

"Six guards are dead," he said. "Too bad they didn't capture the two terrorists so we could put them on trial and see their faces."

"Yeah. Too bad."

It gave me an idea.

"When is the funeral for the six guards? Are they going to have a service?"

"Yes. Sometime next week. But it won't be like any other funeral. The king has declared a national day of mourning. The entire city of Oslo will come to a standstill. Schools and businesses will close. That's why I'm in a race to get to Oslo and drop off my load and get out of there."

My heart burst with excitement. The Crown Prince himself would almost certainly be at the funeral. It'd be in a public place.

I could picture it now.

The prince, surrounded by security. Standing for the procession in the street for the dead guards. Facing the grieving crowd.

This would be my opportunity. The perfect time and place. My best chance to kill the prince.

14

Oslo, Norway
The next day

The following morning, I arrived in Oslo too late to meet with A-Rad at the tiger statue but early enough to conduct some much-needed surveillance. An ambitious plan to kill the prince had formed in my mind. Jamie would probably call it a "crazy" plan, but I'd seen her do things that were even more insane over the years.

As I surveyed the downtown area of the city and saw the heavy level of security, I realized that "idiotic" would be a better word for my plan. Military personnel armed with machine guns were stationed at every major intersection and convoys of soldiers roamed the streets in various military vehicles. I made sure to steer clear of those areas as much as possible while keeping a close watch when I got near enough to observe their activities.

Unlike London, with its extensive camera surveillance system on every corner, Oslo cameras weren't stationary and only used for random controlled temporary checkpoints. I only saw one and it didn't look operational, but I noticed crews preparing to install some along what I had learned was the funeral procession route.

The police were out in force as well. Norway had a long-standing policy that police were to be unarmed with their weapons stored in their police car trunks under lock and key. That policy had obviously been lifted since everyone I saw in blue shirts and gray pants with emblems on their sleeves were carrying standard issue German Heckler &

Koch MP5 submachine guns with Heckler & Koch P30 semi-automatic pistols on their hips. Even SWAT teams, which normally only came out as needed, were occasionally present and carried Diemaco C8 assault rifles.

Jamie used to joke that automatic weapons were overrated, claiming that a well-placed shot from a single bullet was all it took to kill a man. "Only people who don't know how to shoot need automatic weapons," she had quipped with a mix of seriousness and humor.

We had our share of automatic weapons and were well trained in them, but I knew what she meant. She went on to say, "A bullet is a terrible thing to waste. Don't fire a shot unless you're certain you'll hit your target."

"What do I do if there are too many targets to hit them all?" I asked.

"Ask yourself why you are even in that situation and figure out how to get away from it as quickly as possible without provoking a gunfight."

I'm sure that's what she'd say now. She'd scold me for even thinking about going down this point-of-no-return road.

"Aren't you in enough trouble?" I heard her say in my head. "Don't be a fool. Meet A-Rad and get out of Oslo. Regroup. Live to fight another day."

"I don't give up that easily," I muttered under my breath. "The mission isn't over."

In reality, I'm not sure Jamie would give up either, but I could see her arguing for it. What was driving me was what drove her all those years. An obsessive resolve to figure out how to finish what she started. Even against overwhelming odds. It's what made her the best in the world.

The debate raged but took a different turn. "The mission was to save the girls," I heard her say with emphasis in my head. "That's not possible now."

"I can't let those young girls die in vain," I retorted.

"The prince isn't worth it. This is a suicide mission."

But the obsessive desire to kill the prince was already consuming me, gripping my senses and clouding my judgment. The impulse for revenge burned hotter than any rational thought.

Of course, Jamie was right. Security was simply too tight. The plan too risky. It'd be nearly impossible to get close enough to the prince to get off a shot. Even if I could, I didn't have a clear way to escape afterward. I didn't even know if the prince would be at the funeral.

The purpose of surveillance was to get information, so I could make an intelligent decision. Everything inside of me screamed that the plan wouldn't work.

What good does it do to gather intelligence if you ignore it?

If I don't go through with it, the prince will get away with everything. I can't let that happen.

The conflicting thoughts tore at my sanity, leaving me feeling defeated and trapped. The prince had already won in so many ways. If I quit now, he'd go about living his pampered royal life. It already felt like I was a girl on the run. Without a home. The CIA wouldn't take me back. More than likely, I was too hot for AJAX to handle as well. I was a liability to them now.

What if A-Rad was dead? Then I'd really be all alone.

I couldn't let my mind go there. I'd sink into a depression if I did.

The mood of the city only added fuel to the fire of my already frayed emotions. As the trucker who had given me a ride to Oslo mentioned, the entire city was consumed by the so-called terrorist attack on the royal family, and he wasn't exaggerating.

I couldn't shake off the weight of grief and tension in the air.

The streets were filled with people on edge. Unsure how to act. The government had warned of possibly more attacks. Norway had one of the lowest murder rates in the world. Some of the locals walked around like they were in a state of shock. Unbelief that their peaceful city had been turned into a war zone.

A sea of guilt flooded my soul even though I knew it wasn't my fault.

Along with the collective fear etched on the faces of most of the residents was the obvious grief for the dead royal guards that seemed to be on everyone's minds. Makeshift memorials lined the streets. Occasionally I saw someone wiping away tears.

It brought tears to my eyes. Tears mixed with my own grief and anger, but for different reasons. I had my own losses to deal with, and I knew things they didn't know. When I saw people crying, I wanted to tell them what those six guards were doing when we killed them.

"They were guarding kidnapped girls! Holding them prisoner!"

"For your beloved prince!"

"He's a murderer!"

How dare they cry for such despicable individuals?

My heart burned with rage at the unfairness as I thought about their misplaced sympathy. I felt even more hopeless when I realized that they wouldn't believe me even if I did tell them. My words had no meaning without solid proof.

Thinking about it disgusted me and made me angry that they considered me the bad guy. I was in hiding. The one who had to watch my every step, avoiding the police and staying out of sight. Later that night, I'd have to check into a seedy motel in a dangerous part of town.

The only thing that helped me keep from sinking into a depression was focusing on the surveillance, so I poured myself into the effort. Since preparations for the funerals had already started, it made my movements around the city more difficult. Certain roads were already closed around the palace and along the funeral procession route.

It probably wasn't a good idea to show my face around the palace, but I couldn't resist. I had to see it for myself. Not that I could see it. Normally, people could walk the path to the front of the palace and congregate around the Karl Johan monument, but two police cars and three armed policemen in blue shirts blocked the way.

That's the closest I came to anyone noticing me. They saw me loitering and commanded me to move on. I tried to look inconspicuous. My red hair was tucked under a baseball cap, and I wore oversized sunglasses, too big for my face, but perfect for evading facial recognition software.

To blend in, I had stopped at a shop and purchased a set of clothes that would help me go unnoticed. Black leggings and sneakers for running if the need arose and a gray university sweatshirt with a hood, which I didn't put over my head. The sun beat down on me and a hoodie would seem out of place, which was why I went with the baseball cap.

I couldn't be too careful. Soldiers would be on the lookout for anything suspicious. The baggie sweatshirt also concealed the weapon tucked in my waistband and I was thankful the policemen didn't conduct a search of me. They mostly ignored me since I looked like one of thousands of University of Oslo students.

After leaving the royal palace, I made my way to the tiger statue, just in case A-Rad had the same idea and was surveilling the area. I didn't see him. If he had seen me, he would've made contact. I'd do the same. No reason to wait until tomorrow when we could meet now.

After scouting the location for a few minutes, it confirmed that the spot was a good and a bad choice. Good because there were many people around and I could easily blend in. Also good in that it had multiple ingresses and egresses, so escaping out of the square was easier and there weren't any places to get trapped.

Bad because it was right across from the central train station where there was a heavy security presence. If the authorities were looking for me, that'd be one of the first places they'd search. Figuring I would try and get out of the country as quickly as possible.

To that extent, I had an advantage. I had no intention of leaving. A-Rad might have a different view, but I was determined to extract revenge on the prince whatever the cost. A risk I was willing to take.

I hung out at the tiger statue for the rest of the afternoon. Somehow it made me feel close to A-Rad. It gave me hope. As if my presence could will him to show up. The tiger statue was a central point for tourists and the area was bustling. The city had earned the nickname The Tiger City. First used by a Norwegian poet in his poem Sidste Sang dating back to the 1800's where he described a fight between a horse and a tiger.

That's all I knew about the statue and wasn't interested in learning more. In different circumstances, I might've been curious to explore a new city and see its sights. For now, I was focused on the task at hand. Staying under the radar so I could meet A-Rad at four the next morning. The worst possible scenario would be getting caught before I had the chance to make contact with him.

Exhaustion was catching up to me quickly. It had been over thirty-six hours since I last slept. A couple of energy drinks and two hot dogs provided a temporary boost, but that's all it was. Temporary.

Getting bored, I found a map with some articles about Oslo. I sat in the sun and read it. I learned that a hot dog was the local food of choice for most Norwegians. The average Norwegian ate a hundred hot dogs a year.

Mine were made from boiled sausages wrapped in a falafel-like potato lompe and I had to admit they were tasty. I went back for two more when my stomach growled after a couple of hours.

As the sun dipped below the horizon, it cast elongated shadows from the tall buildings onto the streets of Oslo. The cooler weather was welcomed but the streets emptied, which made my situation more precarious. My senses sharpened by the adrenaline coursing through my veins, and I felt the vulnerability.

Oslo's chilly night air kissed my skin, a sharp contrast to the heat building within my chest when I went back to take one last look at the well-lit royal palace from a higher vantage point in the city.

I didn't know if the prince was there, but the rage burned like fire again seeing where he lived. Part of me wanted to burst into the palace right then, guns blazing, and get it over with. Our team had infiltrated more secure places than even the royal palace.

But that was the problem that hit me between the eyes.

There was no team.

For the first time in my career, I felt completely alone.

I'd been on solo missions before, and it never bothered me until now. This time was different. In the past, I was never really alone. I could pick up the phone at any time and call for support.

Before, I could phone Alex and he'd have the layout of the royal palace for me within minutes. Brad would know if the prince was even in the palace. If so, I could call the Colonel and he'd have an infiltration plan in place within a few hours.

If I needed the cavalry, A-Rad, Bond, Jamie, Alex, and/or Colonel would be there for me in no time and would storm the palace with me. Or if that wasn't feasible, help me come up with a better plan.

Such as Bond taking up a position in a building along the funeral procession route and taking a long-range sniper shot at the prince. Similar to the one he took out in the sea that helped me escape from the boat.

Brad would handle the extraction and we'd be out of Oslo before the authorities knew what had happened. My heart plummeted to the bottom of my chest as I came to the painful realization that those days were probably over.

I was on my own.

I might not even have A-Rad to help me. I wouldn't know until four the next morning. If he didn't show, I wouldn't know until the morning after that. Or the next morning . . .

If he didn't come, how long would I keep going to the tiger statue before I gave up hope?

Tears welled up in my eyes when I realized that I had no idea how to make that decision and dreaded the possibility that it might come to that.

For my own sanity, I had to get away from the city and find a place to get some sleep and decompress. I found the grimiest motel in the worst part of town. One that took cash. The musty smell of decay, stale cigarettes, and body odor greeted me as I stepped inside the room.

The carpet crunched under my feet with each grimacing step. With a shudder, I pulled back the stained bedspread and climbed onto the mattress fully clothed.

With my gun next to my pillow.

Some operatives slept in a closet in case someone tried to take them out in their sleep. I'd rather endure a gunfight than sleep with whatever creatures inhabited the closet.

Even with the conditions, my eyes slammed shut and I succumbed immediately to the exhaustion. The last image in my head was the submarine as I watched it plunge into the murky depths of the ocean. My mind followed it down to the bottom of the sea until darkness enveloped it and me as I fell asleep.

When I woke up at two in the morning, a surge of hope greeted me. It was electric anticipation. I could feel my insides buzzing like a live electrical wire.

A new dawn of possibilities would replace the despair of yesterday.

Today, I would get to see A-Rad. And everything would be better.

15

Jamie would be proud of me. The fact that I woke up at two in the morning to give myself time for SDR. Which stood for surveillance detection route. It's the method CIA operatives used to detect potential surveillance activities and find out if someone was following you.

It usually involved varying one's travel patterns. In my instance, I did take a different route back to the tiger statue than what I took the night before, but mostly I was using evasive tactics to flush out a tail and make sure I wasn't leading any threats to A-Rad.

While I didn't think anyone was following me, I really didn't know what capabilities the Norwegian military or intelligence services had at their disposal. The peaceful country wouldn't have nearly the resources that most of the bad actors we dealt with had. The Russians, North Koreans, Iran, China, any other number of other countries that funded terrorist activities put billions of dollars into their intelligence operations and were formidable.

Even the United States could be considered a threat to me. I wouldn't put it past the CIA to at least be looking for me. If for no other reason than to track my movements. If I wanted to get paranoid, they might track me to take me out and cover their tracks. Make sure I didn't talk or do something stupid like kill the prince.

If Jamie or Alex were following me, I'd never detect it. They were just too good. Anyone else, I felt fairly certain I could flush them out. Now an hour into the endeavor and I hadn't seen anything. I was safe for the moment. I doubted anyone, even the CIA, had a clue where I was.

Still, I was being overly cautious. Jamie spent a lot of time training me on how to go dark. She'd be upset if I got caught this quickly. Which was why I was going to the effort to do surveillance detection. At least I was doing something right in her eyes.

Why was that so important to me?

Since the day I met Jamie, I'd been trying to win her approval. Like a puppy dog trying to earn treats from a trainer. I thought I was past all that. That I was an equal.

Why did it feel like I had regressed?

What did she think of me now?

Was she utterly disappointed?

Disgusted?

Did she tell Alex, "I told you so." Alex was the one who first stood up for me. Jamie eventually came around and I earned her trust to the point that she brought me into AJAX, but it always felt precarious. Like I was one major mistake away from losing her trust completely.

Was this that mistake?

A sharp hurt stabbed at my heart. I worked so hard to get into the small circle of operatives who were the best of the best. I felt beyond special when they asked me to join them.

Was all that goodwill out the window now?

At least that morning I was taking precautions which would make Jamie happy. She said to do an SDR a hundred out of a hundred times when in the field.

"Even if you don't think you need to," she had admonished on more occasions than I could remember. "All it takes is not doing it one time and you die!"

I'd feel even more guilty if I didn't listen to her this time even if she didn't know it.

The night air was chilly but invigorating and I wasn't going to let my thoughts spoil my mood. The excitement inside of me was filled with adrenaline fueled from the excitement of getting to see A-Rad along with the briskness of the air which contributed to the energy pulsing through my veins like water through a fireman's hose.

I quickened my pace. I couldn't wait to meet A-Rad.

The darkness brought me back to reality. I had entered another bad area of town and most of the streetlights were not working and contributing to the eeriness. I kept my eyes peeled. Looking for anything suspicious. For some reason my senses had alerted me to danger even though I didn't see any.

Jamie said to trust those instincts.

"They saved my life on more than one occasion," she had said.

The streets were empty making my job easier. If someone was tailing me, I had made it more difficult for them. I wore a different outfit than what I wore yesterday. The university sweatshirt was in my backpack. Now I was wearing a black leather jacket and different shoes.

One mistake people made in spycraft was not changing their shoes. That's the first thing I looked for when I was searching for a tail. It's easy to change hairstyle, color, clothes, or jackets, or change your gait and demeanor. Most people forgot to change their shoes which were a dead giveaway.

My hair was in a ponytail. A different baseball cap from yesterday was in my backpack. I threw the other one away. I could change my hair within seconds. I could take off the scrunchie and let my hair relax down to my shoulders. I could pin it up. A barrette readily available in my backpack could pin my bangs to either side or part it in the center.

I could turn my jacket inside out and almost instantly be wearing an off white jacket.

I obviously didn't wear the same sunglasses from yesterday, but I did have a pair of reading glasses in my backpack that I could slip on in seconds.

And I wore different shoes. I wouldn't make that amateur mistake.

Jamie called disguising your appearance shapeshifting. I'd never heard the term until she used it in a conversation with Alex. We were on a mission preparing for the day. I sat at a kitchen table cleaning my gun. Alex was pacing around the room like a caged tiger, wanting to leave even though we were early. Colonel was going over the written plans. A-Rad was in front of the television chilling. Bond was on the phone with someone.

Jamie had changed her dress for the third time and Alex was annoyed.

"What are you doing?" Alex asked. "That's your third outfit. Choose one."

"I'm shapeshifting," she answered almost whimsically.

"What's shapeshifting?" he asked, semi-roughly.

"It's the ability to physically transform into another shape or form."

"Like a werewolf or vampire?" he asked.

Jamie laughed. "No, like octopuses."

The whole dialogue made me look up. I forced back a smile and pretended I wasn't listening to the conversation.

"Don't you mean octipi?" Alex asked, with a smug grin.

Jamie twisted her lips to the side in a disapproving manner. "No Alex. That's a mistake a lot of uneducated people make."

"I think octipi is right."

Alex looked over at me and grinned widely. I'd seen this kind of banter between them a hundred times. It's almost like it was their way of relieving the tension before a dangerous mission.

They did have a running argument about who was smarter. Alex was the foremost computer hacker in the world and when it came to computers, it didn't get any smarter than him. When it came to street smarts, Jamie was head and shoulders ahead of us all. Despite her bright naturally blonde hair, she surprisingly had a big vocabulary and book learning as well.

She was about to tell us why Alex was wrong. My money was on her being right.

"The word octopus doesn't come from a Latin word and doesn't have Latin endings," she said.

Alex asked the question that had popped into my mind. "Okay, I'll bite. What's the origin of the word?"

"I'm glad you asked," she said, as she slipped on her shoes. "Technically, octopus is a Greek word. The plural would be octopodes. But we're not Greek. We're English. So we use the English ending, octopuses."

"Thanks for the English lesson," he mumbled, as he checked his weapon for the umpteenth time.

"I'm going to make a scholar out of you yet."

"Hey! I'm already a scholar."

"Scholar *is* a Latin word. It means one who learns from a teacher. That's me. I'm the teacher, you are the pupil."

"Pupi," Alex said.

Jamie laughed as did I. "The plural of pupil is pupils," she said.

"I thought you said it was Latin."

"It is. But not all Latin plurals end in i."

"I'm confused," he said.

"Would you like me to unconfuse you?"

"No. I'd like you to finish getting dressed. Finish my shapeshifting."

"What does shapeshifting have to do with an octopus?" I asked, my curiosity piqued. "More importantly, what does it have to do with octopuses?"

"An octopus is an amazing creature," Jamie explained as she stood and walked over to the table. "It can change color, shape, and behavior to blend into the environment. It's how it protects itself from predators. When you're in the field, consider yourself an octopus. Constantly on the lookout for predators. With the ability to adapt at all times."

"I didn't know that about octopuses."

"A mimic octopus can even change its form to look like a predator. It can take the shape of a flounder, lionfish, or sea snake. So a predator thinks it's one of his own and won't eat it."

"Shut up!"

"I know!" Jamie went back into teaching mode. Something she rarely got out of. "You can learn a lot from the octopus, Kaley. You need to learn to think like the bad guys. Get in their heads and anticipate their every move. That'll put you a step ahead of them. When you're in the field with them, learn to adapt and change your appearance."

She flipped the ends of her hair. "I'm blonde. That sticks out in a crowd. A bad thing for a spy. We don't want anyone to notice us. You have red hair. The same problem. You need to constantly vary your appearance so you can go undetected."

"I'll try."

I always darkened the red when I went on a mission for that reason. To not stand out in a crowd. Jamie and I were both fairly attractive. Another disadvantage in the field. Men and women took second looks at an attractive person and remembered them.

It warmed my heart to think about those days when we were all together. The banter was constant, and I missed it. What I wouldn't give for another one of her lectures. I didn't appreciate her constant instructions at the time but did now.

The analogy of an octopus shapeshifting rang true in my mind at that moment. I could see what Jamie meant. I had blended into the nighttime, with my choice of black jacket, black leggings, and black shoes. Meeting at four in the morning was also a good idea. Someone would have a hard time following me in the dead of night. If I sensed a threat, I could disappear into the darkness, and they'd never find me.

I just had to make sure I didn't walk into a trap. I was careful around alleyways. Parked cars got my attention. A car drove past me then changed lanes for no reason. I watched it until it was out of sight, but recorded the make, model, and color in case I saw it again. If the same car drove past more than once, I'd really be suspicious.

I looked for anyone loitering. Leaning against a building or standing on a corner for no apparent purpose. I even gave a worker truck a second look when it passed by. It disappeared down the road without giving me any pause.

The only thing I saw that gave me the least bit of concern was an older man walking a dog. It seemed out of place at three in the morning. Especially for that neighborhood. Which didn't feel safe even though no one was around. He approached me and barely made eye contact.

I passed him without speaking and determined he wasn't a threat. He was cursing under his breath, which made me chuckle. He was annoyed that his dog had woken him to go out that early in the morning.

His shoes were also a clue. Slippers. I couldn't imagine someone tailing me and thinking to wear those.

About a half hour later, I was ready to head for the tiger, satisfied that no one was following me. Almost as soon as I made the decision, I abruptly slowed down before I even realized why. Something had caught my eye and my mind had processed a situation before I could recognize it.

A woman was standing at a bus stop on the other side of the street. About half a football field ahead of me. She looked like a working girl. At first, that's what I thought I had noticed. My training was to spot and rescue prostitutes and girls who were sex trafficked.

The acceleration of my heartbeat told me to take a closer look.

Something in the shadows had caught my eye. I spotted them when I got closer. Four men were hiding in close proximity to the bus stop. I had to squint to even make out the figures. Something had triggered their presence in my mind. Maybe a belt buckle caught the light and I saw a reflection out of the corner of my eye. Perhaps one of them moved slightly and I noticed it.

Regardless, it seemed odd. The men were eyeing the girl. Or at least it seemed like it. They weren't just loitering in the shadows. They were crouched down. Trying hard not to be seen.

Was the woman in danger?

Should I ignore the threat? At least warn her?

My instincts screamed at me to intervene. It's what I was trained to do. Protect girls from predators. Eliminate threats.

But what about A-Rad? I had to meet him in less than an hour.

16

The decision was made. The choice was clear. I had to help the woman in potential danger. If I missed A-Rad today, I could always meet him tomorrow morning at the same time.

It's how I was wired. It's what I trained all those years to do. My desire to rendezvous with A-Rad at the tiger had been sidelined at the unexpected sight of the woman being followed by four men.

The thought of waiting another day tore at my heart. Not knowing if A-Rad was dead or alive weighed heavily on my mind. That unanswered question threatened to consume me, but I pushed it aside.

With a silent set of angry words stuck in the back of my throat, I walked past the bus stop where the woman stood, and I continued down the road on the opposite side of the street until I was out of sight. Then I circled back to avoid being seen by the men.

Now I was the one lurking in the shadows, posing a potential threat to the goons who had no idea I was sneaking up on them from behind. My intention was to confront them and scare them away before the woman had a clue what was happening.

Moving closer, I got to within twenty feet and they still didn't notice me. From my vantage point, I could see the woman still standing at the bus stop wearing headphones completely oblivious to the danger.

Before I could act, I froze as a distant rumble filled the air, signaling the arrival of an approaching bus. The bus stopped and the door opened. The four men tensed, still in the dark, crouched like tigers about to lose a prey.

The woman disappeared inside the bus, and I let out a quiet sigh of relief, prepared to back away now. The woman was safely on the bus, and if I hurried, I still had time to make it to meet A-Rad. My heart lurched when the four men sprang out of the shadows and yelled for the bus driver to keep the door open.

No!

Indecision hit me. Should I follow them? Who were these men and why were they following the woman? What did they intend to do to her?

Did she still need me? Was she safe now that she had the bus driver to protect her? What if the men got off at her stop and attacked her?

But A-Rad!

I still have time to make it.

But could I live with myself not knowing what happened to her?

Before I had time to process the debate in my mind and come to a decision, the door to the bus started to close. I reacted and ran toward it, right before the driver was about to pull away. He saw me in time and opened the door.

I muttered an apology and inserted some money in the slot, not even knowing how much it cost or how much I put in. I made my way down the aisle to the back, carefully assessing my surroundings without it appearing like I was doing so.

The woman from the bus stop sat in the front on the second row. The four men were four rows behind her, joking among themselves. Acting like junior high kids who were up to some sort of mischief and enjoying it.

When they saw me board, their eyes collectively widened, and they looked me over. Probably wondering where I came from. Perhaps sizing me up to see if I was potential prey.

I dare you.

One of them even spoke to me.

"Hey beautiful. You can sit by me."

I didn't answer, causing his friends to tease him for being rejected. That brief interaction confirmed my suspicions. My instincts were right. They were up to no good. I could feel it. I sat down in the last row with my back to the rear, so no one was behind me.

The only other person on the bus was a woman dressed in hospital scrubs, either coming off a shift or going to one. The four men eyed her as well, but their main focus was on the other woman. What probably seemed like easier prey to them.

Maybe I should've sat down next to the guy when he offered. I could've taken their attention off her and onto me. I wanted them to come after me instead. I had a lot of pent-up anger I wouldn't mind taking out on them. Namely missing my meet with A-Rad.

The woman from the bus stop had her back to me but I had sized her up when I first entered the bus. She appeared to be in her late twenties, too thin as if she needed a good meal. She'd be considered above average attractive if not for the toll her lifestyle had taken on her appearance. I decided she was probably a stripper rather than a streetwalker.

She likely was following a set routine. Her ten-to-twelve-hour shift at the strip club was probably over at three. Time enough to walk to the bus stop and catch the same bus every night. The men targeting her may have been tracking her movements for some time or perhaps they spotted her by chance that night and decided to follow her.

Either way, I was certain they intended to attack her at some point. Probably not on the bus since people were around, but they might attack her when she got off or follow her home and force their way into her house.

I desperately hoped I was mistaken and the four men remained on the bus when she got off. If they did, I'd get off on the first stop and rush downtown praying every minute that A-Rad was there and stay fifteen minutes past four as we had agreed.

My stomach twisted into a knot and I felt a grimace come on my face when the bus turned away from downtown and started heading in the other direction, taking me further away from the tiger statue. Further away from A-Rad. The disappointment turned into shock when I saw the camera at the front of the bus next to the driver.

I'd been so focused on the woman and her potential attackers, that I hadn't noticed it when I boarded. I immediately tilted my head down and turned it to the right while grabbing the baseball cap out of my backpack. After slipping it on my head, I made sure to tuck my chin down so the camera wouldn't capture a clear image of me.

But deep down, I knew it was probably too late. My face was most likely already on the security footage and now I regretted getting involved in this situation more than ever. I'd worked so hard the day before trying to keep my face off any security cameras, but here I was, unknowingly walking straight into one.

Nothing I could do about it now. A few minutes ticked by in tense silence. The extra time gave me the chance to further size up the four men a few rows ahead of me. From their looks, I estimated their ages to be between twenty-two and twenty-six. All four were fairly well dressed and wore expensive, I presumed, stolen watches.

All were wearing black leather jackets similar to mine. Each had similar thick, dark hair, slicked back with an excessive amount of product, giving off a vibe of trying too hard to be cool.

I could loosely call them a gang as they also had identical dragon tattoos on the sides of their necks. Real gang members I had faced down in the past would laugh at me. They'd make quick work of these inexperienced ragamuffins, as I intended to do if the need arose.

These four were probably local boys from a poor part of town who came into some money by stealing from others or dealing drugs. While this probably wasn't their first time to target women, they clearly weren't experienced and had made numerous mistakes. One being that they didn't seem to care about being caught on the security camera.

At first, I thought maybe I had misjudged them based on that. Then I realized that the four did know enough to target a sex worker.

If assaulted, working girls didn't call the cops unless they were badly beaten or severely injured. No one would ever be searching security footage for the men's identities. The woman would take whatever they dished out and be thankful they hadn't killed her. Assuming they didn't.

Such a shame that she felt so powerless and might even feel like she deserved it. In my mind, this woman had already been violated and taken advantage of by multiple men today, even if it was consensual. The fact that she made the choice to engage in these acts didn't lessen the damage to her soul. Even if she couldn't see it now, she would someday, when the guilt and shame overwhelmed her emotions.

They already had.

How did I know? Jamie had taught me to read a woman's soul through her eyes. Prostitutes had a certain look. Trafficked women had an even deeper and more profound pain present in their eyes. There's no doubt that this woman was suffering and the four men wanted to inflict more damage upon her.

I wasn't judging her. I was there to help her.

Norway had weird prostitution laws. It was illegal to buy sex acts but not to sell them, so she wasn't doing anything the authorities would arrest her for. The purpose of the laws baffled me and I never really understood why countries didn't do more to stop the practice altogether. Even sex trafficking was a rarely investigated or prosecuted crime.

They made it too easy for her to stay in it. While I'd like to get her out of the profession altogether, that wasn't my main goal for tonight. If these four guys did try to assault her, I intended to teach them a lesson they would never forget. If I really wanted to, I could make it to where they could never do anything with a woman, consensual or otherwise, ever again.

A loud screeching sound filled the inside of the bus as the driver applied the brakes and brought the bus to a sudden stop. He looked back at the girl, like he already knew this was her stop, confirming she had followed this routine many times. She unknowingly made herself a target and needed to vary her routine for her own safety.

A hissing sound signaled the opening of the door. The woman in scrubs didn't move. The woman I was there to help was through the door with a slight wave of the hand in the bus driver's direction.

I held my breath as I waited to see what happened next. I tried to will the four men to keep their seats, but of course, they didn't. They stood in unison and rushed towards the door. That's when I knew for sure that I had made the right decision to get on the bus. Even if it did mean missing A-Rad for another day.

Rising quickly to my feet, my heart started to pound in my chest in anticipation of the inevitable confrontation. By the time I was off the bus, the woman was already twenty yards ahead of me and had a good head start on the four men.

Perhaps she had sensed the danger, as she was walking with more urgency. With determined steps, the men caught up to her, their intentions clear.

I trailed closely behind making no effort to conceal myself. The men were so fixated on the woman that they still hadn't noticed me. As I closed in, I caught a glimpse of something bulging from the back of their jackets, confirming my worst fear.

Guns!

They were armed and even more dangerous than I had initially thought.

Without hesitation, I reached for my weapon, in a cold calculated move I'd practiced thousands of times. My heart had slowed and was beating normally now. A strange phenomenon that few of us had. Jamie and I both grew calmer as the danger intensified.

I wasn't going to take any chances. The men could never get a chance to draw their weapons. The gun felt good in my hand and I was confident. My finger curled around the trigger as I prepared to dictate the terms of this encounter.

17

Ending this confrontation quickly by bringing my gun to the party was my plan. This wasn't the first time I had been in a situation like this where one wrong move and everything could go downhill fast if I let them pull their guns as well.

Still, something was holding me back. I needed confirmation of their intentions before any shots were fired. While I suspected I knew what they were there for, mistakes did happen.

What if they weren't predators at all? Did I really know for sure? All I knew was that they were acting strange. That wasn't a crime. I couldn't proclaim a death sentence on them and then find out they were the girl's cousins or merely her bodyguards. Or coincidentally lived in the neighborhood.

So I needed to let this play out.

Another worry had entered my mind. If I used my weapon, even if justified or necessary, it'd draw unwanted attention from the authorities. With all the heat already on me, I couldn't afford any more trouble.

I had to find a way to scare them off without causing them too much harm. The fact that the area was well-lit compared to where we had just come from only added to my frustration. If I had taken them out when we were still in the shadows before they ever got on the bus, it would've been better.

The woman abruptly stopped and spun around, her eyes meeting her attackers with fierce determination. "What do you want?" she said, her tone laced with defiance and fear. "Why are you following me?"

One of the men laughed mockingly. His intentions clear even with his back to me.

"Do what we say and we won't kill you," he sneered, his words dripping with malice, giving me all the confirmation I needed to do whatever it took to stop them. Even if it meant pulling my gun again and killing them.

The woman's eyes filled with fear. Her defiance vanished as she cowered back.

"Don't hurt me," she pleaded.

I stepped closer and she saw me for the first time. Her eyes widened and her lips twisted to the side when she saw me and my gun, which I was in the process of putting back in my waistband.

Her reaction caused one of the men to turn and look in my direction. I had stopped a couple of feet away from him. Close enough to spring into action immediately, but far enough away to give myself room to operate.

The element of surprise was gone, and I was going to have to figure out how to take all four of them out at once. They might think they had the upper hand, but I was still prepared to strike them with swift and ruthless force they wouldn't see coming. My resolve was especially firm after I heard the threats to the woman which fueled my determination to protect her even more. Regardless of the cost.

But I'd do it with the other weapons at my disposal. My hands and fists. My knees and elbows. The heels of my shoes. I could kill these men in a hundred different ways with my bare hands. Or leave them eating their food out of a straw for the next six months, if I wanted to show them mercy and didn't kill them.

My plan of attack was already mapped out. The one talking would feel the full weight of my palm driving his nose into his brain. How far depended on how angry he made me. Right now, I was so furious that he had threatened to kill the girl and he made me miss A-Rad, that I might not hold back at all.

The guy to my right would be next. The heel of my right foot would deliver a devastating strike to his groin or stomach. Perhaps a crippling blow to the shin if I needed to pivot quickly to take out the other two threats to my left.

Those two would be the most problematic. I'd have to act quickly. The closest one would take an elbow to the head. The other would be disabled with a swift kick from my other leg to a vital area. I hadn't decided which one.

At least that's how I had pictured it happening in my mind. Of course, in the heat of the moment, the order might be different depending on what was demanded. A different part of my body might be used. The result would be the same, which was all that mattered.

It rarely happened the way I envisioned it, but somehow I knew what to do when the time came to act. When faced with multiple attackers, my actions were driven purely by instinct. The men would be writhing on the ground before I even realized all of what I had done to them.

Before I could make a move, the leader spoke up. "Hey. I saw you on the bus. What do you want?" he snarled, trying to sound menacing.

"I think the lady asked you that question first." I gestured at the woman, hoping they'd look toward her. If they did, I'd take the initiative while they were distracted and recapture the element of surprise.

The leader chuckled but didn't look back at the woman who was frozen in place from the fear. He kept his eyes warily on me, trying to determine if I was a threat.

"Her? Lady? Haha. She's a two-bit whore. She's no lady."

"Neither am I," I said roughly. "And if I were you, I'd walk away while you still can."

Jamie told me to avoid confrontations whenever possible, especially when guns were involved. A lot could happen. An errant or lucky shot could kill the woman or me just as surely as a skillfully fired one.

The best thing would be if the men would walk away, but I didn't see that happening. And deep down, I knew that even if they tried to leave, I wouldn't let them. What would prevent them from coming after the woman tomorrow night? Or any other night? I wouldn't be there to protect her. I couldn't risk it.

"You're the one who should walk away. This ain't none of your business," the leader said.

"I'm making it my business," I replied firmly.

The man on his right got a weird and lustful look on his face. "No TJ," he said. "Don't let her get away. This could be fun. The more the merrier. Two birds with one stone. I'll take her first. You can have the other one."

As he finished his sentence, he reached out to touch me on the shoulder. I slapped his hand away. He's lucky I didn't break his wrist.

"You're right. She's feisty," TJ said. "I like a girl that fights back a little. We'll take turns. I want some of her too."

"You're about to get more of me than you bargained for."

I threw in the most derogatory Norwegian term I knew at the end of the sentence.

TJ's expression changed and his eyes glowed like blazing coals, suddenly filled with a hot rage. His fists balled. I'd struck a nerve, which was a good thing. An opponent acting out of emotion was less effective than one with the ability to channel those emotions into destructive and effective actions.

"You talk big for a girl," he said mockingly. "What are you going to do little darling? There are four of us and only one of you."

I'd heard enough. I didn't like him calling me a girl. Or darling. If A-Rad were here, he'd kill the man on the spot for calling me that.

My weight shifted to my left leg and I coiled the muscles in my right leg like a spring. Before any of the four of them could blink,

I lifted my right leg and propelled my foot with lightning speed into the groin of the man to my right, leading with the one-inch sharp heel which I wore for that reason.

The order had changed. The one who touched me deserved the first blow and I didn't hold back.

A sickening but satisfying cry of agony filled the air as the man doubled over in pain, clutching his crotch. Or what was left of it.

"Hey! What the . . . " TJ's shocked voice added to the chaos.

"I tried to warn you," I said. "You should've walked away. Now it's too late."

He had just witnessed the brutality I was capable of and was confused, which was a good thing for me. It caused him to hesitate, unsure what to do. He further compounded his mistake when he started to reach for his gun. A foolish decision. The back of the pants was a stupid place to keep a gun. It took too long to draw and his hands behind his back left the front of him exposed.

In a surge of my own fury, I lunged forward two steps and drove my palm into his face under the bridge of his nose. In the perfect spot and angle to do the maximum damage.

The impact caused a burst of bodily fluids as blood, cartilage, crushed bones, snot, and soft tissue flew through the air. I had anticipated the gruesome mixture and had taken two steps back immediately after the blow was delivered. I'd had the spray from a blow to the nose get in my mouth and in my nose before and was determined to never let it happen again.

It also allowed me to put myself in position to strike the other two men who were staring at their leader falling to the ground. The man's head cracked when it hit the sidewalk and made a satisfying sound that echoed through the air distracting them further.

The woman let out a scream that pierced through all the other sounds and overwhelmed them.

As I expected, the other two men also reached for their weapons, not learning a thing. Didn't they see how that worked out for their leader? With the precision Jamie taught me, I drew my gun again, having it in the firing position before they could get their arms around from behind their backs.

Pop. Pop.

The sound of gunfire shattered the night like a thunderclap.

The order didn't matter, but I fired one shot into the man on the left's heart, not even wasting a second to go for a headshot. Jamie said I was better shooting from left to right so that's what I went with unless I wanted to practice shooting the other way.

The second guy was dead with a bullet between his eyes before the first one hit the ground.

I looked over at the woman to make sure she was okay. She was frozen in place, staring back at me with wide eyes, her breaths coming in short gasps. She raised her hands in surrender like I was going to harm her.

"Get on out of here," I said. "You're safe now. Forget you ever saw me."

Without hesitation, she turned and ran without looking back, which was for the best considering what I was about to do.

Emotionless, I stood over the leader considering my next move. He was probably dead, but I put a bullet between his eyes anyway, even though I saw no movement or sign of life.

Under normal circumstances, I might've just left. But since two were already dead, I couldn't leave any potential witnesses alive. So I did what I had to do and killed the other one as well who was still writhing in pain on the ground and never saw it coming.

As I looked around the area for any potential witnesses, the magnitude of the disaster left me no time for regret or reflection. I had saved the girl but created a trail of destruction and death in my wake. The police would be called. There'd be an investigation.

Could it be traced back to me? The ramifications tried to invade my mind, but I pushed them back for another time.

With a swift turn, I broke into a full out sprint, the opposite direction from the woman. My heart pounded in my chest within seconds from the adrenaline and the sudden movement. The route led me back toward the bus stop and the main thoroughfare, but I changed course, wanting to stay on the side streets until I could get further away from the scene.

My feet pounded against the pavement as I kept up the sprint until I was a couple of blocks away. From there, I headed toward the main thoroughfare where I could catch a taxi and get away from the area as fast as possible. It's possible the authorities might question ride services in the area to see if they picked anyone up around that time, but it was a better alternative than trying to get away on foot.

Panic surged through me when I heard sirens blaring coming from the direction I was headed.

What?

How could the police have gotten here so fast?

My mind raced with possible explanations and worst-case scenarios. I came to the conclusion that the police presence was a coincidence. They weren't coming for me. They didn't have enough time to react this fast.

I had to know for sure, so I rushed to the main thoroughfare and hid behind a weathered fence just in time to see the patrol cars speed by. My stomach dropped when they pulled into the street where the dead bodies lay.

And then it hit me.

The bus driver.

He called them. He saw the men following the woman and worried for her safety.

I suddenly remembered my face on the security camera and my throat constricted into a muted scream of disbelief.

18

Jan Sealy had been a member of the Norwegian police force for more than thirty years and had risen to the rank of politiadvokat, the Norwegian word for "police lawyer." No other police community in the world had exactly that system. Essentially, he was both an investigator and a prosecutor with the primary authority to make charging decisions.

The unique system eliminated a layer of bureaucracy and effectively streamlined prosecutions, but it also gave immense power to the police lawyer. Some might argue too much power, but not in Sealy's mind. He relished seeing a case through from beginning to end. It allowed him to be at the crime scene shortly after the murder occurred and remain involved until the final verdict was delivered.

His focus was exclusively murders and he was well-known for solving and prosecuting them. He rarely lost a case. Not many crimes were left unsolved on his watch and very few people went free once they got in his crosshairs.

He voluntarily worked the night shift because that's when most of the murders in Oslo occurred. Although admittedly, murders in the city were rare. In the past eleven years, Oslo had an average of 23 to 33 murders a year, with 2013 being an anomaly when it reached the unusually high number of 44 for no apparent reason.

Sealy was amused when he heard some of the statistics coming out of America, like forty-one murders in a single weekend in Chicago. Why would any civilized country tolerate such high levels of violent crime? It defied all logic. It wouldn't if he was in charge there.

When the call came through about a quadruple homicide on the east side of town, he couldn't believe it. He thought there had to have been some kind of mistake. In all his years, he'd rarely investigated a homicide with multiple victims, and never more than two deceased at one time. Those were usually domestic violence or something like a murder-suicide.

He recalled an incident when two thugs in rival gangs shot each other. One was pronounced dead at the scene; the other died two weeks later. He considered that a multiple homicide, although he had nothing to really investigate and no one to prosecute.

Sealy sped to the scene of tonight's quadruple homicide with his blue light flashing on the dashboard of his unmarked car. As he stepped out of the vehicle and approached the scene, the senior officer was already walking toward him with a black notebook open in his right hand. He was pleased to see the proficiency of the local police who had secured the area.

The officer greeted him with a grim but professional tone. "We have four young men confirmed dead from gunshot wounds, sir," he said gravely. "My officers arrived shortly after the shooting occurred. Suspect fled the scene. I have a dozen men looking for her."

Sealy's right eyebrow raised in the air at the mention of a female suspect. The officer had also used the word "suspect" in the singular. Meaning one gunman or gunwoman in this case. He expected multiple assailants.

How did one person, especially a woman, kill four men? Were the men armed?

"The four deceased had weapons on the ground next to them," the officer continued, as if he were reading Sealy's thoughts. "A witness only heard four or five shots, so I don't believe any of the deceased had a chance to fire their weapons. One of the victims also sustained a severe injury to the face."

Sealy raised his hand in the air. "Hold that thought," he said. "Let me take a look at the scene myself first, so I can draw my own conclusions. Then I'll let you fill me in on the rest."

This had become his standard mode of operation. He preferred to form his own initial opinions without being influenced by others. Even if his impressions were wrong, he still wanted to draw his own conclusions, then fill in the blanks later.

He walked past the officer to the four bodies. Before he observed them, he scanned the surroundings in every direction. It was still dark out and the sun wouldn't be up for a couple of hours, so the conditions then were likely similar to when the incident occurred.

Typical residential neighborhood for that part of town. Modest homes. Not an area known for violence. Many of the residents in that area were elderly. He noticed an officer talking to an older woman across the street.

Was she the witness? Did she see the shooting as it happened? Did she give a description of the perpetrator, possibly a woman?

The officer had followed Sealy and must've noticed him eyeing the elderly woman because he said, "She was sitting on her porch and witnessed the whole thing. According to the witness, a woman got off a bus. Over there."

He pointed to the main thoroughfare about fifty yards away. Sealy could see the bus stop from where he stood. He looked back over at the elderly woman. If she was standing in front of her house and that was her porch, then she would have an even better view of it.

"The four men got off the bus as well and were walking behind her," the officer continued.

This time, Sealy didn't stop him from sharing his information. He obviously was anxious to keep going and Sealy might as well get it over with. Sealy wasn't sure if the man was trying to impress him or simply wanted to save him some time. Either way, the details were useful. Eyewitnesses to murders were rare. Especially in the middle of the night.

A scenario had already formed in Sealy's mind. He voiced it as much for his own benefit as that of the officer's.

"So four men exited a bus and began following a woman, possibly intending to harm her. She sensed it and turned to face them. She had a gun and threatened them with it. They pulled their own weapons and she shot them. Good for her. That sounds like self-defense. Case solved."

A nagging question clawed at his mind after a slight chuckle at his own quip. *Why did she flee?*

"That's not how it happened," the officer replied coldly.

"How do you know?"

"According to the witness, there was another woman. She had the gun."

Sealy's heart lurched in disbelief. That's the last thing he expected to come out of the officer's mouth.

"There was another woman?"

"Yes."

"Two women?" His voice rose with emphasis.

"Yes."

"Why didn't you say so?"

"I was getting to it."

"Go ahead." The words came out more like a demand than a request. But as the officer continued things made even less sense.

"The first woman exited the bus. Four men followed her. Shortly after, a second woman got off and followed the four men. With her gun drawn at their backs."

A number of questions swirled inside his mind. *Did the two women know each other? Were they working together? Why did both women flee the scene? Did they split up or are they still together?*

"The old woman said she ambushed them," the officer added.

"Did she shoot them in the back?" Sealy said. That would explain how one woman could kill four men. "Never mind. I'll see for myself."

He abruptly turned his back on the officer and looked at the bodies for the first time. All facing in the same direction. Feet towards the bus stop. Meaning they stopped walking at some point and turned around. Fell backwards when they were shot, which matched the eyewitness account.

The woman was behind them.

Though one man's face was battered and almost unrecognizable from a severe blow that looked to come right under the nose.

What?

"She had a gun but got close enough to deliver a blow to his face," Sealy muttered to himself.

The man on the sidewalk had a noticeable bullet wound between his eyes.

"This man wasn't shot from behind," Sealy said roughly to the officer.

"I didn't say he was."

"You said the men were ambushed by the woman following from behind."

"Perhaps 'ambushed' wasn't the right word to use."

"Did the witness say ambushed?"

"Not exactly."

This was why he always preferred to see the crime scene first.

"Just tell me what the witness said she saw."

"Not much more than I've already relayed to you. When she saw the gun, she went inside and called 112. That's when she heard the gunshots."

"So she didn't actually see the woman shoot them?"

"That's correct."

Sealy rubbed his forehead in frustration. He'd have to question the old woman himself.

"Did the witness get a good look at either of the women?"

"She said the first woman was dressed like a prostitute. She lived in the area. She'd seen her many times around that same time of night. She shouldn't be hard to find. My men are working on it now."

"Good."

"The witness also gave me a fairly good description of the one with the gun. Younger. Late teens, early twenties. Five six or seven. Athletic looking. Wearing a black leather jacket."

The four men lying on the ground were wearing black leather jackets. Sealy wondered if that was a coincidence, or if she knew the men and had specifically targeted them.

Were they all part of the same gang?

"Color of hair?" Sealy asked.

"The old woman couldn't tell in the dark."

"But she definitely saw a gun?"

"That's what she claims."

"If it was dark, how could she tell it was a gun?"

The officer shrugged his shoulders.

The area was fairly well lit with streetlights around where the men were shot, but the woman was a fair distance away. She might have trouble with her eyesight. Sealy had been in this line of work long enough to anticipate every possible defense tactic that could be used by a slick lawyer to discredit the witness if it went to trial.

"Maybe she only thought she saw a gun," Sealy said.

"I'm not sure. She seemed sure of what she saw."

"I'll ask her myself," Sealy said and stepped closer to the four bodies arranged in a somewhat semicircle.

He made a mental note to ask if the officer knew the identities of the men but didn't want to interrupt his observations of the bodies. The man on the sidewalk who'd taken a blow to the face was most likely already dead when he was shot because there was minimal blood around the entry wound.

She killed him with her bare hands. What type of blow would it take to kill a man his size? Why would she shoot him if he was already dead?

He answered his own question. *To be certain he was dead.*

The body to Sealy's right was interesting because he was positioned oddly. A somewhat fetal position with his hands around his crotch area. He'd been shot in the side of the head, likely while he was on the ground. A pool of blood had formed on the ground around his head indicating he was still alive when he was shot.

The woman is cold-blooded whoever she is.

Sealy couldn't help but wonder if the woman had delivered a blow to his privates before shooting him. Maybe a kick. He tried to picture it in his mind.

She followed them off the bus for whatever reason. Maybe a Good Samaritan, concerned for the other woman's safety. She was packing heat and had skills, so she wasn't afraid of them. She confronted them from behind. Maybe to ascertain their intentions. They turned around. Saw her gun and pulled their weapons. She took them down.

After striking the first guy in the face, kicking the second guy in the crotch, then shooting all four of them.

It seemed far-fetched.

If that's what happened, she'd have to be highly skilled to take out four armed men at once. Sealy took a handkerchief out of his suit coat pocket and picked up one of the weapons and smelled the end of it. It had not been fired. He repeated the process with all four guns. None had been fired.

He looked behind him for any traces of blood. Anything that might suggest to him that the woman had been injured in any way.

Nothing.

If nothing else, he was impressed by the suspect's efficiency. She had managed to kill four armed men and escaped without a single scratch.

He scolded himself for already jumping to those conclusions without all the facts. He hadn't even questioned the witness or finished examining the four bodies. He didn't know for sure she was even the one who shot them. Maybe the second woman pulled a gun.

But the men were between her and the second woman.

He leaned each man to the side and didn't see any bullet wounds to the back. In fact, the two men on the left didn't have any noticeable injuries other than the bullet holes. One had been shot in the chest. The other in the head.

The woman was clearly proficient with a weapon. Controlled and precise. Nerves of steel. The bullets seemed to hit right where she intended them to go.

A professional job?

Who sends a woman to do a professional hit on four punks?

He took another good look at the four dead bodies sprawled on the ground, wearing identical black leather jackets with the same dragon tattoo on their necks. Likely part of the same gang, although he wasn't familiar with the insignia. He had no doubt they were up to no good. What he didn't know was if they deserved their fate.

What did he have on his hands? If the woman did shoot the men, she may have done the city of Oslo a favor or she may be a cold-blooded serial killer. He wouldn't know until he found her.

Which he would.

He'd seen enough.

A game plan had formed in his mind. The first thing was to interview the witness. He doubted she had any more to add since she didn't actually see the shooting. But he'd talk to her anyway.

He also needed the identity of the four dead men as soon as possible. The senior officer needed to get on that. It shouldn't be hard to find out if they lived in the neighborhood. If they didn't, then the woman with the gun was probably right to follow them off the bus. If they lived in the area, then that's another story.

He also needed to retrieve the footage from the bus's security camera. Assuming it was on and in working order. The cameras were notorious for malfunctioning. If it was working properly, he would be able to see all those involved and their actions, their behavior, and when and where they boarded the bus.

Did the two women get on together? Did they communicate with each other? Did either woman have any interactions or confrontations with the men on the bus?

The bus driver might even be able to give him more information.

He'd also have the senior officer contact the taxi companies and see if anyone picked up a ride in this area around that time.

The sun threatened to rise soon, and his shift would end, but a surge of adrenaline coursed through his veins making sleep impossible.

A quadruple homicide.

The case of a lifetime. One that made careers.

He needed to see what was on that bus security camera as soon as possible.

It could be the crucial evidence to crack this case wide open.

19

Two days later

Desperate times called for desperate measures.

I couldn't imagine my situation being more dire. A-Rad wasn't at the tiger statue this morning and added to the uncertainty since I didn't know why.

Was he still in custody? Or worse, had something unspeakable happened to him? I couldn't shake off the feeling of unease as I tried not to imagine all the reasons why he didn't show up.

I took hope in the fact that A-Rad was skilled. The lady who interrogated me was capable, but was she really a match for A-Rad and his abilities? I didn't think so. She couldn't hold him this long without him escaping. But if he had escaped, why didn't he show up at the tiger statue?

Something had delayed him and my thoughts were in disarray, torn between hoping for his safety and fearing the worst. Since I didn't know, I had to quit dwelling on it. I had my own chaos to deal with. After killing the four thugs, my situation had deteriorated considerably.

The police flooded the scene that morning with a tsunami of sirens and blue lights, along with a deafening warning that they'd soon be looking for someone. Namely me. It wouldn't take them long to fan out and search the area like a swarm of angry hornets. Anyone walking around that early in the morning would be stopped and questioned immediately.

My mind had raced through possible escape routes, but I didn't know the area well enough to maneuver through the labyrinth of back-streets to safety. The odds of them finding me were great and, if I was searched, they'd find the weapon I used to kill the men.

So, I decided the best thing for me to do was to find a ride out of the area as fast as possible. When I spotted an empty taxi parked at a nearby convenience store, I waited for the driver to emerge from the store with a cup of coffee and asked him for a ride knowing it was a risky move. Any investigator worth his salt would question all the ride sharing companies to see if they picked anyone up in that area around that time.

When he hesitated, my heart began beating even faster as this was my best option. "I'm about to go off my shift," he mumbled tiredly.

I thought about offering him more money but all that would do was raise suspicion in his mind, so I flashed my best look of disappointment. He let out a sigh for my benefit, then reluctantly agreed. I had him drop me off at the downtown train station in case he was questioned. My hope being that the investigator would think I caught a train and left the city. It might be wishful thinking, but maybe he'd quit looking for me in town.

The train station was across from the tiger statue, so I was able to see that A-Rad wasn't there, even though I was certain he wouldn't be. The plan was to wait fifteen minutes after the designated meeting time of four a.m., and I didn't arrive until after four-thirty.

A-Rad would follow the protocol perfectly. Jamie had drilled that into both of us. Even if he was tempted to stay beyond the designated time, he wouldn't. I'd put the protocol in place for a reason. Someone lingering around the statue for longer than fifteen minutes would be suspicious.

Even though I had anticipated him not being there, when it actually happened, it felt like a gut punch. It left me paralyzed with indecision for a few minutes. I waited about fifteen minutes and then left, feeling as despondent as I had since the mission started. With no place to go and no plan of action. With more questions than answers.

This was the definition of a mission going horribly wrong. Jamie had warned me that someday it could, probably would, happen.

"Hope for the best, plan for the worst," she had warned.

This worst-case scenario was worse than I could even imagine it'd be.

The sun rising spurred me to action and gave me some new hope. Rather than wallowing around in self-pity, I used the burst of adrenaline to motivate me to start making progress toward my mission to kill the prince. Needing fuel so I could sustain the new-found energy, I stopped at a local diner and ordered some coffee and breakfast, while keeping my eyes peeled for threats.

The jolt of caffeine and the food in my stomach cleared my head. A things-to-do-list formed in my mind. One decision was easy to make. I wasn't going to spend the day holed up in the disgusting hotel room, even though that might've been the more prudent thing to do.

So with desperation clawing at my chest, I decided to do the last thing I was supposed to do. I decided to call Brad. I left the diner and made my way to a side alley behind the diner. With my hands shaking slightly, I took out the burner phone and dialed the number I knew by heart.

Only to hear the robotic voice of a disconnected line.

"Dang it!"

Rage bubbled up inside of me like molten lava as the obvious hit me between the eyes. Brad and the CIA had abandoned me. While I was technically still on a mission for AJAX and the CIA, they had officially cut me off.

Frantically, I called Jamie next. The cold monotone of a dead line greeted me for a second time.

What?

That I hadn't expected. Brad and Jamie had sent me on this mission. It was their idea, not mine. How could they forsake me now? Toss me out like a piece of unwanted trash?

Was I that disposable?

Jamie's voice filled my head.

"You shouldn't be so surprised. I told you this would happen if you screwed up."

"This isn't my fault."

"Regardless, you know what you signed up for. The CIA will deny they ever knew you."

"What about you?" I had asked her on one occasion. "Are you going to forsake me as well?"

"Never," she said emphatically. "AJAX is a family. We will always have your back."

And yet her phone was disconnected as well. So much for cheap words. There was obviously a limit to everything. Even Alex and Jamie would choose their own skins over mine.

Jamie was right. I shouldn't be surprised. That had already become perfectly clear when Alex and Bond sped past me in the yacht leaving me behind.

After getting the disconnected lines, that's when I did something even more desperate. I went to the CIA safehouse located outside of Oslo.

There I was, outside the house, torn between walking right up to the door and knocking, or getting away from there as quickly as possible. If the house had been empty, I would've picked the lock and gone inside already.

To a casual observer, it might look like no one was home, but I knew better. A slight flicker of light bounced off one of the blinds telling me that Charlie Mason, the housekeeper, was inside and trying to avoid any contact with me.

The housekeeper was a CIA operative in charge of maintaining a local safehouse during a mission. His main purpose was to assist A-Rad and me if we needed him. I desperately needed his help now, but I was the last person he wanted to see, and I was sure he had been instructed not to help me.

But I didn't have any other options, which was why I hadn't left yet.

A car drove by reminding me how foolish it was to loiter outside the house. Standing around outside in broad daylight was not a wise move. My indecision was putting us both at risk. So I walked toward the back door.

The breakfast in my stomach churned as I approached the house. For a number of reasons, I dreaded seeing Charlie. His reaction would tell me everything I needed to know about my standing with the CIA.

Would he confirm that my career was over? That I had no life in America to go back to?

When I reached the steps, I hesitated. Charlie might even have orders to detain me on the spot. I wasn't sure what my next move would be if he greeted me with the barrel of a gun.

Would I fight back or go voluntarily?

The CIA was the most powerful organization in the world. They could literally make me disappear off the face of the earth and erase any trace that I even existed.

That's the chance I had to take.

With one last glance around in every direction, I tapped out the code on the back door: three knocks, a pause, one knock, another pause, and then two gentle raps.

I held my breath as I waited. My head moved closer to the door as I listened for any movement on the other side. When the door didn't open, I didn't bother doing it again. If Charlie hadn't heard the knocks for some reason, he had certainly been alerted to my presence by the security cameras.

So I impatiently proceeded to pick the lock. Before I could finish the task, the door flew open. Charlie's eyes raged with anger as he grabbed me by the lapel of my jacket and jerked me inside. Quickly closing the door behind me.

"Are you crazy? Have you lost your mind?" he growled.

I found myself in the kitchen. While this was my first time in the house, I had studied the layout in the mission plan.

"I think we both already know the answer to that question," I said jokingly, trying to ease the tension. "Anybody who does what I do has to be crazy."

Charlie was anything but amused. His voice was strained and his body tense, coiled like a wire about to snap.

"You shouldn't have come here," he said, while striding over to the window and peering out the blinds towards the back yard. "It's reckless."

"I took precautions," I spat out, my voice filled with its own rough and ragged tone. "I wasn't followed. I may be crazy, but I'm not some bumbling idiot. I know what I'm doing. I wouldn't let anyone follow me here."

I had been meticulous and resented the undertones of his accusations. I spent nearly forty-five minutes on counter surveillance techniques even though it was clear within ten minutes that no one was tailing me.

"If you get caught here, you put us all in serious jeopardy!"

I ignored the tone. "I need help."

"You made a serious mistake coming here. I can't help you anymore. That ship has sailed and you're too late to catch it."

A picture of Bond and Alex on that yacht and me not on it flashed into my mind, stoking the mixture of pain and anger I felt. The hurt buried deep inside of me suddenly boiled to the surface.

"I'm still on the mission!" I said through gritted teeth, my voice shaking from the anger. "My partner is missing, and I have nowhere else to turn. Brad disconnected his line."

"Where is A-Rad?" he asked in a softer tone.

I replied. "I was hoping you had heard from him."

"Last I knew, he was taken to Mostad. Same place they took you."

"They separated us. I managed to escape. I don't know about A-Rad."

Charlie was pacing now.

"We have a meeting point set up," I added. "He didn't show up this morning."

Charlie didn't know the details of where we were supposed to meet and at what time and didn't need to.

"I assume the worst," he said.

"I never assume anything," I said with more resolve than I felt.

The anger on his face faded. "What do you need? Are you hungry? I can give you some food and supplies and then you'll have to leave."

Even though his tone had softened, mine remained stern.

"I don't need food! I'm perfectly capable of fending for myself. I'm here because I need to talk to Brad."

"That's not possible."

"Then I need to talk to Jamie."

"Look Kaley, don't think I don't sympathize with you. This isn't entirely your fault."

"No, it's not. And you're the housekeeper here. Your job is to support me on this mission."

"There is no mission. It's over. I've been told to stand down. You're on your own now."

I tried to control my anger but couldn't keep it in check. "The mission is not over! The prince is behind the sex trafficking!"

"I know."

"How long have you known?" I demanded, accusingly.

"What's that supposed to mean?"

"You work this area. When did you know that the prince was involved in the sex trafficking?"

"I didn't know. I swear. We've heard rumblings about the prince, but I just thought he was a playboy. I had no idea he was caught up in something like this."

"Yeah, well he is. He's a monster. He killed those innocent girls. He sank the submarine and buried them alive. I intend to make him pay."

Charlie shook his head violently from side to side. "You need to leave the country as fast as possible and go dark for a couple of years."

"A couple of years!"

"Until all this blows over."

"Not until I kill the prince."

"Listen to yourself. You can't kill the prince. The CIA doesn't authorize killing a sovereign head of state, even if he does deserve it. You know that."

"You said it yourself. The CIA no longer authorizes this mission. I'm taking matters into my own hands. Don't worry. I'll make sure it doesn't fall back on you."

I walked away from him toward the door that led to the cellar.

"What are you doing?" he asked.

"I need a sniper rifle."

I opened the door. He came up from behind me and his hand gripped my arm tightly causing my fist to ball and my body to recoil. "I don't recommend you do that again," I said.

"I can't let you take a sniper rifle."

I turned and faced him.

"How are you going to stop me?" I said in a threatening tone.

He immediately backed away with his hands held up in surrender. "You know I'm only administrative. I don't have the skills you have."

"That's right. So stay out of my way. I don't want to hurt you, but I will if you try to stop me."

His tone turned to pleading but only fueled my determination. "Please don't take a sniper rifle. I'll get in huge trouble."

"Blame me if you want. Tell them I forced you to give it to me."

"Aren't you in enough trouble already?"

"Maybe. But it's something I have to do."

"You won't get within two miles of the prince."

"I have a plan."

I wasn't about to reveal my plan to him. He'd tell Brad. At this point, I didn't know who I could trust. I wouldn't put it past the CIA to tip off the Norwegians.

I flipped on the lights and went down the stairs to go through the stash of weapons. A sniper rifle would be there, but the question was if there'd be a suitable case to hide it in. I couldn't exactly walk down the street openly carrying the rifle. It needed to come apart and be able to be hidden in a violin or cello case.

Charlie followed me down the stairs.

"Did you kill those four guys?" he asked, out of the blue stopping me in my tracks.

At the bottom of the stairs, I turned to face him again, trying to maintain a calm facade while my heart raced with panic. "What four guys?" I asked.

How much did he know?

"Don't be coy with me. I already know you killed them."

He must've heard it from Brad who saw the police report. Now I wanted to know how much they actually knew.

"I don't know what you're talking about."

"It's all over the news."

"The news?"

Of course it would make the news.

Charlie chuckled. "You haven't seen the news?"

"No. I've been a little preoccupied."

"So you obviously don't know."

"Know what?"

"The police are onto you," he said gravely.

"How do you know?"

"Because your face is plastered all over the television."

The world seemed to suddenly tilt on its axis as I struggled to keep my knees from wobbling.

"You're the primary suspect," Charlie said. "There's an all-out manhunt for you."

It felt like I had just been struck by a taser gun, as I was suddenly unable to move or speak.

20

Only a few people knew exactly how many CIA safehouses there were around the world. The locations were one of the most highly guarded secrets in the CIA system. Considered highly classified, "need to know" type of information.

Each house in the system was given a name and designation, either defensive or offensive. Defensive meaning it was only used to hide people. A defensive location could be nothing more than an apartment in a downtown city with a bed in it.

"Eagle's Nest" was an offensive safehouse in a suburb of Oslo. It was equipped with advanced technology and had been used for covert operations, stashing supplies and weaponry, and even interrogations for years.

Strategically located in a secluded cul-de-sac surrounded by mature trees, the house looked like any other on the block. Inside, however, the decor was sparse and utilitarian, with few personal touches. The furnishings were functional but not designed for comfort.

Eagle's Nest was a working house. Millions of dollars had been poured into it. Offensive safehouses were often elaborate. This particular house had reinforced walls, a state-of-the-art surveillance system, and closed-circuit cameras with motion detectors inside and outside the house.

Two-way mirrors were present which meant it could be used for interrogations. I hadn't seen all the rooms, but I had no doubt one of them was set up for intense interrogations, if necessary. Torture, some might call it. Waterboarding and the like.

Not all safehouses were set up for encrypted communications, but thankfully, the one in Norway was. While Norway wasn't considered a hot area, the safehouse was a fairly active rendezvous point for operations run in other parts of the world where things were more volatile such as Russia, North Korea, Pakistan, Iran, and similar adversarial countries.

Over the years, it had been utilized for numerous operations including this one and even a number of defectors had passed through there. Major intelligence gathering operations had been run out of that house.

So, fortunately, it had everything in it I needed.

When Charlie Mason told me that my face had been broadcast on every television station in Oslo, I almost didn't believe it, and wanted to see it for myself. He took me upstairs to the control room in the back of the house where the communication equipment was kept. He sat down in front of the computer and with a few clicks fired up the main computer monitor.

"I recorded every broadcast and they are still pulled up," he said. "I just sent them to Brad."

I winced at the mention of Brad's name.

My mouth flew open as I watched my own face appear on the oversized screen a few seconds later. As I feared, the shot was of me sitting in the back of the bus right before I exited to kill the four thugs. The camera had captured my face the exact moment when I looked up and spotted it and was staring directly into its lens. It didn't matter that I turned away immediately or that I put on a hat so it couldn't capture my face again. The damage had been done.

My image was now part of a larger news story circulating nonstop on all the Norwegian news stations. According to them, I was the primary suspect in the brutal killing of four men, although the police had only labeled me a person of interest.

"Let me sit there," I said to Charlie who was still in the chair. I was standing behind him, looking over his shoulder and had a sudden and desperate urge to use that computer.

"I can't let you do that," he said.

"Oh, for heaven's sake. Get up out of that chair right now. I've got something I have to do."

He hesitated.

I smacked him across the back of his head. Not hard, but with enough force to get his attention.

"Hey! What did you do that for?"

"Quit being ridiculous. I need the computer. I still have my clearances."

"What are you going to do?"

"Need-to-know basis," I said, mockingly.

When the mission first started, Charlie was assigned to my team, and I was considered his superior. He never would've gotten away with disobeying an order from me.

How things had changed. I wasn't sure where I fit into the chain of command now. Probably at the very bottom of the food chain. Lower than the lowest shrimp on the ocean floor.

That's where certain people in the CIA and the Norwegian officials wished I was right now.

The thought almost caused me to chuckle.

Even though I had insisted, Charlie still hadn't moved from the chair. Confirming he wasn't at all concerned about my former status as mission commander.

"I'm in charge of this safehouse," Charlie said defiantly. "I need to know everything you're doing while you're here."

"Are you sure you want to know? I don't think you do."

He let out a groan in response.

"I suggest you make yourself scarce for a few minutes," I said. "Go grab me an energy drink and power bar and pour yourself a cup of coffee. Wait for me in the kitchen. That'll give you plausible deniability."

"I don't have a choice, do I?"

"No, you don't."

"Then I guess you're right."

He stood from the chair and left the room, closing the door behind him. The first thing I did when I sat down in his place, was pull up his email, and send Brad a one-word message.

Jerk.

I thought I'd feel better after sending it, but it only caused a fiery dart of disappointment to shoot through my heart. I loved Brad. He had been more than just a boss to me. He brought me into the CIA and believed in me enough to have Jamie Austen train me and hand pick me to take her place.

While I meant what I said in the message, I couldn't help but feel like I had let him down to some extent. He was the Assistant Director of the CIA and usually had our backs at every turn. Why the sudden change? I couldn't help but wonder if it came down to saving me or saving his reputation and career.

Rather than wallow in the speculation, I was anxious to get to the real reason why I needed to access the computer. I focused my eyes on the computer screen and let my fingers flail away on the keyboard logging me into the dark web.

Alex taught me how. He trained me the ways to navigate into the dark recesses of the internet where most people never go and would be horrified to know existed. Through a gateway, I pulled up a website Alex had constructed for our benefit. After logging in, I was relieved to find that my password still worked.

The website had email capabilities and I was about to do something that terrorists had been doing for years. Every email sent through the internet was captured by one or more governments including the

United States. In order to avoid that, terrorists and other malicious individuals would go into an email account on the dark web and create a draft message that was actually never sent. Anyone with access to the site could log in and read the draft and either respond or delete it and no one would ever know about it except them.

This was their covert way of communicating, avoiding an electronic paper trail and away from the prying eyes of the United States government. The CIA had been trying for years to figure out how to break the system, but to no avail. The only way to detect it was to know the existence of the site and hack into it. Nearly impossible considering the size of the web. Like looking for a needle in a haystack.

My heart leapt when I saw a draft message in the folder. My hand trembled on the mouse when I opened it.

The author and intended recipient were immediately clear.

Jamie sent it to me!

My mind raced with disbelief and excitement, hardly believing what I could see right in front of my eyes. I began to read it slowly and deliberately.

Kale.

A smile came on my face when I saw my nickname. Jamie used to call me that all the time during my training at The Farm. At the time, I resented it. Now it made me feel warm inside.

I'm sorry this has happened to you. I'll do what I can to help, but it won't be much. Sorry.

"It's okay," I whispered under my breath.

Just knowing that Jamie hadn't abandoned me, sent a burst of euphoria running through me like water through a firehose.

I'm praying for you and our friend. I hope he's okay.

She meant A-Rad. That told me she hadn't heard from him either.

"Me too," I said out loud.

The last line in the message was what I had hoped to see.

SHCC. #51.

I silently thanked Jamie and brushed away a stray tear out of my eye before it could fall down my cheek. I erased the words in the draft and typed, *TY KP.*

Jamie would know I had read the email and left the message thanking her for her help.

I let out a huge sigh of relief and logged off.

Charlie was in the kitchen, a power bar and energy drink sat on the counter. Despite not needing the extra boost of energy, I devoured them anyway. Jamie's words had invigorated me more than a dozen power bars ever could.

"Did you get what you needed?" Charlie asked.

"Yes I did. I'm leaving now."

"What about the sniper rifle?"

"I won't be needing it."

"That's a relief. Looks like you finally came to your senses and took my advice to leave town."

"Yeah. That's exactly what I'm doing."

Charlie didn't need to know that I had no intention of leaving town. Of course, he would probably tell Brad everything, including what I said about leaving town, but I didn't think Brad would be fooled.

Didn't matter. Nothing Brad could do to stop me.

"Thanks for the help," I told Charlie, trying to sound as sincere as possible.

"No problem," he replied.

"Well, I'll be going now," I said, after an awkward moment of silence.

He peeked out the blinds and gave me an all-clear sign as I waited before opening the back door. "Good luck" was the last thing I heard as he closed the door behind me.

Jamie's voice erupted in my head. It felt good to have her back there in force. This time not condemning me.

"You don't need to rely on luck, Kaley. Luck is when opportunity meets preparation. You are fully prepared for what lies ahead."

"Yes, I am," I said, softly but confidently to myself.

"In our line of work, we make our own luck," Jamie added. In a voice that sounded satisfied that our plan had worked, and that she had gotten the message to me.

Jamie was right. I shouldn't doubt my skills or second guess myself, even in this dangerous game of unknowns. Where every decision I made could be a matter of life or death.

Like my decision to come to the safehouse. It turned out to be a good move. One of the few good decisions I had made so far.

It wasn't luck that Jamie left me a message or that I knew how to find it. That came from meticulous preparation and training. Anticipating problems and creating solutions was better than luck.

I felt a new bounce in my step. The message was a lifeline from Jamie. A glimmer of hope in an otherwise bleak situation.

I couldn't wait to find out what was behind the message.

21

The message, SHCC #51, was part of a larger plan devised by Jamie. Combined with the ability to communicate on the dark web through draft email accounts, this was a way we could stay connected and provide each other with necessary resources should we run into significant problems in the field during our missions.

Such as now.

Missions were fraught with risks and unknowns. We could be arrested and interrogated by a foreign government. We could mistakenly kill an innocent civilian. In almost every mission, we broke some kind of law in that country. Even operating in most countries was illegal unless the CIA notified the government of our presence before we went there.

And in the event of a worst-case scenario, the CIA had already told us they would deny they knew us if it were in their best interests to do so. I'd been told many times that if I was arrested in a foreign country like Russia or Iran, little or no efforts would be made to free me. I'd either have to escape on my own, or rot in jail for the rest of my life.

With that fear looming over all of us, we needed to have a way to get resources to each other. SHCC stood for Southern Hills Country Club. I arrived there within twenty minutes of leaving the safehouse. The rideshare driver dropped me off a block away and I walked to the entrance. At the same moment I arrived, a man drove up in a flashy red Porsche convertible causing the valet to become preoccupied and providing me with a welcomed distraction.

"Welcome back, Mr. Roberts," the preppy brown-nosing valet said with a wide and admiring smile as he opened the door for the tanned and fit sixty-plus-year-old, who proceeded to hand him the keys and some denomination of money.

Both of them ignored me completely which was fine by me.

With my head turned back for one last glance at them, a walking perfume store brushed my shoulder and pushed past me, her eyes fixed on the man getting out of the Porsche.

"Hello, Ed, darling," she cooed as they exchanged air kisses on each cheek.

The woman was decked out from head to toe in expensive clothes and accessories. Her hair was expertly styled, and her face seemed to be frozen in time by Botox injections.

I didn't hear the rest of the nauseous display because I had more important things to consider. Specifically, the pressing matter of discovering the contents of the locker.

Fifty-one was a locker number in the women's shower and changing room. Jamie had no doubt put something in there for me. Sometimes she rented a locker in a train or subway station if it was safe. If it wasn't, she chose a fitness or country club or even the equivalent of a local YMCA or community rec center as long as they had permanent lockers she could rent.

In this case, she rightly decided to go with a private country club where security was lax. Obviously, it wouldn't be as safe for me now to show my face inside a train station or airport.

The woman working at the front desk was also preoccupied with helping another wealthy member and didn't notice as I confidently walked through the lobby and into the women's locker room without being seen by her or anyone else. To my relief, the locker room was empty, simplifying things for me.

My gun was tucked in my waist, but I didn't want to brandish it. However, if someone recognized me, I would draw it as a last resort because I wasn't leaving that country club without the contents of that locker. Even if it meant causing a scene.

What difference did it make anyway? The police already had my picture. So what if I was spotted at the country club? It had security cameras and I avoided looking directly into them, but I wasn't that worried. Alex had likely hacked into the system and would erase my image before anyone could see it.

Even if the authorities learned that I had been there, they'd be even more confused, and my actions would raise more questions than answers. What was I doing at the country club? How did my image get erased off the camera?

The thought of confusing the investigators brought a smile to my face, although my main goal was to enter and leave with the package without them knowing I was ever there. I hoped things would continue to go smoothly and Murphy's law didn't enter the equation like it had already in this ill-fated mission.

My heart started racing as I approached the locker. The combination was seared in my memory.

41-25-36.

Jamie's idea of a joke. My small, A-cup breasts barely filled a sports bra. It'd take a skilled surgeon to get my breasts to a size 41 and he couldn't do so without making me look like a freak.

My figure was far from hourglass or curvy and I'd never once been described by anyone as voluptuous. Nor did I want to be.

According to Jamie, and verified by my own experience, smaller breasts were more practical in the field anyway where a larger bust could become a hindrance during a gunfight or physical confrontation.

I glanced around the room before I entered the combination, my stomach twisting with anxiety, more related to the contents of the locker rather than worry about someone entering the room. My heart fluttered when I saw there was something inside. A backpack.

One was on my back already. I slipped it off and sat it on the bench behind me. With shakier than normal hands, I quickly took the one out of the locker and shut the locker door, spinning the dial to reset it even though I doubted I'd ever be back there and it didn't matter if it remained unlocked.

My initial instinct was to get out of there as quickly as possible and look at the contents later, but my curiosity won out. Rather than opening the backpack in plain sight, I had the presence of mind to go into one of the stalls of the immaculately clean bathroom. The toilet had a lid, so I closed it, and sat down.

Excitement bubbled within me as I unzipped the backpack, like a kid unwrapping gifts on Christmas morning. Inside an outside compartment was a passport, credit card, and some cash.

I couldn't hold back my laughter when I opened the passport and saw a doctored picture of myself. My name was now Mary Alice Broadcastle and I looked like someone who would fit right into this country club.

Jamie had outdone herself, giving me blonde hair, long lashes, heavy makeup, and ridiculously gigantic boobs.

How am I supposed to make myself look like that?

I had a strong suspicion that I'd know as soon as I saw the contents of the larger compartment. Confirmed when inside I found a fancy red dress and a pair of six-inch stiletto heels.

I can't walk in those, Jamie. You know that.

During my training, Jamie had attempted to teach me how to take on the persona of a sexy and sophisticated lady. She said I might need those skills in the field someday. I never quite mastered the art of gracefully walking in high heels or flirting for that matter. If I were ever tasked with acting like a floozy and seducing a target in the field, Jamie and I both knew I'd be in trouble.

Jamie, you think you are so funny!

Another burst of laughter escaped my mouth when I found a bra at the bottom of the backpack. It was unlike anything I'd ever seen before. I held it up in the air and inspected it. It had to be every bit of a double D-cup and made of sturdy material with wiring sewn in for support. Two silicone inserts were meant to fill up the cups since I obviously couldn't.

Inside was also a blonde wig. I grabbed it and placed it on my head. Scoffing aloud as I did so.

I'm going to look ridiculous!

Jamie was a blonde and I was a redhead, and we had a history of playful banter about our different hair colors. I had insisted that redheads were smarter than blondes.

"You never hear any dumb redhead jokes!" I had quipped.

While I had a stable of blonde girl jokes in my arsenal, I rarely used them. Jamie was not only stunningly beautiful but also one of the most intelligent individuals I had ever met. The dumb blonde jokes didn't really fit her.

That didn't stop Bond and Alex from letting the jokes fly.

A-Rad and Colonel sat on the sidelines with me. It wasn't in their nature to joke around like that, and I adopted that same mindset. I didn't have much of a sense of humor anyway.

Jamie's was better than mine and she had told me on more than one occasion to lighten up. Banter eased the tension. She encouraged it on missions.

I had to admit that the outfit had caused my shoulders to relax from the levity I felt inside. Leave it to Jamie to interject humor into a difficult situation. All joking aside, this was her way of helping me and it was welcomed and brilliant. The disguise was exactly what I needed to get around Oslo now that I was famous in the area.

In the last compartment, I found a set of paperwork and a key to a private plane with directions to a nearby airport. The message was crystal clear. Get out of Norway as soon as possible.

The idea was tempting. Even with the disguise, staying in Oslo was a risky move. It made sense to leave immediately and wait for another time to exact revenge on the prince.

I would have considered it except for one thing; A-Rad. I couldn't leave without knowing what had happened to him. I'd keep going to the tiger statue every morning until he showed up. And if he didn't, I'd spend my days searching for him.

The decision to leave Norway didn't have to be made right away so I dismissed the thoughts out of my mind. I quickly returned everything into the backpack and got ready to leave the women's locker room and the country club.

I momentarily considered putting on the disguise but decided against it. It wasn't something I was looking forward to. As much as it made sense, I hated the thought of wearing it. I couldn't imagine anything less like me or more uncomfortable to wear. I might have to wear it every day for the foreseeable future, so I'd put it off as long as I could.

The plane was something I was thankful for. At least now I had a way of escaping out of the country if I ever needed it. It'd also have supplies and weapons including a sniper rifle. Along with internet access to plan any potential operations. I could even sleep there if I wanted, although I preferred to be closer to the tiger statue so I could walk to it.

Using the ride services was becoming problematic. The risk of someone recognizing me was greater the more rides I took. It'd be helpful to have some kind of reliable transportation of my own. With the passport and disguise, I could rent a car and have freedom to navigate the area more freely.

The contents were back in the backpack, and I was ready to go. Just as I was about to exit the bathroom stall, the noise of a door opening froze me in my tracks.

Two women entered the locker room, engaged in a passionate conversation. Apparently, someone in the country club was getting a divorce and the juicy details flowed off their lips like slobber off a bulldog.

From the sound of things, I wasn't sure how long they'd be, so I sat down on the toilet stool to wait, careful not to make a sound. About ten minutes later, they left for their mid-morning massages. When the door closed behind them, I slipped out of the bathroom stall and verified that the room was still empty. Before the sigh of relief could escape my lips, the door swung open, and a woman entered.

Our eyes met.

We locked gazes.

Recognition flashed across her face. She immediately turned and bolted for the door before I could react. Panic flooded through me along with frustration. I'd come so close to getting out of there without anyone recognizing me.

I weighed my options, which were few. There was only one exit out of the locker room, and the windows were up toward the top of the high ceiling and didn't open from the inside.

I needed to act fast.

The lady would immediately go to the front desk, and they'd call the police. I calculated that it'd take the police about twelve minutes to get there. The country club might also have an armed security guard who could be summoned. If I tried to exit the front, it might create a confrontation with him. Something I needed to avoid at all costs.

I figured he'd wait until the police arrived. Or so I hoped.

An idea popped into my head.

I didn't like it.

22

Right before I attempted to sneak out of the locker room, a member of the country club walked in and recognized me, then abruptly turned around and left obviously with intentions to inform someone that a fugitive from the law was in the building. This left me with few viable options to escape unnoticed.

I could resort to pulling my gun and waving it around in a threatening manner if someone tried to stop me from leaving, but that went against everything Jamie had taught me. She made it clear that I should never brandish my weapon unless I was willing to use it.

For obvious reasons, I couldn't. What if a security guard was on the other side of the door and had a gun pointed at me? I couldn't risk harming an innocent man only doing his job.

What if he didn't give me a chance to give up and opened fire? He could miss and hit another innocent civilian. Or he might have good aim and put a bullet in me.

Although it wasn't my first choice, the best option was for me to do something I didn't want to do, but probably should've done to begin with. With a resigned sigh, I reluctantly returned to the toilet stall and took the disguise out of the backpack.

Stripping off my clothes, I began by putting on the massive bra and stuffing it with the two silicone inserts which were heavier than I had imagined them to be. When the bra was in place, it felt like I had two coconuts hanging off my chest.

My lower back hurt already.

Next, I took the dress out of the backpack and slid it onto my body, questioning Jamie's color choice. I never wore red because I thought it clashed with my red hair.

Then I remembered the blonde wig. Getting used to the different hair color might be the biggest adjustment.

No. The breasts. I'll never get used to the set of dumbbells on my chest.

Trying to maneuver the dress over them was a chore. I don't know how she did it, but Jamie had picked the perfect sized dress. It was tight and form-fitting which only exaggerated the chest area. It barely fit over the massive fake honkers, but it did work, although they pulled on the dress, making it more of a mini than the intended midi. I could envision having to constantly pull it down and being extremely self-conscious.

Stop being such a prude. This might be fun.

Wait until A-Rad sees it!

He'll keel over laughing. If he doesn't have a heart attack on the spot.

Ignoring the picture in my head of A-Rad making fun of me, I took out the matching red stiletto heels and reluctantly slid them onto my feet, muttering curses under my breath towards Jamie for making me wear them. It took a few seconds to find my balance. The huge breasts had thrown off my equilibrium.

"I thought spies were supposed to blend into the environment, Jamie," I said aloud to with an angry undertone. "How many times did you tell me to make myself unmemorable? Everybody is going to notice me. And not in a good way."

Being inconspicuous was one of the golden rules of espionage. Jamie struggled with it her entire career because she was so gorgeous. She had somehow learned how to make it work to her advantage and she could get away with wearing such an outfit.

I'd been told that I was attractive in a girl-next-door kind of way, but I never found it hard to tamper down my look. Growing up a tomboy I could easily put on that persona and blend into any environment with no trouble.

This was going to take some getting used to.

The person I was trying to portray now was so out of character for me, that I didn't even recognize myself and it felt strange. Which was sort of the point and why Jamie chose this outfit. While she clearly meant it as a joke, sometimes the best strategy was to hide in plain sight. By appearing so unlike my normal self, no one would ever be able to recognize me.

With a sense of urgency, I slipped on the wig and burst out of the stall to look at myself in the mirror. It felt like a stranger was looking back at me.

I felt more like a clown than a glamorous lady.

It really was a good disguise if I allowed myself to admit it. There wasn't enough time to apply makeup, but Jamie had included an oversized pair of sunglasses that I slipped on my head and would use to cover my face if necessary.

She also included a holster for my gun that fit tightly on my inner thigh. The thought of drawing it sent shivers down my spine. The only thing that could make my situation worse was for an innocent bystander to get caught up in the crossfire and die.

I had to avoid that at all costs.

Inside the backpack was an expensive designer handbag with delicate gold clasps and a signature logo. Inside the bag was an assortment of accessories—a large fake diamond ring that sparkled under the light, an expensive looking necklace, and a pair of dangling earrings.

I put them on quickly.

A problem developed immediately as I prepared to leave the locker room. I couldn't walk out carrying two backpacks and a handbag. Especially since the backpacks didn't match my outfit. Fortunately, the oversized handbag was big enough to hold the contents of both the backpacks, so I emptied them and stuffed them in the trash.

I inhaled sharply and put the expensive handbag over my shoulder while walking briskly toward the door, building confidence with each step. My heart raced as I exited the locker room half expecting an armed security guard on the other side of it.

But, to my relief, no one was outside the locker room. Instead, a crowd had gathered around the front desk. I removed my sunglasses from my head and held them in my hand as I walked towards them.

"Excuse me," I said in perfect Norwegian, although for some reason it came out sounding British. "I just came from the women's locker room. The girl who shot those boys? The one on the news. I believe I saw her in there."

The woman who had seen me in the locker room, raised her eyebrows and her mouth gaped open. For a moment, I was afraid she had recognized me.

"I saw her too," she exclaimed, clearly not.

"We've called the police," the front desk attendant informed me. "They're on their way."

"Brilliant," I replied before swiftly turning and walking away. I kept waiting for someone to figure it out and shout for me to stop, but no one did.

My plan worked perfectly.

And just in the nick of time. As I stepped outside, I could hear distant sirens approaching. Time was running short.

I motioned to the valet, who was standing off to the side. He didn't seem to be aware of the situation unfolding inside.

"My car, please," I said in my developing posh British accent.

He looked puzzled and asked, "Which car is yours?"

"Actually, it's not my car. It belongs to my uncle, Ed Roberts. The red Porsche over there." I pointed to it, relieved that it was parked in an easy-to-access spot at the front.

"Can you grab the keys for me?" I requested politely but firmly.

He hesitated.

"My uncle left his tennis racket at the house and sent me to get it."

Still unsure, he replied, "I didn't see you arrive with him."

I let out a disapproving sigh. "And I didn't see you at your post when I arrived. But now here we are. My uncle is inside. You can go and ask him yourself if you want."

He still seemed hesitant, so I added sternly, "He's not going to be very happy with you if you don't give me the keys. You know how he is."

If the valet did go inside, I saw that as a perfect opportunity to steal one of the cars.

But then he surprised me by saying, "That won't be necessary."

He walked towards a box mounted on the wall and retrieved a key from inside. With a press of the fob, he confirmed that it was indeed the keys to the right car.

He dutifully held the door open for me before I jumped into the driver's seat and started the engine. I waved a quick thank you as I sped away. The sirens were growing louder and more urgent behind me.

I wondered how long it might take them to figure out I had stolen the car.

After about three miles, I spotted a parked car on the side of the road. Without hesitation, I switched the license plates. When the police did figure it out, the mismatched plates would throw them off my trail if I was spotted.

Satisfied with my quick thinking, I drove to a hotel in downtown Oslo, confident that hiding in plain sight was my best option. The valet at the hotel would safely tuck the car away in their parking garage, where no one would think to look for it.

"Thank you, Mr. Roberts," I muttered under my breath. I didn't feel guilty about borrowing it; after all, he was wealthy and had insurance. It might be a minor inconvenience for him, but he probably had another fancy car waiting at home. Besides, he'd get this one back soon enough.

The important thing now was that I had transportation and a plan. If A-Rad didn't show up at the tiger statue tomorrow, I would head to

Mostad to look for him. The Porsche would get me most of the way there.

The friendly lady at the front desk asked if I had a reservation.

"No. My flight just arrived, and I didn't get a chance. Do you have a room available?"

"Absolutely."

"How about a suite?" I asked. Since the room was on Jamie's dime and she could afford it, I'd get the most expensive room available. I could justify it. When A-Rad arrived, we'd need something bigger than a small room with two beds.

She asked for my passport and credit card already in my hand, giving them a quick glance before swiping the card then returning them to me. "Do you have any luggage?" she asked.

"No," I replied smoothly, thankful that the card had worked even though I knew it would. Jamie was meticulous when it came to these details. A mistake could be disastrous.

"Unfortunately, the airline lost my luggage," I replied, having already anticipated the question. "Can you believe it?"

Seeming satisfied with my answer, the woman handed me my room keys and discreetly pointed out that I was on the top floor—the penthouse. A word popped out of my mouth without thought, "Brilliant," I said.

I'd heard Bond say the word a thousand times. He was British and had a heavy rogue. Jamie and I often talked to each other in a fake British accent. A skill that was coming in handy at the moment.

I thanked the lady and made a straight line to the elevator.

As soon as I entered the luxurious room, I shed my disguise and hung up the dress to avoid wrinkles. Tomorrow, I'd try to find more dresses and maybe a pair of shoes with lower heels.

While I needed to focus on our mission and should probably go get clothes now, I also desperately needed some rest. As Jamie had said on many occasions, "Sleep and eat when you can."

With a contented moan, I crawled into bed. The designer sheets enveloped me in comfort.

My last thought before darkness engulfed me was the tiger statue, A-Rad, and Mostad.

Where are you A-Rad?

I have to find you.

23

The investigation into the shooting of the four gang members on Oslo's east side had become the most perplexing and confusing case of Jan Sealy's esteemed career. Just when he thought it couldn't get any stranger, his secretary informed him that Hefina Rosser, from the Royalty Protection Unit, was waiting to speak with him about the case.

From what he understood, Rosser was responsible for the safety of the prince of Norway. Why did she want to meet with him? How was the royal family connected to these gang related killings? Could it have something to do with the recent terrorist attack on the prince and the murder of his six bodyguards?

That's the only thing that made sense. Perhaps the woman he was pursuing was somehow connected to both incidents.

Before he had a chance to contemplate any more of his questions, Rosser appeared at his office door. He immediately stood to his feet and came out from behind his desk to greet her. She flashed him an obligatory smile and shook his hand when he offered it. With such surprising strength and intention, the arthritis in his hand announced its displeasure.

He gestured for her to take a seat in one of the chairs across from his desk. Rather than sit in the chair next to her, he returned to his seat behind the desk to maintain a position of control over the conversation.

Why was he so nervous?

She may be a powerful woman, but this was his territory and his investigation. For some reason, he felt a defensiveness creeping up on him even though she hadn't spoken a word. He couldn't seem to shake the nagging feeling that he might not like the tenor or nature of this conversation.

Rather than continue to dwell on it, he decided to get straight to the point. "What can I do for you today, Ms. Rosser?" he asked, in the friendliest tone he could muster.

"I'm here regarding the woman who murdered the four men."

He found it interesting that she used the term "murdered." While he suspected that the woman was indeed the person who shot them, he was going to keep an open mind until he had all the facts. His main priority was to find the only eyewitness to the shooting itself. The woman who had been followed by the dead men. The woman the old lady had described as a prostitute and saw getting off the bus first.

He wouldn't use the word "murder" yet. The shooting might've been in self-defense. The thugs pulled their own guns. If they pulled theirs first, the only thing he could probably pin on the woman was leaving the scene of the crime. Assuming her gun was properly registered. If not, he might be able to throw in a gun charge, although he doubted he'd pursue either crime that diligently.

It's possible that the woman did the city of Oslo a favor.

One of the most frustrating parts of the investigation was that the prostitute still hadn't been found. The bus's security camera didn't actually capture her face. All he could see from the footage was the back of her head as she boarded and sat down in the first row. The camera angle also didn't capture her face when she got off the bus.

It did clearly show the four gang members following her off, followed by another woman, the presumed shooter.

"I understand that you're the one who released the woman's picture to the media," Rosser said while he was still deep in thought and had failed to respond to her telling him why she was there.

"That's right."

"That was a foolish thing to do." Her words dripped with vitriol that he hadn't seen coming.

Instantly, anger boiled up inside of him as fast as a roaring flame from a blowtorch. He despised others questioning his decisions, especially from someone he didn't even know. Even if it came from the head of the Royalty Protection Unit, the very pinnacle of law enforcement in the hierarchy of command. His fists clenched under the desk, and it took every bit of self-control not to lash out at the comment as he fought to contain his temper.

"First of all, I don't know for sure that the woman in question shot the men."

"She shot them!" Rosser countered.

"I've designated her as a person of interest. I want to bring her in for questioning before I decide that she 'murdered' them."

"You and I both assume she did, which is why you released her picture."

He couldn't help but feel defensive. "I'm not sure how you investigate crimes in your department, but I like to deal in facts, not assumptions. Until I have enough concrete evidence I can use to convict in a court of law, I will withhold making any judgments."

"You have a witness. An old woman. She saw the suspect follow the men off the bus and pull a gun on them."

He tried to mask the surprised look he felt form on his face. "How did you know about the witness?"

"I make it my business to know."

The only explanation he could come up with in that short of time was that she had accessed his computer somehow and read through his investigative notes.

"You say you make it your business to know," he said, "but why do you care about the shooting of four low level gang members? Don't you have more important things to concern yourself with?"

She ignored the question.

He added a remark to provoke her. "I would think you have enough on your plate dealing with how someone could attack the prince since it's your job to protect him."

Her face remained composed, and she didn't give away whatever emotions she was feeling inside. If she had any feelings. Her demeanor was cold and steely. She spoke bluntly. With condescension. Almost like he was nothing more than a bother to her.

"Tell me what you know," she said, matter-of-factly. "I understand that there's another witness. A prostitute. Have you found her?"

"Alleged prostitute. And no, we haven't found her. We're working on it."

"How hard could it be? She had to live in that neighborhood. Why else would she get off at that bus stop at that time in the morning?"

While he had the same questions, he couldn't help but answer defensively.

"My men have gone door-to-door. So far, we haven't determined who she is or what she was doing there that night."

"Any leads on the shooter's whereabouts?"

Rosser leaned forward in her chair, her eyes fixated on his. Trying to stare him down. Attempting to intimidate him.

Why was she being so combative? He still didn't know why she cared so much. Why was she so anxious to find this woman?

"No, I haven't. That's why I decided to release her picture to the public and see if anyone recognizes her."

"Have you got any leads on the tip line?"

"Many. We're following up on them. You know how it goes. Some of the calls are from people looking for a reward. We get a good number of calls from the crackpots who always call in. We know who they are, but it takes time to sift them out. Then you have the pranksters. Like I said, it's a process."

"Do you think she's still in the city?"

Her voice quivered as she asked. For some reason, Rosser was desperate to find this woman. What was she so afraid of?

He decided not to ask the burning question in his mind. *Are you afraid that she's still on the loose or afraid that she might get caught and reveal what she knows?*

"I don't know where she is," he said sincerely. "A taxi driver picked up a woman matching her description not too far from the scene and around the same time."

"That has to be her," she said excitedly.

"Most likely. He dropped her off at the train station in the city."

"Maybe that means she left the country," she said, almost sounding relieved.

"Perhaps. Like I said, I deal with facts. I don't assume anything until I know for sure."

"If she is located, she's not to be questioned. Contact me immediately."

"Do you have some jurisdiction here that I don't know about?"

The woman pointed her finger at him. "I can pick up the phone and call the king, so I'd say my jurisdiction is halfway up your incompetent you-know-what."

He felt his temper flaring again, and he had to bite his lip to keep from snapping back at her. Instead, he said, calmly but firmly, "With all due respect to you and His Royal Highness, I can assure you that I am extremely good at my job. I've been doing it for more than thirty years. And until someone explicitly tells me otherwise, I'm in charge of this investigation. So, if you'll excuse me, I'd like to get back to it."

"I'm telling you otherwise," she said, mockingly. "That's why I'm here. You're no longer in charge of the investigation. I'm removing you from it immediately and taking over. Effective now. I want all of your records and files handed over to me."

He was shocked and almost fell out of his chair.

"I'm going to have to talk to my boss about this."

She sat back in her chair and crossed her legs while pointing at the phone on his desk. "Be my guest. Call him. He already knows."

Sealy picked up the receiver and dialed the extension of the director. The conversation didn't take long. He confirmed what the lady had so confidently stated.

"She's taking it over. Cooperate with her in every way," his boss said. "If they want the can of worms, they can have it."

"But I'm making progress, and I would like to see it to the end."

His boss raised his voice. "You heard what I said! This is above our paygrades. Give the lady what she wants so she doesn't make trouble for us."

How could she make trouble for them? Why did it feel like he had done something wrong?

He hung up the phone slowly. "I'll gather everything together and have it brought to your office," he said to Rosser, who had a smug expression on her face that irked him even more.

"No. I want to leave with them right now."

"That might take a few minutes."

"I'll wait."

She sat forward again.

"And I want everything deleted off your computer after you save it for me."

"Why?"

"It doesn't matter why," she said harshly.

"Does the woman we are looking for have something to do with the shooting of the prince's bodyguards? It wouldn't surprise me. She has impressive skills. Does she work for the CIA?"

"You ask too many questions."

"I'm trying to understand why."

"Why doesn't matter. What's important is that you do what you're told."

"I've invested a lot of hours in this. I know the case backwards and forwards. I'm working on a few leads. What do I do about those?"

"I guess I haven't made myself clear. You and your entire department are off this case. You are to cease all efforts. Do not pursue any leads. Do not conduct any interviews. Stop all searches for the shooter or the prostitute. Have I made myself clear?"

"Perfectly. What if someone recognizes her on the television reports and calls in the tip line?"

"That line has already been disconnected and I have notified the media to discontinue any stories. Like I said, that was a foolish thing to do."

Rosser clearly didn't want this woman to be caught. At least by anyone but her. He could speculate why, but that's all it would be, pure speculation. Better to drop it and do what he was told to do.

"Do you understand what I am saying?" she demanded.

"Yes."

She leaned forward again and rested her elbows on his desk. Her voice took on a menacing edge. "Let me give you a word of advice. I want you to forget everything about this case. Do you hear me? When I walk out this door, I want you to erase it from your memory."

"What if I worked with you on it? I could be of some help to you."

She let out a huge disapproving moan for his benefit. "I don't think you're hearing me. I don't want you anywhere near this case. You're getting close to retirement, right?"

"It's a few years away. But yes."

"Do you want to retire with your pension?"

Was she threatening him now?

"Yes."

"Then stay out of my way. If I find out that you're still working this case, I'll have you arrested."

"On what charge?"

"Obstruction for starters."

He decided it was best not to argue the point. He had no doubt that she wielded the power to make something like that happen.

After he finished gathering all the files, he placed them on his desk in front of her and handed her a thumb drive.

"This contains everything from my computer files including the murder book."

"Excellent. Now wipe everything off your computer."

"I already have."

With a few strokes on the keyboard, he had deleted the file, although he had a file on his home computer as well. He'd decide later if he was going to keep it or not, but for now, he wasn't going to mention it.

He probably wouldn't keep it. Rosser was right. He couldn't do anything to jeopardize his career or his pension. It wasn't worth it.

He felt relief when Rosser eventually left his office. She wasn't gone for ten minutes when his phone rang.

"They spotted our girl," one of his investigators on the case said.

"Which girl?"

He wasn't sure if he meant the shooter or the prostitute.

"The shooter."

"Where at?"

His heart was suddenly racing.

"She was spotted in the women's locker room at Shadow Hills Country Club. The police were called, but she disappeared before they got there. I'm headed there now. Can you meet me there?"

He hesitated. Rosser's warnings were still freshly etched in his mind.

"I need you to back off," he finally said.

"It's only been twenty minutes. She might still be in the area. This is our best lead so far."

"I told you to stand down. We're no longer on the case."

"What! We've got hundreds of man hours on this."

"It doesn't matter why."

He didn't provide an explanation because he didn't have one. After hanging up the phone, he leaned back in his chair. This sudden turn of events was bewildering.

How were the prince and the woman connected?

More importantly, what was Rosser trying to cover up?

24

Later that afternoon
One day before the funerals

A loud bang shattered my deep slumber. It had been a long time since I had slept that soundly. I hadn't had a really good night's sleep since I started working with Jamie. Because of her, my life had been a whirlwind of danger and tension since the day she brought me into AJAX. I'd been living on the edge for nearly two years and my sleep had suffered as a result.

The soft luxurious sheets and comfortable mattress in this five-star hotel were a far cry from the rat-infested, shouldn't even be called a hotel, sleep-killing, stinky armpit I had stayed in the first few nights after arriving in Oslo. The thought occurred to me that my present situation was also a lot better than a Norwegian jail cell which was why I needed to find the source of the noise.

More bangs were louder this time. Deep, resonant thuds that seemed to vibrate through the walls. It sounded like it came from outside, but I couldn't be sure. The gun I kept under my pillow was already in my hand, even though I didn't remember picking it up. The cold, hard metal felt reassuring in my grip as I bolted out of bed and walked quickly toward the door in the living room area of the suite.

My senses were on full alert as I was now fully awake.

Another loud screeching sound echoed through the room. It sounded like major construction was happening right outside the hotel. Despite my suspicion, I put my ear to the door anyway and listened, even though I was fairly certain the sound wasn't coming from the hallway. Just to be sure, I looked through the peephole but saw no one.

Satisfied, I went to the window and pulled back the curtains. On the street level below was a flurry of activity. A group of workers dressed in orange vests were everywhere, moving with the precision and the urgency of a well-coordinated team. Some were installing concrete barriers between the streets and the sidewalks, while others were blocking off roads and setting up equipment.

The funeral.

The realization hit me suddenly. That was tomorrow. These must be the preparations being made. I knew the funeral procession was set to run through downtown Oslo, but I hadn't realized that my hotel was adjacent to the route.

My heart ached at the thought of the missed opportunity. I hadn't made any progress toward my goal of killing the prince. If he attended the funeral, it would be a prime opportunity to take him out while he was in public view. Missing this chance could mean I might not ever get another.

A loud sound brought me back to reality. This time the noise was more of an obnoxious clanging. Workers were pounding, drilling, constructing something significant just outside my view.

I had to see what was happening.

I hastily put on my disguise and left my room with the intention of heading towards the street level. When I stepped into the elevator, I remembered the lady at the front desk mentioned that the hotel roof had a happy hour around this time. It struck me that the roof, being the tallest point in the area, would provide the best vantage point to see what was going on without the risk of running into any authorities or workers who might ask questions.

So I pushed the button to go up and the elevator ride to the roof was over in a matter of seconds since the rooftop was only one floor above the penthouse suite. As I waited for the door to open, I couldn't shake the feeling that something monumental was unfolding outside, something that could alter the course of my mission.

Would the prince be at the funeral? Riding in a vehicle? Would the top be down? Would he get out to greet the crowd or the families of the victims?

The thought of seeing his face exhilarated me. Putting a bullet in his head was the most satisfying image I'd had in a long time.

I scolded myself for jumping ahead. I was a long way from getting a shot off at the prince. Too many questions remained, and I needed to answer them.

Some were obvious. The prince would surely attend the funeral, but security would be tight. Maybe impossible to penetrate, especially with no time to plan. The prince might ride in the funeral procession, but there's no way the top would be down. In fact, he'd more than likely be in an armored car with bulletproof windows.

I couldn't imagine that the security team would let him get out of the vehicle and greet the crowd, especially knowing that I was still on the loose and I'd already killed four other men. If they were stupid enough to let him, how could I possibly get close enough to take a shot?

When the doors finally opened to the roof, my hopes had dissipated as fast as a tiny rain cloud on a sunny day. When I stepped out of the elevator, I was met by a fairly large group of people in a lively mood. Music blared from speakers, and the scent of grilled food wafted through the air. People were laughing, drinking, and chatting, oblivious to the commotion below.

I quickly scanned the crowd for any potential threats and noted that the crowd seemed to be business professionals and mostly older than me. Almost immediately, a fortyish man approached and offered to buy me a drink. I waited for him to give my fake breasts a good look before I answered.

His approach was friendly but not pushy, and I politely declined without shooting him down too hard. In my current situation, the last thing I wanted was for anyone to remember me.

How would people not remember me with these massive twin grapefruits hanging off of the front of my body?

They weren't exactly hanging since the wire meshing made them stick out like two pointed objects that could put an eye out. It was a different feeling for me. This was the first time in my life that I had the biggest breasts in the room.

Too bad I didn't have time to see if I liked it.

The sounds I was curious about were coming from the left side of the roof area and brought my mind back to the purpose at hand. I discreetly made my way over to the edge and peered down. From that vantage point, I could see everything happening below.

A surge of adrenaline rushed through me when I saw what they were building. It appeared to be a viewing stand and the major construction was already completed. Chairs were being arranged beyond what appeared to be reinforced, bulletproof glass. That could only mean one thing: someone worth protecting would be sitting behind those partitions.

Obviously, this was where the dignitaries were going to view the funeral procession.

The prince.

The viewing stand was a clever move. If the king and his family attended, their movements could be controlled and their location secure.

I could picture the seating chart in my head. The king, the prime minister, and other high-profile figures would undoubtedly be in the front row. Their bodyguards would be strategically positioned around them. If the prince attended, he would likely be seated in the second row, just behind the main dignitaries.

If they were smart, they'd keep the prince as far away from the event as possible. I didn't think they would. He was the future king.

This was the funeral of his dead bodyguards who had given their lives for him.

How could he not attend? It'd make him look weak and afraid. The press would eat him alive.

If only the people knew how big a coward he really was. A deviant who preyed on young girls and held them hostage. Forcing them into unwanted sexual acts.

What I wouldn't give to take him out.

I could envision taking the shot. Seeing him slump in his chair.

For the girls.

I'd do what they couldn't do. Their revenge would finally be fulfilled by my hand.

Was it possible? Could I get off a shot? If I did, could I get out of there without getting caught?

I cared about getting caught, but I'm not sure how much. I seemed more concerned about getting off the shot than how to get away. I was willing to take tremendous risk to make this happen. I already had. I could've easily driven to the plane and flown out of the country.

But I wasn't like the prince. I wasn't a coward. I wasn't weak and afraid. Killing him was worth whatever risk came with it.

And it wasn't even that risky, I decided. I had the disguise and a car. I could take the shot, ride the elevator down to my room, and wait it out. I'd no doubt be questioned, but I had my passport.

Why would anyone suspect me?

Or even better, I could ride the elevator down to the parking garage, drive the Porsche to the plane, and fly out of the country. It meant leaving A-Rad behind for now, but I'd come back for him once it was safe. The thought of successfully completing the mission and exacting revenge caused my spirits to soar.

My focus was broken when a second man interrupted those thoughts and offered to buy me a drink. He was a little more persistent, but so was I and I firmly rejected him. When he finally got the hint and I was able to refocus on my planning, my heart sank as I realized that shooting the prince through the protective glass would be nearly impossible.

The plane wouldn't have any bullets that'd pierce that glass. Even if I did have access to some, generally it took more than one shot, and the prince would be rushed to safety before I could make a deadly shot with the rifle.

My mind raced as I continued to survey the scene. After further inspection, hope returned when I noticed the entrance at the back of the viewing stand. There was a covered walkway and three steps that led down into the viewing area. As they entered, their heads would be just above the glass, creating a small window of opportunity for me.

Could I get a shot off in that brief moment?

It would be an incredibly tight window and I'd have less than a split second to make the shot. I estimated the distance to be a manageable shot for someone of my skill level, though not without its challenges. Someone like Bond could make it in his sleep, but I was no Bond.

I'd have to factor in the external elements like the wind and also the angle of descent. Another variable was how fast the prince walked. I'd have to time the shot and pull the trigger at exactly the right moment, even milliseconds before he actually came into the kill zone. And what if there were others between us, such as his mother or another dignitary? I could never risk hitting them.

I reminded myself to take a deep breath. I didn't have to figure everything out at once. I could play it by ear as the situation unfolded. Assuming I could get into position, I'd just have to hope everything went as planned.

The most important thing was that I had a glimmer of hope. I could pull it off if everything went perfectly. So I turned my thoughts to escaping. Even if I shot and missed, I'd have to get out of there as quickly as possible, while chaos and confusion took over the scene.

Contemplating the potential reaction of the royal protection unit, I began to doubt the probability of success. All my assumptions to that point had been that I could get into position. It suddenly dawned on me that it might not be possible.

The security team would surely realize the risk and have guards strategically placed on every rooftop in the area. Snipers, spotters, and other security personnel would be stationed to prevent exactly the kind of attempt I was planning.

First things first.

I needed a sniper rifle, and it was stashed away in the plane at a private airfield outside the city. Leaving the hotel was risky with the increased security, but I had no other option. The authorities would no doubt be looking for a red Porsche by now, but I hoped every available officer was involved in the security preparations and busy elsewhere.

Making my way to the lobby, I exited the hotel and asked the valet for the keys to the Porsche. He inspected my parking ticket and then gave me a cursory look right before taking off running in the direction of the parking garage. When he returned with the car, he handed over the keys without comment although he did give my breasts a long ogle.

I was starting to get used to it.

The drive to the airfield was tense. Every traffic light and every slow-moving vehicle felt like an obstacle conspiring to delay me. Thankfully, I didn't see any police. When I finally arrived, I parked the car and made my way to the small hangar where the plane was stored. My credentials easily got me through security.

"Are you leaving us today?" the administrator asked.

"Not today. Tomorrow," I answered, hoping upon hope that I was speaking words of prophecy.

"Your aircraft is fully fueled and our maintenance team gave it a good once over."

"Excellent."

"That's a fine plane you have there," the man said.

"Yes, it is," I answered, although I didn't even know which one Jamie had left for me.

It seemed like the man wanted to continue chatting or perhaps just wanted more time to savor his preoccupation with my breasts. It felt strange to have so many men notice me in this way. Eventually, I pried his eyes off my chest and was able to enter the hangar.

The rifle along with dozens of other weapons and supplies were hidden in a specially designed compartment within the plane's fuselage. Retrieving it was a quick process.

It's almost as if Jamie could read my mind and knew that my next move would be to try to kill the prince. She had left me the sniper rifle I trained with along with a discreet carrying case and the bullets I needed. It even had a specially designed scope should I have to take a long shot.

With the rifle secured, I made my way back to the hotel. The return trip was equally nerve-wracking, but I managed to make it back without incident. I decided to park the car in the self-parking rather than leave it with the valet, in case I needed to make a quick getaway tomorrow.

Once back in my room, I laid out the rifle and began inspecting it. Each component clicked into place with satisfying precision.

I mentally went over the plan again.

The dignitaries would arrive by vehicle at a location behind the stand. They'd walk in through the back, giving me two brief windows to take the shot. Either while the prince was entering or when he was leaving. I would need to position myself perfectly on the roof, somewhere I wouldn't be immediately spotted by the royal protection unit.

I went back to the roof and was greeted by the next obstacle. The door leading out to the roof was locked. A sign was displayed that read, *The rooftop bar will be closed tonight and tomorrow. We are sorry for any inconvenience.*

How am I going to get on that roof?

With less than twenty-four hours to figure it out.

25

The next morning

Two hours ago, Jan Sealy sat in his office, still fuming over his recent confrontation with Hefina Rosser from the royal protection unit. Not only had she taken over the case which in and of itself was bad enough, she had also disparaged him, questioning his competence in the process.

Where did she get the nerve? He prided himself on his tenacious investigative skills, honed by years of working the streets, being among the first to arrive at the scenes of gruesome crimes, and enduring the horrific images that haunted his nights.

Rosser, in contrast, worked in the luxurious royal palace, serving as a glorified nanny for a spoiled prince. Admittedly, Sealy had little respect for the prince, who seemed more interested in partying than attending to his state duties. If this impudent brat was Norway's hope for the future, he feared the country was in serious trouble.

Rumors about the prince's wild escapades were rampant. The police had been told to look the other way on multiple occasions when the prince caused problems that would have landed any ordinary citizen in jail. Sealy was a man who stood by his principles; he firmly believed that no one was above the law, not even royalty.

Something about this situation didn't feel quite right to him. Rosser hadn't been forthcoming about her motives for wanting to get involved in the killing of the four gang members or why she was so adamant about taking over the case and shutting down his investigation.

Further confusion reigned when the tip line was abruptly disconnected and stories in the news media about the shooting and the search for the person of interest were buried. It almost seemed like Rosser didn't want the woman brought in for questioning.

His curiosity had been sparked, and against his better judgment, he found himself at the bus stop where the rumored prostitute, four gang members, and the person of interest had disembarked, about a football field away from where the shooting occurred.

Checking his watch, he was right on time. Three thirty in the morning was about the time the incident occurred. He was going off a gut feeling, hoping that the woman might have a routine and get off work at the same time every night.

If he got lucky, he might get the chance to talk with her.

Or unlucky, if it cost him his job and pension. Despite the risks, Sealy was consumed by a need to uncover the truth of that night.

When he spotted the bus in the distance, his heart skipped a beat. Standing about twenty yards from the bus stop, he didn't want the woman to see him until she was off the bus. He stamped out his cigarette with his foot and waited, his breath coming heavily in the crisp night air.

The bus approached, and his mind raced with endless possibilities. Was she on the bus? Would he actually go through with it and question her? If he did, how could he keep it from getting back to Rosser?

The bus slowed to a stop, its doors opening with a hiss. He saw someone get up from the first row and move toward the exit. He held his breath in anticipation.

A woman stepped off the bus, looking weary and cautious, her eyes darting around as she surveyed her surroundings. He was safely in the shadows where she couldn't see him. She wore the same headsets as the person seen in the security camera footage, and his instincts screamed that this was the person he was looking for.

He didn't move until she started walking away from the stop, then he started to follow, keeping a safe distance. He had tailed suspects before, but this felt more personal. He knew he was risking everything by being there, but the stakes were too high to back down now.

The woman's pace was brisk, and she walked with a purpose, not even bothering to look over her shoulder, so she didn't know he was there. He considered turning back, but the obsession gnawing at his soul drove him to continue following her.

She turned a corner, heading down a side street. That's when she saw him.

He immediately responded by quickening his pace, closing the gap between them. She was headed toward a small but quaint white house. She looked back nervously, her eyes wide with fear. With several large bounding steps, he caught up with her before she could enter the house.

"Please don't hurt me," she begged.

"I'm sorry to scare you, miss," he said. "I'm a police lawyer and I just want to talk." He flashed his credentials. The porch of her house was dark so he doubted she could see them. She also probably couldn't clearly see his face, which might be a good thing if someone asked her to identify who she had spoken with.

"What do you want?" she asked, her tone had turned chilly.

"Like I said, I'm with the police." He thought it best not to mention his name or give her his card. "I'm not here to arrest you. I just want to know what happened the night of the shooting."

The woman looked at him with a blend of fear and suspicion. "I have no idea what you're talking about."

"Why are you lying to me? I know you were there. I have your face on the bus's security camera."

He actually didn't, but she didn't know that.

"A witness also saw you. She said you got off the bus first. Then four gang members followed you. A second woman exited the bus after you, armed with a gun. All I want to know is what happened after that."

"The witness is lying. I wasn't there. I heard about it on the news, but that's all I know. You must be looking for someone else."

"I think you're the one who is lying," he said, gruffly. "Would you like to do this down at the police station? Perhaps your memory might improve if I put you in a jail cell for a few hours."

The police station was the last place in the world he would take her, but she didn't know that, and the ploy worked.

"Alright, I was there. I got off work and the four boys started following me."

He started to ask her where she worked but decided not to interrupt her. She just started talking and he didn't want her to clam up.

"They got on the bus at the same time as me," she said. "I was hoping they would leave me alone, but when I got off at my stop, they followed me."

The woman became overwhelmed with emotions. Her voice quivered, and tears welled up in her eyes.

"Why were they following you?" he asked.

"Why do you think?" she replied bitterly. "I knew what they wanted. I just wanted them to get it over with."

Sealy gave a sympathetic nod. "I'm sorry you had to go through that. It must've been terrifying." He said it softly, to encourage her to continue.

"They said they'd kill me if I didn't do what they said."

His suspicions were confirmed. The men were dangerous and ruthless. Anyone who would prey on a young woman was the lowest of the low in his eyes.

Did they deserve to die? It depended on what she said next.

"I was lucky to . . ."

"Let's back up. When did you first notice the other woman on the bus?"

"She boarded right after the boys."

"Do you know her?"

"No, and even if I did, I wouldn't tell you. You can take me to jail if you want but I'm telling the truth. I don't know her, and I hope you never catch her."

"I'm not going to take you to jail. In fact, this conversation is strictly between us. Okay? Don't tell anyone we talked. Other people might try to talk to you."

Her eyes widened with fear.

"Who else knows about me?" she asked in a panicked tone.

"I'm not sure. But if I can find you, so can they."

"What do they want from me? I haven't done anything wrong. I don't even know the woman. She just appeared out of the blue."

"I believe you."

Her face softened slightly. Her shoulders had been tense and her forehead burrowed. She seemed relieved.

"Don't worry about the other people. They probably won't try to talk to you. As far as I know, I'm the only one who knows about you. And I'm not going to tell anyone. You're right. You did nothing wrong. You were a victim."

She brushed away tears that had escaped out of her eyes.

He felt guilty for trying to manipulate her, but he was covering his own tracks. He doubted she'd stand up to pressure if Rosser did confront her.

Nothing he could do about it now.

"What happened when everyone got off the bus?" he asked.

"I actually didn't know the girl got off until I turned to confront the boys. That's when I saw her and . . . she had a gun."

Fear flashed across her face as she recounted the horrific event. He was a good judge of witnesses and could tell when they were lying. This woman was telling the truth and had no reason to lie.

"I was petrified," she admitted. "I was afraid they'd kill her and me too. There were four of them and only one of her. The main guy, the one doing all the talking, pulled his gun. I screamed."

"But she shot them first," he stated.

She shook her head vigorously from side to side. "Actually, she had already put her gun away. I'm not sure why . . . " Her voice trailed off as she said it.

"But yeah, when he pulled his gun, she didn't hesitate," she continued, with renewed strength. "She was amazing; fearless, not afraid at all. She stood right up to them. I wish I had her courage."

The woman took a deep breath and her story spilled out more freely now. Like it was helping her to get it out.

"She hit the main guy in the nose. Like a ninja. She was lightning fast. I heard his head crack when it hit the sidewalk. It was sickening. Then she kicked the next guy in his bits. No. Actually, she kicked the guy first. Then hit the main guy. It all happened so fast."

That confirmed why the one guy was on the ground in the fetal position. Seally had deduced as much looking at the scene.

"I was cheering her on, but then the others pulled their guns. I thought they were going to kill her . . . and then me."

He opened his mouth to ask a question, but she kept talking.

"She pulled her gun and shot two of them point blank. Bam. Bam." She raised her hand and mimicked the motion of firing a weapon with her finger.

"What happened next?"

"She told me to get away from there as fast as possible and not to tell anyone about what happened. She told me I was safe and that she only did this to help me. To keep them from hurting me. I took off running. I heard two more gunshots, but I didn't dare look back. I went home and didn't tell anyone. Until now. I didn't even get a chance to thank her."

"You did the right thing by telling me. Your secrets are safe with me. I promise. I'll protect you if I can."

"You should protect her too. She's a good person. I can tell. She saved my life. That's all I know. And all I care about. When I saw the picture on the news, I didn't call in. Because I owe my life to her."

"Sounds like she's a hero."

"She is."

He thanked her and told her to get inside before anyone saw them. He waited until she disappeared into the small white house, the door closing softly behind her.

He remained frozen in place for what felt like a couple of minutes, absorbing the weight of the night's revelations. The woman's account had confirmed his suspicions but had also complicated things. His involvement in this case was a delicate balance of personal curiosity and professional duty. He couldn't afford to make any mistakes and wasn't sure what to do with this information.

As he walked back to his car, his mind raced. The mystery woman was an enigma. She had taken out four, armed gang members singlehandedly. This wasn't just someone who happened to be carrying a gun. She was trained, skilled. A professional.

But who was she? And why did she decide to intervene that night? Was she simply a Good Samaritan who happened to be at that place by accident?

No. She was more than that. She was important to Rosser in some way.

A car appeared out of nowhere.

It screeched to a halt next to him.

Rosser got out.

His heart was now a lump in his throat.

"You're a fool," she said. "I told you to stay away from this case."

"I don't like loose ends," he said. "I needed to talk to the prostitute and find out exactly what happened. I figured she might get off the bus at the same time again. Obviously, you thought the same thing."

"Get in the car," she ordered.

He didn't think he had a choice, so he got in. He hoped he didn't regret it.

26

Sleeping again was impossible, so I didn't even try. My mind was too wired for the events that would unfold tomorrow. At four in the morning, I planned to go to the tiger statue and desperately hoped that A-Rad would be there as well. It could be risky to venture out with heightened security in the area, but I had to take that chance. The thought of sitting in my hotel room wondering if he was there would drive me mad.

Avoiding risks wasn't in my nature and had never been my style. Even before I joined the CIA.

Besides, my disguise was working perfectly. I went out earlier that day and purchased a laptop, then spent a couple hours in an internet café meticulously planning my attack on the prince. Satellite images gave me a full layout of the area, including entrances, exits, hiding spots, trouble areas to avoid, and the road layouts.

I even found the funeral procession route and warnings about which roads would be closed. From that information, I was able to map out an escape route from the hotel to the airport.

My confidence in the plan grew by the minute. Reports confirmed that the royal family would be in attendance, including the prince. Media outlets even showed footage of the viewing area where the royal family and dignitaries would be seated.

The king was scheduled to address the crowd via live broadcast to various locations around the city, carried by all the news outlets. What

I had planned would be carried out on live television and watched by millions of people around the world.

That wouldn't deter me.

The only potential issue I could see was sneaking onto the roof of the hotel undetected. According to the sign, the roof was closed. I didn't know if that meant that the door was locked and no one would be on the roof, or the door was going to be manned by guards.

I hoped the former. The lock wouldn't be a problem. I could pick about anything. If nothing else, I'd bust it open somehow.

Guards would be more problematic, although manageable when I allowed the most optimistic thoughts to fill my mind. I could easily overpower a guard at the door. The trick would be to take him down without alerting the other guards. They'd have radios.

I'd have to be quick. Once on the roof, there'd be more guards stationed around. I could envision where they might be positioned, or at least where I would put them if I were in charge of security.

Whatever I did had to be done without harming them. They weren't my enemy. The prince was.

If I could successfully deal with the guards, I needed to act fast to get into position. The ideal spot for a shot was on the northwest corner of the hotel roof. I could hide there and wait for the perfect opportunity to fire the shot.

Being the tallest building in the area gave me an advantage. I could make it to the hiding spot without being seen since I didn't have anyone looking down at me from an adjacent building. The disadvantage was that snipers in the other buildings would probably notice if one or more of the guards were missing.

Further, the guards on the other buildings would be on the constant lookout for threats. As soon as I lifted my head and raised the weapon, snipers would be trained to take me out. I would have a split second to take the shot, and about the same amount of time to keep from getting my head blown off.

The challenge was how to see the viewing stand so I could time the shot. I'd have to be able to monitor it without being seen by anyone in any nearby buildings. Studying satellite images of the roof helped me to identify a potential spot, but I wouldn't really know until I got up there.

Despite my detailed planning and growing confidence, fear of failure still gnawed at my gut. One wrong move could lead to capture or death. But my desire to fulfill the mission outweighed those thoughts. Jamie had warned me that stoking the fire of revenge could make me do something foolish.

I could see that playing out now.

Once I was done planning, I had nothing else to do and the hours became agonizingly slow as I waited for four in the morning to arrive. I found myself pacing the room like a caged jaguar in a zoo. Ready to pounce but constrained. In my instance, by time.

At precisely half an hour before four, I finally could put on my disguise after taking two showers during the night to pass the time. I had time to put on makeup and looked like a real decked out floozy.

If A-Rad was at the tiger statue he might take one look at me and pass out on the spot. Or fall down on the ground from laughing so hard.

Once outside the hotel, I navigated through the quiet streets towards the tiger statue. Protocol demanded that I implement counter-surveillance tactics to check if anyone was following me, but practically won out.

The less time I spent outside the hotel the better. My goal was to go directly to the statue, and time it so I arrived exactly at four. If A-Rad wasn't there, I'd wait fifteen minutes and head straight back to the safety of the hotel and prepare for the funeral.

The increased security in the area due to the funeral had its pros and cons. The streets were closed off and free of cars, which meant there were fewer people around compared to the other mornings.

On the other hand, I couldn't help but feel like I stood out like the proverbial fish out of water. I felt uncomfortably conspicuous. The darkness was my only ally, cloaking my movements as I made my way to the rendezvous point trying to stay mostly in the shadows.

Walking the streets gave me another advantage. I could see with my own eyes what I'd seen in the satellite images. From the narrow alleyways to the major thoroughfares, every detail was now imprinted in my mind.

The planned funeral procession route and road closures were committed to memory. Being able to see them firsthand allowed me to be certain there hadn't been a last-minute change in plans.

As I walked in the moment of solitude, the weight of the mission hit me hard. An eerie anticipation filled the air. It's what it would feel like to be in an empty football stadium the night before the Super Bowl.

Only the stakes were so much higher for me.

As I approached the tiger statue, my mind was a whirlwind of strategies and contingencies. Every step brought me closer to knowing if A-Rad was there. My soul was filled with mixed emotions. I was hopeful, but I could already feel the extreme disappointment that he probably wouldn't be.

I took a deep breath, steeling myself for what lay ahead. The night was calm, but I sensed it was the calm before the storm. As I rounded the corner into the square where the tiger statue was prominently displayed, my heart began to do cartwheels in my chest.

The anxiety had turned into utter jubilation.

A-Rad was standing a few yards from the tiger statue. While I couldn't see his face clearly, I'd recognize that form anywhere.

I couldn't believe it.

He made it back to me!

I always had faith he would and chastised the cruel doubts that had gnawed at my confidence.

Would he recognize me in my disguise? When I saw the smirk form on his face, I knew he did.

I strode past the statue and continued walking. He left his location and came up beside me. I noticed that he was limping and struggled to keep up with me, so I slowed my pace.

"You look breast-taking," he quipped.

"If you say one more thing about my outfit," I said, half-joking and half-seriously, "I'll break your other leg!"

"You are a breast of fresh air," he said, ignoring the admonition.

"I'm warning you. I'm not in the mood."

"It's good to see you too," he said, sarcastically. I could hear the weariness in his voice. By his disheveled looks, he'd obviously been through quite an ordeal to get there.

I softened my tone to match his. "I'm sorry. I really am happy to see you. But right now, I'm focused on getting us safely to our hotel. It's not safe out here."

"I noticed downtown was crawling with cops yesterday."

"You were here yesterday?"

"Yeah. I arrived here in the afternoon. Needed to check things out."

"I wish I'd known. They're having the prince's bodyguards' funerals today."

"I figured that out. And I assume they're looking for us."

"You have no idea how true that is."

"How much farther is our hotel?"

"Not far."

We walked the rest of the way in silence. A-Rad was really struggling. He must've injured his leg badly.

When we got back to the hotel, we had a lot to talk about. I couldn't wait to tell him everything I'd been through over the last few days. How I managed to escape in Mostad. The killing of the four thugs. My plans to kill the prince.

I had countless questions for him. How did he escape? What happened to his leg? Was he going to help me with my plan?

I'd already decided that I wouldn't blame him if he didn't. What I was doing was reckless and I knew it. That wasn't going to stop me, and I wasn't going to let him talk me out of it either. If he had any reservations at all, I would encourage him not to participate.

As we walked back, the streets seemed even emptier than before. The silence between us was thick, but it felt comfortable, one filled with the unspoken happiness that we were together again.

I could sense it from him, so I reached for his hand. Then I linked arms to provide support while we climbed the hill to our hotel.

Each step felt heavier, each breath a reminder of the gravity of what I was planning. As we got closer, I began to feel the familiar knot of anticipation in my stomach.

I almost dreaded telling him about my plan and killing the thugs. Afraid of being judged.

Would he scold me for getting caught on a security camera? Would he say I was crazy for even thinking about killing the prince?

I wasn't sure how I'd handle the rejection without getting defensive. I could picture him refusing to help me. Not willing to participate in my foolish endeavor.

Which was fine. He could go back to the plane. If things didn't go well, he could leave without me and get away safely.

I just didn't want him to go away angry with me. After all we'd been through, I didn't want our first hours back together to be filled with strife.

It's even possible that the next few hours may be our last. There were no guarantees that I'd get out of this alive. My heart ached at the thought of being separated again, even though I knew it'd be the best thing for him.

It was settled in my mind. That's what I would urge him to do. Even command him, since I was still the mission leader.

Inside the hotel, we made our way to the room without incident. The hallways were deserted. Once inside the room, A-Rad collapsed onto the couch, wincing in pain. I got him some water, which he devoured in a couple of gulps.

"Tell me everything," I said, my voice barely above a whisper. "What happened to you? How did you get away? How did you hurt your leg?"

A-Rad took a deep breath, his eyes locking onto mine. "Escaping wasn't hard," he began. "After they separated us in Mostad, they put me in a makeshift interrogation room. They even tied me up although it wasn't hard to get out of. Some woman came in and started asking questions."

"I had a woman asking me questions!" I said, excitedly. "I found her on the internet. Her name is Hefina Rosser. She's in charge of the prince's security. A better description is that she's his fixer. She cleans up his messes."

"I figured as much. She told her men to hogtie me when I wouldn't answer her questions. That wasn't going to happen."

A smile came to my lips. I could imagine what he did to the guards. I'm sure they still regretted it.

"Yeah. It didn't turn out well for them," he said, noticing my smirk. "I got out of the room easily enough and ran into the woods. I was going to circle back to help you escape. But I slipped on a rock and messed up my knee. Pretty bad. It hurts like a son-of-a-gun. It's an old football injury. I'll probably need surgery."

"I'm so sorry," I said, sympathetically. It warmed my heart that he was coming back for me. I had done the same thing. Tried to get away so I could come back and help him. I realized it wouldn't have mattered if I had tried to look for him. He had already escaped as well.

"That's why it took me so long to get here. I had to walk all the way. I'm sure I made my knee worse."

I sat down next to him on the couch and ignored the putrid smell. He clearly hadn't taken a shower or brushed his teeth in days, and I resisted the overwhelming urge to kiss him to make him feel better.

He gestured to his injured limb, a grimace crossing his face. "But I managed to elude them all the way to Oslo. Barely."

My heart ached at the thought of what he had gone through alone. The trucker gave me a ride. I couldn't imagine walking all that way. Surviving the elements.

"I'm sorry, A-Rad. I wish I could've been there to help you."

"I saw you," he said, surprising me. "I mean . . . I didn't see you, but I heard you. I heard them chasing after you. I heard the dogs. I tried to catch up and help you but couldn't with my leg. I thought maybe I could lead the dogs away from you, but they were too far ahead of me. Anyway, I was cheering for you. Praying you would escape."

I filled him in on my own details, the tense moments traversing through the woods. How I returned to the yacht. How Bond and Alex helped me escape by disabling the guard's boat. He didn't seem that surprised that they had helped me or that they left me behind.

I didn't mention killing the thugs. What difference did it make now? This would all be over today. One way or the other.

"You should take a shower," I said. "I have everything you need in the bathroom. I got you toiletries."

He traced his full beard with his fingers.

"I could really use a razor."

"I got you one of those, too. Although, scruffy A-Rad is kind of growing on me."

"I hate it," he grumbled.

I'd never seen him anything but clean-shaven except occasionally when we were on a mission, and he had no access to a razor for a few days. The moment he could, he always shaved off any hair on his face and chest.

"There are some clothes for you in the closet. Are you hungry?"

"I'm starving."

"I'll order room service. What do you want?"

"Everything on the menu," he said, weakly.

I forced a laugh. "That's my A-Rad." He could eat more in one setting than any man I had ever known.

I helped him to his feet. He let out a groan.

As he walked toward the bathroom, he stopped and pointed to the bed.

"What's that?"

My heart did a lap around my chest.

"It's a sniper rifle," I said.

"What's it for?"

"After your shower, I'll tell you."

A-Rad gave me a long intense look, nodded, and continued toward the bathroom. By the time he finished his shower, I had a feeling he would figure it out.

27

A-Rad spent more than an hour in the shower and bathroom. I couldn't blame him. I remembered what it felt like to finally enjoy the luxury of a hotel room after being out in the field.

The room service food had arrived and was getting cold, but we were used to eating cold meals on missions. After the room service attendant left, I quickly changed out of my disguise, grateful to be back to my normal self.

I doubted I'd ever have to wear that outfit again. Certainly not to kill the prince. It was too restrictive, and the shoes weren't conducive to a quick escape.

A thought caused me to laugh out loud. I pictured myself trying to hold the rifle and firing. I doubt I could even manage it around those two fake melons.

The bathroom door opened, and A-Rad emerged, looking fresh and clean with a newly shaven face and dressed in the tidy clothes I had gotten for him. The weariness remained in his eyes, but his handsome face almost took my breath away.

I rose from the couch and walked over to him, planting a big kiss on his lips before rubbing my hands across his smooth cheeks.

"This looks more like the man I know," I said, playfully.

"And you look more like the woman I know," he teased, looking me up and down. His smile had turned to an exaggerated fake frown.

"You sound disappointed."

"I can't lie. I liked the new look," he said, trying to hide a smirk. "If that hadn't been you by the tiger statue, I might have asked that girl for her number."

I patted his broad and solid chest. "What is it with men and breasts?" I questioned.

"I admit it. We are shallow creatures. Do you remember that time we had to dress up for the party in Singapore? You were decked out then. I kinda liked it."

"My disguise had padding in my bra then too, but nothing like what I was wearing this morning."

"We made quite a couple.

"I remember. You looked handsome in your tuxedo. I barely knew you then."

He nodded. "Maybe we should dress up more often."

"Let's do it sometime when we aren't getting shot at."

Brad had sent us to Singapore, where we were to pose as a married couple for nearly three months. That's before our relationship took a romantic turn. The whole thing was a disaster. We were constantly at each other's throats, fighting like a lot of typical married couples.

One evening, we had to attend an event at a large corporate center while targeting a notorious arms dealer and sex trafficker flanked by a team of armed bodyguards. We barely got out alive. That night was probably the first time I noticed that I might have feelings for A-Rad. Surviving a dangerous situation together can bring you closer.

We formed a bond that night that had only strengthened with time. Looking back, that night in Singapore was probably more dangerous than what I was planning now.

There, I didn't have the element of surprise. The mark was aware of us, and it turned into a cat-and-mouse game to see who killed who first. We were both constrained by the hundreds of innocent people who attended the gala.

This time, I had the safety of the hotel, which provided cover and multiple exits. I also had a car and an airplane. In Singapore, we didn't have any of those resources.

I think Brad planned it that way. He wanted to test our abilities to improvise under pressure. I was a young operative, and A-Rad, though skilled and more experienced, was accustomed to running missions with Jamie, not me.

Somehow, we survived the night. Hopefully, we'd survive today as well.

A-Rad took another glance at the sniper rifle and asked, "So what are you planning?"

"Let's eat first," I said.

He didn't object and walked to the dining table laden with a smorgasbord of food. I hadn't ordered everything on the breakfast menu, but almost. We had six different breakfast meals in front of us.

A-Rad was already digging in. I picked up the menu and read from it.

"We have an omelet with sausage, bacon, ham, and cheddar cheese. Just like you like it. No mushrooms, tomatoes, or onions."

"Perfect," he said with a full mouth.

"It comes with a side of whole grain toast and jelly. We have buttermilk pancakes, French toast, and a Belgian Waffle with pure maple syrup."

"Yum."

"I know you like all three, so I figured I'd let you choose."

"I'll eat all of them."

He was alternating between them, barely stopping to breathe between bites.

"There's also eggs benedict."

He made a disapproving face.

"That'll weigh me down for what I figure you got planned. I don't want to be fattened up for the slaughter."

I grimaced at the word "slaughter." He was right though. I'd want to take a nap if I ate the eggs benedict.

"There's a side of home fries."

"Now you're talking."

"And sweet potato hash."

"Any chicken sausages?" he joked, while biting into one.

"You got coffee, tea, and me," I said, sitting down beside him.

I decided to eat as well. Even though I wasn't hungry, the Jamie mandate was to eat and sleep when we could since we never knew when we might get another chance.

Depending on how things went, this might be our last good meal for a while. Hopefully, we'd be feasting on the plane later today, which I was sure was well-stocked with food and beverages.

"How's your knee?" I asked once we started to slow down and our mouths weren't continually full.

He pulled back the leg of his pants to show me a swollen knee, twice its normal size.

"A-Rad! That looks awful. I can't believe you even tried to walk on it."

"You ordered me to escape and meet you at the tiger statue. I had no choice."

"What can we do about it?"

"Don't worry about me. I'll be alright. It's not as bad as it looks."

I knew that wasn't true.

"Alright," he said, his tone serious. "Tell me what you're planning."

I took a deep breath. "The prince is attending the funeral tomorrow," I began. "It's my chance to take him out. The plan is to get onto the roof of this hotel, find a good vantage point, and take the shot. It'll be broadcast live around the world."

A-Rad's expression hardened. "And you thought you could pull this off alone?"

"I've mapped everything out," I insisted. "I know all the entrances, exits, and where I think the guards will likely be positioned. I don't expect you to help. Your leg—"

"Forget my leg," he interrupted. "I'll manage. I'm not going to let you do this alone. If we go down, we go down together."

His words hit me hard, and for the first time, I seriously considered abandoning my plan. Foolishly putting my life at risk was one thing but making him do so was far worse.

"I want to do this," I said. "But if you don't think it's worth the risk for us, I won't."

Tears welled up in my eyes at the thought of not going through with it. "After everything the prince has done... the girls... I feel like I owe it to them," I said.

A-Rad reached out, his hand covering mine. "I get it. Believe me, I do. But this isn't just about revenge. You need to survive this, too. The risk has to be worth it."

A pang of guilt shot through me. "That's why I think you should stay with the plane. You can leave if things go south."

"We have a plane?" he asked with his eyes widening.

"Alex and Jamie left it for us. That's where I got the sniper rifle."

"I thought that thing looked familiar."

"I also have a car in the hotel parking garage. It's a red Porsche."

"Nice. That might come in handy in a chase."

"Here's what we should do. You take a cab to the airport and stay with the plane. I'll kill the prince and then drive the Porsche to the airport. We can be in the air within an hour. They might close down the airspace, but that has never stopped us before."

"I'm not leaving you," he said firmly. "Not again. If you're determined to go through with this, then we'll figure it out together."

A surge of gratitude and relief washed over me. "Thank you," I whispered. Deep down, that's what I was hoping he would say.

He squeezed my hand. "But we need to be smart about this. Minimize the risks as much as possible."

I nodded, feeling a renewed sense of determination. With A-Rad by my side, my plan seemed more feasible.

"Let's go over your plan in detail," he said. "We have to be prepared for anything."

I filled him in on the specifics: the timing, the escape routes, the potential pitfalls. A-Rad listened intently, occasionally asking questions or offering suggestions.

I showed him the satellite images of the area, which he studied closely. Neither of us were experts at developing mission plans. Colonel did most of these types of plans for the AJAX team. But we had watched him enough to learn some things.

Despite the gravity of our situation, a sense of camaraderie settled between us. We were back together, facing impossible odds once again. It's so much easier when we know we have each other's backs.

"Look at this," he said, pointing to an elevator on the roof.

"What's that?"

"That's the service elevator. There's a bar on the roof that serves drinks and food. The food is brought up from the kitchen on that elevator."

"That's where we need to enter the roof," he said excitedly. "By that elevator. That way, we avoid the guard at the door."

"What if that elevator isn't working? They'll probably have it shut down."

"I thought about that. All we need to do is get to the shaft and climb up the ladder. We can open the door to the roof."

"You can't climb an elevator shaft with your leg."

"Don't worry about me."

For two more hours, we planned. It seemed feasible. I was still worried about A-Rad's physical limitations, but I knew his will would overcome them.

We sat on the couch and relaxed for the first time. I leaned my head against his shoulder. We both closed our eyes and drifted off for a few minutes.

"We're really going to do this, aren't we?" I asked after waking up, searching his eyes for any sign of hesitation.

A-Rad stood and poured himself a cup of coffee then limped over to the microwave. He heated it without answering my question, making me wonder if he was having second thoughts. When it beeped, he took out his coffee and took a long sip.

"Kaley, I know you too well. Once you've set your mind on something, there's no turning back. And given what's at stake, I understand why you feel this has to be done."

I nodded. "I've considered every angle, and every potential obstacle. I know it's incredibly risky. And the ramifications afterwards . . . " My voice trailed off as I thought about them.

"That's putting it mildly," A-Rad said, leaning back in the side chair he was now sitting in. "We have no idea what we're walking into. Probably trained snipers, high security, and the eyes of the world. One mistake, and we're dead."

He took a long and contemplative sip of his coffee before speaking again. "Even if we're successful and kill the prince, you know the fallout is going to be off the charts. We'll be on the run for the foreseeable future. Maybe the rest of our lives. There'll be a global manhunt for us. The CIA will never take us back."

The weight of his words hung heavily in the air. "I know. I've thought about that. But the prince's death will send a powerful message. It will give us a chance to expose the corruption and atrocities he's committed. No telling how many other world leaders are like him."

A loud and urgent knock on the door jolted both of us out of our seats. I reached for my gun, but A-Rad gestured for me to stay calm.

"What is it?" I asked through the door after I rushed over there.

"Maid service," came the response.

Was it really? Could it be a trap?

I looked through the peephole and confirmed it was the maid. A noticeable sigh rose to the back of my throat.

"We won't be needing it today," I said. "Thank you." My grip on the gun loosened.

A-Rad and I both sat back down at the table, the tension momentarily broken. A-Rad reached for a piece of toast and devoured it in two large bites.

"Kaley," he said softly after washing it down with a huge gulp of orange juice. He reached over and took my hand. "Whatever happens, know that I'm with you. To the end. I love you."

I squeezed his hand, my eyes meeting his. "Thank you, A-Rad. I couldn't do this without you. I love you, too."

That's the first time I had said those words and I knew they were true.

He smiled, a glimmer of the old A-Rad shining through. "You don't know how long I've waited to hear those words."

"Then let's make sure we come out of this alive so I can say them many, many more times."

We embraced and kissed passionately. It seemed like we had turned a corner in our relationship. We'd gone past the point of no return. I realized that he was my future. Whatever it might be. Fifty years. Ten years. One year. Or a few more hours.

I'd live the rest of my life with him.

The fear and uncertainty were still there, but they were overshadowed by a steely determination and a new-found bond cemented in love.

The funeral service for the bodyguards was at eleven, and we watched the broadcast on television. Hearing the speakers praise the bodyguards sent a rage through me. Those men weren't heroes. They weren't "wonderful men." They were protecting the prince and his depraved operation. They were complicit in the prince's diabolical scheme. They were the ones who guarded the girls.

And some of those in attendance knew the truth and yet chose to cover it up, including Hefina Rosser, whom I spotted among the crowd. When the camera panned and captured the prince, my blood started to boil, and I almost became unglued.

We had planned to get into position before the procession began. We figured the guards wouldn't be on as high alert since none of the royalty were there.

But I decided I couldn't wait anymore, so I stood up and picked up the rifle.

"Are you ready?" A-Rad asked, his voice steady and resolute.

I nodded, my heart pounding with a mix of fear and anticipation. "I'm ready."

28

Jan Sealy was, for all practical purposes, under house arrest. Hefina Rosser from the Royal Protection Unit had snatched him off the street in the middle of the night after he met with the prostitute who witnessed the shooting of the four gang members. She took him directly to his house with strict orders to remain there until further notice.

"What right do you have to detain me?" he had asked defiantly.

"Test me and you'll find out. You're lucky I don't take you directly to jail. I told you to stay out of my investigation."

He decided not to press the matter. She had warned him that he could lose his job and pension. He wasn't entirely sure if she had the authority to arrest him, but he didn't want to push her far enough to find out.

What disturbed him most was seeing Rosser's goons drag the prostitute out of her house. They put her into a second car, and he had no idea where they took her.

"She doesn't know anything!" he had cried out when the scene unfolded before his eyes.

"She saw the shooter."

"But she doesn't know who she is."

"I told you to stay out of it. When will you learn to do what I say?"

Defeated, he slumped down in the back seat of the SUV, riding the rest of the way to his house in silence, mentally berating himself for his foolishness. Not only had he jeopardized his career, but he had also put the prostitute in danger.

He had no idea what Rosser was covering up or what lengths she would ultimately go to protect it, but she seemed to think she was all powerful and he wondered to what extent she was.

"I promise I'll protect you," he had reassured the young woman only minutes before they took her. "No one will know who you are but me."

She must surely think he was lying, that he set her up. He felt worse about that than any repercussions he might face. If the worst happened to him, he could handle it. He had been poor once and had worked his way out of it through his own hard work and determination. While he didn't want to start over in a new career, he could if necessary.

He wasn't married anymore: that union ended after twenty-four years. They had one daughter together, who he put through college. She was on her own now and doing well, married with two kids. Although he rarely saw her or the kids and couldn't remember the last time he'd spoken to his ex-wife.

The stillness in the house was something he was used to, but today it added to his anxiety. What disturbed him most was having a guard outside his door. It's not that he had any place specifically to go, it's the lack of freedom that bothered him.

Normally, when he got off a night shift, he went straight to bed. That's what he should be doing now and would be, had he not been ambushed by Rosser. Since he couldn't go anywhere, he had the obsessive urge to leave the house.

The point was that he should be able to leave if he wanted. He was a prisoner in his own home. Even if he wanted to leave, his car was parked on the street in the neighborhood where he talked to the prostitute.

He called the police impound lot and had them tow it to his office. He'd catch a ride over there, whenever he was allowed to leave. Which had to be later that evening when his next shift began. Surely, Rosser couldn't keep him from doing his job.

Why would she want to? He hadn't done anything wrong, and he resented being treated like a common criminal.

Sealy tried to sleep but tossed and turned in the bed. Eventually, he got up and powered up his laptop. All the case files were still there. He thought it best to get rid of them. He could envision Rosser storming his house and searching it, seizing his laptop along with other electronic devices.

It pained him to do so, but he permanently deleted all the files. It was the right move. This case was too hot for some unknown reason. He needed to heed Rosser's advice and stay as far away from it as possible.

He looked over at the clock. The funeral for the bodyguards was about to start, and he had it on in the living room with the volume up so he could hear it in the next room. As he was about to log off his computer and go watch it, an email notification from an unknown source popped up on the screen. He hesitated since his policy was not to open something if he didn't know who sent it.

For some reason, he was drawn to the email. The subject line read: Why the Prince Wants You Off the Case.

Should he open it? Did he really want to know what was in that email? Wasn't he in enough trouble already?

Curiosity got the best of him. He couldn't resist the temptation to open it. Unanswered questions had always plagued his investigative mind and insatiable curiosity. His tenacity and stubbornness drove him to be a relentless pursuer of the truth. Looking back, the biggest frustrations in his life were when the truth escaped him.

It often took him too long to give up. He spun his wheels when his efforts would be better served elsewhere.

He stared at his computer screen and indecision set in. Should he delete the email or open it? The questions flooded his mind like a raging river that had overflowed its banks.

Who sent it? How did they get his private email address? Whoever sent it obviously had inside information. Not many people knew he was on the case and even fewer knew he had been taken off it.

Against his better judgment, he decided to open it. Who sent it was unclear and the cryptic message immediately raised more questions than it answered.

Things are not as they seem, were the words that jumped off the screen.

That's all it said.

That's weird.

When he was about to delete it, he paused. The email had an attachment. He had instinctively decided to delete it without opening it. Now he was having second thoughts.

His hand quivered as he hovered the cursor over the mysterious attachment. He wasn't worried about inadvertently opening himself up to a virus. Because of his job at the police department, he had sophisticated anti-malware protection on his personal computer as well.

He was worried that it might be a trick. That Rosser might've sent him the email to test him.

I've come this far. If I'm going off the cliff anyway, I might as well get it over with.

With his hands still shaking, he opened the file and a picture appeared on the screen. He blinked twice to make sure what he was seeing.

The prince was in the picture along with four young women. They looked to be college age girls.

What?

The women were in various stages of undress. Clearly caught in some kind of sexual activity. Was the photo real or was it doctored? If it was real, then who took it? More importantly, why did they send it to him?

Upon further inspection, he noticed a blurry figure in the mirror behind the girls taking the picture with a phone. Behind her were more girls. He felt a rush of excitement. He struggled to see the face of the person taking the picture. He tried to blow it up. It came into focus enough to recognize who it was.

The woman! The shooter. The person Rosser was so desperately looking for.

He examined the image more closely to be certain. The picture was grainy, but it looked like her. By the time he had studied it from every angle, he felt confident it was her, but was unsure what to make of it.

What did it mean? Was Rosser trying to cover up one of the prince's indiscretions? The public wouldn't be shocked to learn that the prince had participated in an orgy with a group of women. Although, the tabloids would probably pay a bunch of money for that photo, and the scandal would be of national importance.

Things started to make sense.

The woman who shot the four gang members had caught the prince in a compromising position. She had photos that she intended to sell. Perhaps she was even blackmailing the prince.

The shooting seemed unrelated, but Rosser didn't want the woman's picture out there in case she got caught by him or someone else. The woman might give up the picture and embarrass the prince which was why Rosser was in full out damage-control-mode.

Yet something about the picture didn't align with his theory. It nagged at him, but he couldn't put his finger on it. The girls' expressions were off. They looked horrified rather than entertained.

It didn't seem like they were having a good time. He dismissed the thought. After all, they were probably freaked out about having their picture taken.

But the room also seemed odd. Not like a palace or a hotel, but dark and seedy. Would the prince go someplace like that?

Of course he would, to maintain anonymity.

He zoomed in on one of the girl's faces. Her eyes looked distant. Troubled. He'd seen that look in victims.

Another girl looked horrified. What was she afraid of? The prince, the woman, or both?

Sealy leaned back in his chair, staring at the screen. Something clicked in his mind. Something familiar. He leaned forward and looked closer at the photo. He thought he recognized one of the girls.

He excitedly got out of the email and did a search for missing college girls. The stories had been all over the news for months. An unsolved mystery that had riveted the country.

The stories appeared from the search. He clicked on one. The pictures of all the missing college students appeared on the screen. Seven of them. He almost fell out of his chair.

Returning to the email, he compared those missing girls to the ones in the photos.

It was them. No doubt about it.

The photo shattered any lingering doubts he might have had about staying involved in the case. He rubbed his temples, trying to process what he'd just seen. The implications were staggering, and his mind raced with possibilities.

Was the prince behind the kidnappings?

He could see now with glaring clarity why Rosser wanted him off the case. The woman had more than provocative photos to sell to the press. She had incriminating evidence that could destroy the prince and possibly even the monarchy.

He considered his options carefully. Turning this photo over to Rosser wasn't one of them and would likely lead to immediate retaliation. She had already shown that she had no qualms about using force and intimidation to control the situation.

Sealy knew he needed to be cautious, and that the image also gave him leverage. As he contemplated his next move, another email notification popped up on his screen. This time, it was from a familiar address—someone he trusted implicitly, his old friend and confidant, Detective Liam Massey.

Sealy opened it without giving it a second thought. He read it out loud, his voice tinged with tension. "Jan, I heard about your situation. Be careful. Rosser is more dangerous than you think. I've dug up some information on her. Let's meet."

He stared at Liam's email, his mind whirring with questions. He closed his laptop and decided to ruminate on it before he decided what to do with the information.

He suddenly felt tired. He walked into the living room and sat down on the couch. The television was broadcasting the funeral procession of the bodyguards. The solemn scene starkly contrasted with the turmoil roiling inside him.

The king was addressing the nation from a viewing stand. Sealy wondered if the king knew about the prince's activities. Probably not. That's why Rosser was trying so hard to cover it up.

The six hearses of the bodyguards were stopped on the street in front of the viewing stand. The camera panned across the somber faces of the attendees. Dignitaries, family members, and colleagues stood in silent tribute. The prince was there, sitting on the back row of the grandstand, his expression a mix of grief and stoic duty.

His thoughts drifted back to the disturbing photograph. He cursed the prince under his breath. Angry that he had been pulled into such a mess. He could never cover it up. It wasn't in his nature.

The women in the picture haunted him. The terrified looks on their faces were permanently etched in his memory. Rage boiled at Rosser for being willing to hide such depravity. It's almost as bad as the crime itself in his mind. It certainly made her culpable. She was the one who should be arrested.

Suddenly, a sharp crack shattered the air. Sealy recognized it immediately.

A gunshot.

He knew the sound of gunfire like he knew his own voice.

The crowd on the screen responded almost in unison, confusion morphing rapidly from disbelief to terror. The camera swung wildly, desperately trying to capture the source of the chaos.

His heart thundered as he leaned closer, his eyes glued to the screen.

"Oh my, God," he muttered, a sinking feeling of dread pooling in his stomach.

The camera finally zeroed in on the prince, or what was left of him. He was slumped in his chair and half of his head was missing, obliterated by the bullet's impact.

Survival was impossible.

An assassin!

Could it be her?

The mysterious woman?

The one who killed the four thugs. The one who took the picture!

Screams erupted as pandemonium engulfed the scene.

Jan remained frozen, struggling to grasp the full magnitude of everything that had happened to him over the last two hours.

29

The spray of bullets from the sniper rifles in the building across from the hotel had me momentarily pinned down. The deafening sound of gunfire ricocheted off the concrete walls, sending chards of debris raining down on me.

As I had suspected, the snipers spotted me, and I barely got my head below the ledge before meeting the same fate as the prince.

I crouched low, my body pressed against the wall, heart pounding in my chest. My next move had to be quick and decisive. I was safe there for the moment, but it wouldn't take long for the police to swarm the building and trap me in.

The prince lay dead, but there was no time to celebrate. I could hear the shouts and screams of chaos coming from the streets.

The buildings where the snipers were positioned were lower than the hotel, a small advantage but one that would save my life. Once I got away from the ledge, they had no angle to take a shot at me.

With a sense of urgency, I duck-walked away from the ledge, keeping low to avoid any stray bullets that might come my way. My muscles tensed and strained as each step was calculated. Once I thought it was safe, I bolted up and sprinted toward the service elevator, my designated escape route.

Halfway there, the main door to the roof burst open with a resounding bang. A guard appeared, weapon drawn, and eyes filled with determination.

Our gazes met briefly.

I raised my handgun and his eyes widened in fear.

The sniper rifle, my instrument of assassination, was left back at the ledge. Since they knew where the shot had originated from, and they couldn't trace the weapon back to me, it made sense to leave it. Carrying it would only impede my escape, slowing me down at a time when speed was of the essence.

My fingers tightened around the grip of the handgun. I fired a single shot over the guard's head, a deliberate miss. I couldn't bring myself to harm him; he was just an innocent doing his job. I'd surrender before I caused him any serious harm.

The warning shot worked as intended, and he ducked down and took cover behind a pillar without returning fire, giving me the precious seconds I needed to reach the service elevator.

When I got to the elevator, a new problem presented itself. The elevator wasn't there; it had no doubt been summoned to the first floor by the police. A logical move, as they would need to use it to reach the roof.

My planned escape route was no longer an option. I remained calm as I weighed other possibilities. I could hear the guard approaching, his footsteps on the concrete floor giving away his position, drawing him closer with each passing second.

That pathway to escape was blocked as well.

Sirens blared on the street below. I had to act quickly, or I might as well give myself up.

I waited for the guard to get closer, then emerged with my hands raised in surrender. My weapon was tucked snugly into the waistband of my pants, strategically placed for him to see it.

"You move, you die!" he shouted at me.

I raised my hands higher in the air.

He inched closer, cautiously, both hands firmly on his weapon. My feet were frozen in place. I didn't want to give him any hint of what I had planned or make any sudden moves that might cause him to pull the trigger by mistake.

He was within a foot of me now. He took one hand off the gun and reached out for the weapon in my pants. A big mistake. He should've made me lie on the ground.

As he reached to remove it, I grabbed his gun with lightning speed and delivered a precise blow to the side of his neck, hitting the exact spot that would knock him unconscious without causing lasting harm. He crumpled to the ground, limp and out of commission. He'd be out for two or three minutes. He'd have a headache tomorrow but would otherwise be okay.

His gun was in my hand now. I tossed it to the side.

An idea came to me. Taking his radio, I spoke into it, "Suspect spotted fleeing the hotel," I said. "Repeat, the suspect is on foot, headed toward the train station."

Hopefully, this would distract them long enough for A-Rad and me to make our escape. If they were searching the train station, it might give us the opportunity we needed to escape.

I was on the move again, sprinting toward the main door, the same one the guard had come through. From there, I opted for the stairs to avoid the elevator and to prevent getting trapped.

When I flung open the door, A-Rad was there, standing at the top of the stairs, waiting for me. Our original plan had been to go to the roof together, by climbing up the elevator shaft ladder to the top, prying open the elevator door, then facing whatever threat was on the roof.

The problem was that the elevator was at the rooftop. Something we hadn't counted on. That meant, we had to ascend the stairs, pull ourselves up onto the top of the elevator, open one of the panels, and drop down inside, then pry open the door to the roof.

A-Rad's injured leg made climbing the elevator shaft impossible. Even if he could pull himself up onto the top of the elevator, he couldn't drop the eight feet to get inside without doing more damage to his injured knee.

We had seriously considered calling off the mission.

"What about the guards?" he had said. "You can't disarm all of them by yourself."

"I'll figure something out. If I get up there and it's too risky, I'll come back and we'll get out of here. I won't take any unnecessary risks. I promise."

"I'll wait in the room for you."

I'll never forget the hurt on his face. I could tell he felt like he was letting me down. Turned out that there were no guards on the roof. Whoever was in charge of security didn't think they needed them. One guard was posted at the locked entrance, and they must've thought that it was all they needed to prevent a threat from accessing the roof.

A critical lapse of planning and judgment on someone's part, and they'd be second-guessed for months to come. I was thankful for the lack of foresight. I was able to make it into position without incident and without being seen. All I had to do was time the shot and execute it.

I was fortunate a second time. The prince was sitting in the back row. He was tall, so his head was just above the protection of the bullet proof glass. Another critical mistake by the people in charge of his security. I didn't have to wait for him to exit the viewing stand. I could take the shot on my own terms.

It wasn't an easy shot, but it wasn't that hard either, and the bullet found its mark. I even had time to duck before the snipers opened fire.

Seeing A-Rad waiting for me on the stairs was a welcomed sight. It saved time not having to go back to the room. The window to escape was closing fast and every second counted.

"All hell is about to break loose," I said to him.

"Let's move then," A-Rad said, urgency lacing his voice.

The plan was simple: take the stairs down to the parking garage where the Porsche was kept, drive to the airport, and fly the plane out of the country.

With adrenaline surging, I took the steps several at a time. But A-Rad's injury slowed him, and I had to adjust my pace to wait for him.

Getting to the garage was going to take longer than I had anticipated. I could only hope my false report had sent the police on a wild goose chase to the train station.

We descended about ten floors, halfway to the parking garage. I slowed again to wait for A-Rad to catch up. I'd feel a lot better once we made it there. If we could just get to the car, we could outrun anything that tried to catch us. If we couldn't make it to the airport, we could find a place to hide and wait it out.

Each floor down the well-lit stairway felt like a victory, a small step closer to freedom. I almost started to believe we were going to make it.

Suddenly, a loud thud echoed behind me, followed by a cry of agony. I turned in horror to see A-Rad on the stairwell landing, clutching his knee, his face twisted in pain. I bounded up the steps to him.

"I think I messed up my other knee," he managed to say through gritted teeth.

"Let me help you up," I offered, but he collapsed under his own weight, unable to stand.

A-Rad was a big man with a large frame, over two hundred pounds of solid muscle, and carrying him wasn't an option. If he couldn't put any weight on his leg, I couldn't even shoulder him out. We still had ten floors to descend.

He slumped to the ground, his face a mask of agony and resignation. "You go. I can't."

"I'm not leaving without you," I insisted, my voice shaking with emotion.

"Kaley, listen to me. Save yourself. Go to the airport and get out of the country. I'll be fine."

Tears welled up in my eyes as I sat down beside him, refusing to leave him behind.

"I'm not leaving you," I said. "You didn't leave me when you had the chance. Remember what you said? Whatever happens, we're together until the end."

He let out an affirming groan, knowing there was no changing my mind. I clutched his arm tightly and rested my head against it, the weight of our predicament settling over me like a shroud.

Oddly, it actually felt peaceful in that stairway.

A few minutes later, the sound of police rushing up the stairs grew louder, their footsteps a harbinger of our impending capture. The worst part of it was that we could've gotten away had A-Rad not had the injured knee.

We had just enough time. Fate had a different idea.

I didn't blame A-Rad. It wasn't his fault.

I tossed my gun away from me, and A-Rad did the same. There was no point in resisting, and I didn't want to give the police any reason to use their weapons on us.

We'd go peacefully, and hopefully live to fight another day. We had escaped from their grasp once before and we could do it again.

The stakes were higher this time. I had killed the prince. There'd be a national outcry against me.

"Did you at least get him?" A-Rad asked, his voice barely above a whisper.

"Yeah. The prince is dead," I replied. My words lacked any sense of triumph to them.

"Good. At least we didn't risk it all for nothing."

"No. Mission accomplished," I said, though the words felt hollow.

Was it worth the price? Only time would tell.

30

Two months later
Oslo Tinghus (Courthouse)

This would be the second time I had seen A-Rad since the shooting of the prince. The first time was in the same courtroom, when we were both arraigned for his murder.

We were transported to the hearing separately. I was led into the courtroom first. My heart leapt to the top of my chest when A-Rad came in shortly thereafter. He seemed to be doing better. During the last arraignment, he had just undergone surgery to repair the damage in both of his knees and was still using a wheelchair.

He hobbled in on crutches today. He moved with a determined grace, if slightly awkward, the metal supports clicked softly on the polished courtroom floor. His face was pale and drawn from pain and exhaustion, but it lit up when he saw me. I couldn't help but smile back at him with what I felt like was a giddy schoolgirl look.

He sat in the chair next to me at the defense table, and despite the awkwardness of our handcuffs and leg irons, we embraced briefly. It was a moment of much-needed connection, a stark contrast to the cold and clinical atmosphere of the courtroom.

I missed him so much.

My days were spent in isolation from the rest of the prison population. The only people I saw were the guards and my lawyer occasionally. Well, less frequently lately since I refused to talk to her and hadn't said a word since the day she came into my cell and introduced herself.

Our attorneys joined us at the table. A-Rad was represented by Dyl Griff, a lanky man with a perpetual five-o'clock shadow and weary eyes that spoke of too many late nights and too few victories. My attorney was Gwenn Poovey, a stern woman with sharp features and a no-nonsense attitude.

She didn't appreciate my aloofness. She thought it rude and unconscionable that I refused to help her with my defense.

We had been assigned these lawyers because we couldn't afford our own legal representation. Or at least that's what they thought. At first, mine seemed excited to represent such a notorious criminal. Arguably, the most famous in all of Norway. But now, she seemed to have lost interest or at least was frustrated to the point that she wanted off the case.

I figured she'd continue to stay on after the judge ruled the hearings could be televised. According to her, every news station in Norway was carrying the events live and that I should be on my best behavior. My low grunt of ambivalence infuriated her.

The bailiff, a burly man with a booming voice, entered the room and commanded everyone to rise. The judge, Erik Wynne, followed soon after. He was a scholarly looking type, with thin-rimmed glasses perched on a nose that seemed perpetually buried in books. His robe swished as he took his seat, exuding an air of authority and solemness.

Formalities were the first order of business. Introductions were made.

Jan Sealy, the prosecutor, rose from his seat and introduced himself, although the judge and our attorneys obviously knew who he was. He presented himself as an exacting and clean-cut man with a worn suit and an air of unwavering confidence.

For the first time, I noticed that Hefina Rosser was in the room. Her presence sent a rage boiling through my veins. She had a lawyer with her who asked to be introduced. She had also been at the first hearing in front of a different judge and my reaction had been the same.

I understood why she was at the hearing related to the prince, but I didn't know why she was in the courtroom today. What did she have to do with the killing of the gangsters?

She was next on my short list of people I wanted to kill. I doubted I would ever get the chance. My attorney had warned that this judge was tough and would likely make things as difficult as possible for me.

As the judge read the charges against us, I tuned him out and let my mind drift to a faraway place. Back to a time when I had a normal life. A career. Friends. A blossoming romance. I squeezed A-Rad's hand to try and feel normal, if only for a few minutes.

The judge's voice droned on in a monotone that seemed to blend with the hum of the fluorescent lights overhead. The words merged into a blur. I did deduce that they were charging A-Rad with the murder of the four gangsters which was why he was there as well. I didn't understand why since he had nothing to do with it. His charges had something to do with conspiracy and accessory to murder.

"He wasn't even there!" I wanted to scream at the top of my lungs, but I forced myself to keep my mouth shut. Maintaining the CIA directive not to say anything if captured.

"Don't even give them your name, rank, or serial number."

Not that I had a rank or serial number, but the admonition was ingrained enough into me that it wasn't hard to keep quiet.

Even as excited as I was to see A-Rad, I made sure my face maintained a stoic demeanor.

"Will the defendants please rise?" Judge Wynne's voice cut through the fog of my distracting thoughts. I stood to my feet and helped A-Rad even though he seemed capable of standing on his own.

"Do you plead guilty or not guilty?" the judge asked sternly and with judgment like we were already guilty. His eyes scanned us over his glasses.

Neither of us responded. The silence stretched out, uncomfortable and heavy.

He asked again, more forcefully. “Guilty or not guilty?”

We both remained silent, staring straight ahead, the courtroom’s silence now thick with uncomfortable tension.

“Counselor?” the judge said, his gaze shifting to our attorneys.

My attorney shrugged her shoulders, looking frustrated. “This is how it has been, Your Honor. My client hasn’t spoken one word to me. She refuses to participate in her own defense.”

“Same with my client, Your Honor,” Dyl Griff added, his voice weary.

“It says on the indictment that the names are Jane Doe and John Doe. Mr. Sealy, can you explain?” the judge inquired, turning to the prosecutor.

“Your Honor, we haven’t been able to identify the two suspects. We don’t know their names or their nationalities. Our searches for fingerprints and DNA in the database haven’t produced a match. That’s why we are proceeding without identifying them.”

He sounded frustrated as well. It felt good that we were disrupting the proceedings in our own way.

“That’s highly irregular,” the judge remarked, his brow furrowing. Clearly perturbed.

“This is a highly irregular case,” Sealy responded, without hesitation.

Hefina Rosser’s attorney stood and requested permission to speak. His presence was commanding, and his suit was impeccably tailored. The judge granted his request.

“As you are aware, Judge, the defendants have also been charged with the murder of the prince of Norway. They are currently awaiting trial and being held without bail. They’ve been arraigned and the trial date has been set. The maximum penalty in Norwegian law is twenty-one years, regardless of the crime. Neither defendant can receive a longer sentence than that. If they are convicted of that crime, I'm certain they will receive the maximum sentence."

"My client hasn't been convicted of the crime yet," my attorney interjected sharply, fiercely advocating on my behalf for the first time.

"I said if," Rosser's lawyer retorted smoothly.

The judge looked thoughtful for a moment. "I'm wondering if this hearing is even necessary at the moment. What would be the purpose of trying them in a separate court, for a different crime, if the maximum they could receive is twenty-one years?"

I understood what was happening. Damage control. The last thing Rosser wanted was a public trial where she couldn't control the narrative. What if A-Rad or I decided to spill everything and implicated the prince in the kidnapping and murder of the girls. This whole matter must keep her awake at night.

Which was the second satisfaction I'd felt that day. Third if you consider seeing A-Rad.

Rosser's attorney confirmed my theory was correct when his eyes flicked towards Rosser and their eyes met in a silent agreement. She was trying hard to mask the anxiety, but the exchanged look told me all I needed to know about who our real enemy was in that room.

The prosecutor directed a displeased look toward Rosser before turning back toward the judge, which surprised me. He seemed annoyed as well. I could sense some kind of territorial battle and power struggle going on between them.

The hearing dragged on for nearly thirty minutes as legal jargon bounced back and forth, technicalities and precedents cited and debated. I didn't mind the length; it allowed me to hold A-Rad's hand a little longer. It felt comforting to touch him, to draw some strength from his presence. His reciprocation warmed my heart.

What I'd give to have time alone with him, to speak freely without fear of being overheard. To kiss him and tell him how much I loved him.

That love had only grown stronger each day in that cold prison cell. The only reason A-Rad was in a similar cell and on trial today was because he loved me and had refused to get away when he had the chance.

When it seemed like the torturous hearing was about to end, Judge Wynne ruled that the trial would proceed under normal processes. With the defendants characterized as John and Jane Doe.

He admonished A-Rad and me to cooperate with our attorneys, but his words barely registered. My mind was already elsewhere, dreading the loneliness of the cell. Counting down the days until our next trial date when I could see A-Rad again.

To my surprise, A-Rad and I were led out of the courtroom together. We were taken to an elevator, a cavernous metal box that hummed as it descended downward. This was different from the first hearing where we were escorted out separately and transported back to the prison in different vans.

The oxygen suddenly seemed like it had been sucked out of my lungs. I couldn't shake the feeling that something was about to happen.

What's going on? Panic surged through my chest and rushed down to the tip of my toes.

Was Rosser trying to kill us? Were they going to make us disappear?

Paranoia had gnawed at me since my first day in prison. Every moment, I feared for my life, knowing that someone could try and silence me for what I knew about the prince and his secrets. The weight of this knowledge felt like a ticking time bomb, ready to explode at any moment.

We rode down in silence. A-Rad and I exchanged knowing glances. He was thinking the same thing. This wasn't going to end well.

The elevator door opened to an underground garage, where a van was waiting with its rear doors open like a hungry predator ready to swallow us. Rough hands shoved us into the back, the doors slamming shut with a chilling finality that sent my emotions spiraling out of control.

Was this how we were going to die?

"What do you make of this?" I whispered to A-Rad.

"I suppose, nothing good," was his grim response.

"How should we play this?"

"Maybe it's nothing. Let's see what happens."

His words were resolute but didn't calm my fears.

The van pulled out of the garage and into the street. I felt like a trapped animal. The city's sounds were muffled, distant, like an echo of another world.

The windows were darkened, and we couldn't see out and no one could see in. A barrier kept us from seeing who was driving the van.

The van's interior was dimly lit, the only illumination coming from a small overhead light that flickered intermittently. I glanced at A-Rad. He looked tense, his grip on his crutches white-knuckled.

"We could use the crutches as weapons," he said. He lifted one up. "This thing would do some serious damage."

"I'm not sure those crutches are going to be much of a match for their guns."

"It's all we have."

We could get out of the chains and handcuffs if we had a couple of hours to do so. The guards had doubled and intertwined them, making it virtually impossible to break free in such a short amount of time.

Whoever was driving took a left, then another right. I realized that we had missed the turn that would've taken us back to the prison. I knew the route because I had memorized it. Something Jamie taught me to do.

We continued driving, each minute dragging on to whatever fate awaited us when the van finally stopped moving. Now I was certain we weren't going back to the prison. The drive there was no more than ten minutes from the courthouse and that's with heavy traffic. We'd been moving for at least twenty.

Something was terribly wrong. I could feel it.

Then, abruptly, the van screeched to a stop. Throwing us against the side.

The back door of the van opened with a creak.

I was prepared to fight to the death.

And there they were—Alex and Bond!

Dressed in uniforms. With huge smiles on their faces.

31

Somewhere over the Atlantic Ocean
A few hours later.

"Ooh! They are so cute!" I said to Jamie Austen.

She was on the other end of a video call, and I couldn't help but squeal in excitement at the sight of her two new babies, Joshua and Ellie. It seemed so surreal.

Two hours ago, I was facing twenty-one years isolated in a prison cell. Now I was on a luxurious private plane, reunited with my friends and colleagues, enjoying all the food and drinks I could possibly want.

One of the babies began to fuss and Jamie excused herself to put the twins down for a nap. Turning to Alex who was sitting across from me in the back of the plane, I expressed my relief at seeing him again.

"I thought maybe you guys had forsaken us for good," I said.

"Never," Alex said. "Our hands were tied which is why it took so long. We were told not to help you at all."

"By Brad, I assume."

His silence was confirmation.

"So he has given up on us?"

"Oh yeah. That ship has sailed. It's not personal. You have to understand that Brad has bigger concerns. National security stuff. Norway is an ally. A founding member of NATO. As you can imagine, the US government can't be associated with killing their heir to the throne. The king's only son."

"I get that. It's hard to swallow though. He sends us on a mission, then abandons us. He didn't know the prince was behind the kidnappings. I don't see how he can blame us for not knowing."

"I don't think he blames you. He'd help you if he could. But you know the drill. That's how it works. We warned you."

"I know. It still doesn't make it any easier to take."

A-Rad decided to change the hurtful subject. "How did you manage it?" he asked. "How were you able to secure the van and break us out?"

"The prosecutor helped us," Alex said. "Jan Sealy."

"Really. How did he help you?" I asked.

Jamie returned to her spot on the video call and answered for Alex. "That picture you sent me, Kaley. It was a smart move on your part to get that picture of the prince on the sub with the girls."

"When Brad told me to give ourselves up," I explained, "I knew no one would believe me if I told them what the prince was doing. That's why I sent you the picture from my phone. As an insurance policy."

"It worked," Jamie said. "Alex emailed the picture to Sealy."

"I did some research on him," Alex said, "and he seemed like a straight shooter. A stand-up guy who wasn't going to compromise the truth. I wasn't sure what he would do with the information, but I was hoping he might be able to help you in some way. I didn't expect him to get you out of jail, but I thought it might expose what the prince was doing."

"Sealy was investigating the murders of the four men," Jamie said, "so he was already on the case and searching for you. He's the one who put your face out on the media."

I let out a groan. "That made it a lot harder to move around the city. Then I woke up one day and the stories were gone. Alex, were you the one who took them down?"

He shook his head. "I took down everything I could find on the internet. Someone else took down the media stories."

"We're guessing it was Hefina Rosser," Jamie said. "She's the prince's fixer."

"That's what I think," I said. "She knew about the girls and what the prince was doing. I think she even knows he killed the girls."

"That's what she does. She cleans up his messes."

"I want to kill her. Can you turn around the plane and drop me back off in Oslo?" I said.

"Oh no!" Jamie, Alex, and A-Rad said in unison. I even heard Bond chime in from the cockpit.

"I'm kidding."

"You'd better be," Jamie said. "We barely got you out of there. Don't push your luck. I don't think we'd risk it a second time."

"Thank you for not abandoning us," I said, sincerely. "It means a lot to me."

Jamie smiled.

"I still don't understand how you pulled it off our escape, though," I said. "Tell me the rest of the story."

"Right," Jamie said. "About a month after Alex sent Sealy the picture, he got an email from Sealy saying, 'I can help your girl.'"

"At first, I thought it might be a trap," Alex said. "So I responded, but I didn't give up my identity. Eventually, I decided to trust him. Although, he still doesn't know who I am."

I took a big swig of the bottle of water in my hand then asked, "How did he help us? He's the one who filed murder charges against me and A-Rad."

"That was part of the plan," Alex said. "Sealy needed a way to get you to the courthouse. He was told not to investigate the shootings of the four men. When he filed the charges, Rosser went ballistic and tried to shut it down, but he stood his ground and got the hearing today."

"We saw that play out in the courtroom," A-Rad said. "There was tension between Sealy and Rosser. Even the judge seemed unsure why he was charging us since we were already facing maximum sentences for killing the prince."

"It was all a ploy. Sealy arranged for your transport from the courthouse. He provided the van and made all the arrangements. After we took off, he took the van to a salvage shop where it's being dismantled and sold for scrap."

"So you've basically disappeared. They don't know where you are," Jamie said. "It's already on the news. You can imagine the fallout."

"So what now?" I asked. "Does this mean we are back working for you now?"

Alex and Jamie were silent.

"Unfortunately, no," Jamie said. "You can't work for AJAX ever again. There'll be a worldwide manhunt for the two of you. Already is. Every intelligence agency in NATO will be looking for you by the end of the day."

Tears welled up in my eyes. "I can't believe it's over. I love what I do. I love working for you guys. I live for getting the bad guys. It's in my blood now. I know it's what I'm called to do with my life. Surely, there's some way we can work things out."

"I do have another plan," Jamie said. "While you can't work for us formally, we can still help you. But it's not a good plan. It's not something you'll want to do. I wouldn't do it if I were you."

"I'll do anything if I can still work for you. I mean . . . with you."

"Tell us the plan," A-Rad said, more skeptically.

Jamie took a deep breath. "There are a lot of bad actors in the world, like the prince."

"That's for sure."

"Alex and I made a list. We counted twenty-three leaders of countries who are dangerous and need to be taken out."

"You're right," A-Rad said, with a disapproving groan. "I'm not sure I like where this is going."

"I don't know where it's going," I said. I sat forward in my seat in anticipation of hearing the rest.

Jamie answered. "The CIA would love to assassinate them, but the law prevents the agency from killing another world leader. That's why you caused so much trouble when you killed the prince."

"I get that."

"You broke every American and international law on the books."

"He deserved it."

"I'm not debating that. Just stating the facts."

"Go on."

"Our plan is for the two of you to assassinate as many of these world leaders on the list as possible," Jamie said.

A-Rad interrupted her, "You mean, keep killing them until we die?"

"Yes," Jamie said soberly.

"You've got to be kidding me," A-Rad said. "How are we supposed to do that? I doubt we could kill one of them without dying first."

"We killed the prince," I said, in rebuttal. "It wasn't even that hard."

"It was so easy, we got caught!"

"We wouldn't have if your knee hadn't been hurt!" I said it more roughly than I intended.

Alex grimaced and I immediately realized how it sounded.

"I'm not blaming you," I said. "I'm saying that if you had been healthy, we would've escaped. Once you're healed up from your surgery, we'll be good to go."

"What leaders are you talking about?" A-Rad said "Are these low-level or are you talking about Presidents and Prime Ministers?"

"All of the above. I'm talking about the worst of the worst. The top of the food chain. North Korea. Iran. Cuba. Even Russia. They're all fair game."

"We can do it," I said excitedly.

"Like Kaley said, killing the prince wasn't that hard. But that's Norway," A-Rad said. "How are we going to infiltrate North Korea or Iran or Russia and get close enough to assassinate their leaders? Sounds impossible to me."

"I didn't say it was going to be easy," Jamie said. "And your life will be forever changed."

"It already is," I said.

"You'll be on the run for the rest of your life," Jamie retorted, starkly. "Every moment of every day, you'll be looking over your shoulder, wondering if it's your last day."

"That's an understatement. Remember these are the most powerful countries in the world," Alex warned. "They can kill you from a drone at any time. Every time you walk outside, you'll be wondering if some bomb is going to drop down from the sky and blow you to smithereens."

"Thank you for not sugar coating it," A-Rad said, sarcastically.

"Did you ever see the movie Bonnie and Clyde?" I asked A-Rad, excitedly. I didn't share his skepticism. The plan sounded thrilling to me. I was ready to start tomorrow.

"No," he said.

"You have to see it. That could be us."

"Bonnie and Clyde were bank robbers," Jamie said, with a chuckle. "I think it's a little different."

"I agree. Our cause will be noble. We'll be doing the world a great service."

"Didn't Bonnie and Clyde die in the end!" Alex said.

"At least they died together," I replied.

"Sounds like you have a suicide wish for us," A-Rad said, the words directed to me.

"No. But I don't want the rest of my life to be wasted. However long it is. I'd rather live two years getting rid of people like the prince and die young than live a long life in isolation and fear. Like Jesus said in the Bible, to whom much is given, much is required. This might be our destiny."

"You can say no, A-Rad," Jamie said.

"And then what?" A-Rad asked. "What happens to us then? Where do we go? Where will we live? How will we support ourselves if we can't work with you anymore in the sex trafficking operations?"

"I don't know," Jamie said honestly. "Like I said, either way, your lives are never going to be the same."

"Where are you taking us now?" I asked.

"To our island," Alex answered. AJAX owned an isolated island north of Aruba.

"You can stay there for a few weeks until we figure something out," Jamie said.

"What does 'figure something out' mean?" A-Rad said. "It sounds like there's nothing to figure out. We're going to be on our own. I'm not saying I don't appreciate what you've done for us, but you're going to cut us loose. Sooner rather than later."

"I'm not going to lie. There aren't a lot of options," Alex said. "You can't come back to the United States anytime soon. Maybe never. You can't stay on the island for long either. The CIA knows about it. Once they put two and two together, they'll come looking for you there."

"You think the CIA is going to be looking for us?" I asked, jolted by the panic.

"Probably harder than anybody," Jamie answered. "They have the most to lose. They'll want to make sure you are silenced."

"You mean kill us?" I said, exasperated.

"I wouldn't put it past them," Alex said.

"That's messed up," A-Rad said.

"Things are different now," Jamie said. "Brad can't protect you. You have a lot to think about. I'll respect your decision either way. If you want to go on the run, we'll help you in any way we can. We can get money and resources to you. But that's about it. We can't run any missions together or bail you out if you get into trouble running your own."

"I'm confused," I said. "You say you can't help us run missions, but you want us to work for you and kill world leaders."

Jamie responded. "It's complicated. It's a matter of risk and reward. We can't take this kind of risk running a low-level operation. But this has the potential to change the course of human history. Alex and I would be taking a huge risk by helping you. But it might be worth it if you're successful. If you can get just one dictator off the world scene, that'd make a huge difference."

"And I know how to keep several layers between us, so it doesn't come back on us," Alex said.

"I can't believe we are in this situation!" I exclaimed. "It seems hopeless."

Despondency had set in. It seemed like we didn't have any good options. A-Rad obviously was against the plan. I wondered if he was going to want to part ways with me as well and go it alone.

"I say we take Jamie up on her offer to kill a few world leaders," A-Rad blurted, doing a complete one eighty and shocking me.

"Are you saying you want to do it?"

He answered, "If we're going to be on the run anyway, we might as well be doing something productive with our time."

"It's a one-way road to death," I said, becoming the one raising the objections. "There's no way it ends well. Like Alex said, Bonnie and Clyde died in the end."

"At least we'll be together. That's all I care about."

"Ahh. That's so sweet," I said. My heart practically broke in two when he said the words. I went over and sat down next to him, taking his hand. "I love you so much."

"I love you, too."

Alex and Jamie allowed the moment to pass. Then I looked at them and said, "Okay. Count us in."

"Great!"

"How will it work?" A-Rad asked. "When can we start?"

"We'll give you the target," Jamie said. "Colonel will draw up the plans, and we'll finance it. Your responsibility will be to execute the plan. After you get healthy again."

"Hopefully, without getting caught or killed," Alex said.

"I think *killed* would be better than getting caught," I said.

Jamie nodded. "You won't be able to count on us rescuing you like we did this time," she said. "We took a lot of risk getting you out of Norway."

"I appreciate it."

"You know what this means," I said, turning to A-Rad.

"What?"

"We have to get married."

"Married?" A-Rad said, his eyes widening to the size of saucers.

"Yeah. I want you to make an honest woman of me. I'm not going to travel the world with you, sleeping in the same hotel rooms, not unless we're married. I have a reputation to uphold."

A-Rad didn't say anything. He had a distant look like he was thinking.

"So, what is your answer?" I asked.

"About what?"

"I'm asking you to marry me."

"You can't ask me to marry you."

"Why not?"

"I already asked you to marry me. Remember."

"I turned you down. That proposal is off the table. My proposal is the only legitimate offer on the table at the moment."

"You guys are too cute," Jamie said.

"I never withdrew my proposal," A-Rad said. "It's valid, until I say it's not."

"There are two offers on the table," Alex said. "Who's going to say yes first?"

A-Rad pulled me close and looked deep into my eyes. "If that's the case, then the answer is yes! I'll marry you. Although I want it on the record that I proposed first."

I squealed with delight. We kissed. Hard. I didn't care that Jamie and Alex were watching. It never bothered them to make out in front of us.

When we were finished, I was out of breath.

I turned to Jamie anyway and said, "Who's our first kill?"

Not The End

GET A SNEAK PEEK INTO FUGITIVES, THE CONCLUDING BOOK IN THE KALEY PRESSLEY SERIES

1

"The president is dead," Brad, the CIA director, said to Jamie Austen, his most famous—though now retired—operative.

"Dead!" Jamie exclaimed in shock and disbelief. "When did this happen?"

"He was assassinated about thirty minutes ago. Did you know it was going to happen?" His tone was almost accusing.

"No! I've been busy taking care of my twins. I haven't had the television on in days."

Jamie had retired a little over two years ago when she became a mother. Her husband, Alex, still ran covert computer hacking operations for the CIA through their cover company, AJAX—a combination of their names, Alex and Jamie.

Since having children, neither wanted to put themselves in harm's way again, although Alex occasionally took calculated risks. So far, he had been skilled enough to survive them without any close calls.

"You had no involvement at all?" Brad asked, sounding skeptical.

"Of course not. Why would you even ask me that question? What's going on, Brad?" Jamie asked with growing concern.

She wasn't sure she wanted to know the answer. When he used the word "assassinated," her thoughts immediately went to A-Rad and Kaley.

Surely not.

"The president was shot and killed by two gunmen," Brad said. "I believe we both know who those gunmen are."

Jamie tried to speak but couldn't find any words. Was Brad really accusing A-Rad and Kaley of assassinating the President of the United States? It seemed unfathomable.

"It could've been any number of people," Jamie finally managed to say.

The question, "Why do you think it was them?" was on the tip of her tongue, but she choked it back. She wasn't sure she wanted to hear the answer to that question.

She hadn't talked to A-Rad and Kaley in weeks and couldn't really vouch for their whereabouts or actions. The thing that gave her pause was that she couldn't deny that they were two of the few people on earth capable of pulling off such a massive feat.

Really, how could they even do it? The security surrounding the president was meant to be impenetrable.

"I know it was them," Brad stated with conviction. "Please tell me you aren't involved."

She assured him, "I'm not involved, and neither is Alex or any member of AJAX."

Brad assumed Jamie had a hand in it because he knew that she and Alex had planned and financed the assassinations of more than a dozen world leaders, using A-Rad and Kaley to carry out the missions. He had indirect knowledge and even silently endorsed them, but never spoke about them, so he could maintain plausible deniability.

For obvious reasons. Brad was the acting director of the CIA, and such activities were against US and international law. Killing the leaders of foreign countries could get them all thrown in jail for the rest of their lives.

Neither of them ever wanted to be on a call talking about the pair or the operations. Brad looked the other way because those missions had been a tremendous benefit to America and the world. But the political fallout would be unmanageable if it got out that the United States, the director of the CIA, was somehow involved or knew about the assassinations of our enemies. So he kept his distance.

Every intelligence agency in the world knew it was A-Rad and Kaley behind the killings, and everyone assumed they were Americans. But that's all they knew. The standard line was that they were rogue and had never worked for the CIA.

Which wasn't entirely true.

Jamie had recruited A-Rad to the CIA and trained Kaley herself. She loved them like they were her own family and would give her life for them. At least back in time before the twins were born.

The covert missions had been her idea, and AJAX funded them. The success of the efforts was beyond her wildest dreams. The brazen pair had taken out some of the most ruthless dictators on the planet without getting caught.

But why would they kill the President of the United States? He wasn't on the list of leaders they were tasked to kill. It didn't make sense.

"I don't think it's them," Jamie blurted after a long moment of silence.

"It is," Brad said, maintaining his confidence.

"What percentage?"

"A hundred percent."

Brad wouldn't say that unless he had undeniable proof.

Could he be wrong? If he was, it might be the first time since she had started working for him years ago. The director of the CIA had more intelligence available to him than anyone else on the planet. If anyone knew, it'd be him.

Jamie needed to convince him she wasn't involved.

"I know nothing about it. I swear," she said.

"Were you aware that they changed their appearances?"

She lied. "No."

She had paid for the surgeries—at least AJAX had.

After A-Rad and Kaley assassinated the prince of Norway, they were caught and put on trial. Alex and Jamie helped them escape, but their covers as CIA operatives were blown and their faces plastered all over the media.

A world-wide manhunt had been going on for more than two years making running missions in foreign countries virtually impossible. With advanced facial recognition software becoming more prevalent, the pair couldn't step foot in any major city or take a plane or train without being detected.

The last time Jamie checked the reward for their capture had reached twenty million dollars. Dead or alive. Preferably dead.

Desperate for a solution, Jamie found a surgeon in India who completely restructured their faces. They didn't even look like the same people. The ploy had worked, and it allowed them to move around the world freely on passports Alex and Jamie provided for them.

She wondered how Brad knew about their new look.

"They were spotted going into Russia two weeks ago," Brad said, interrupting her thoughts. "I've been tracking their movements. As far as I know, I'm the only one who knows about the new look, and I used facial recognition software to find them."

"What are they doing in Russia?"

"That's where the president was assassinated."

Instantly, Jamie felt a wave of relief and disbelief at the same time. She had been worried that the president was killed inside the United States. She couldn't imagine A-Rad or Kaley being stupid enough to come into the US and try such a brazen operation. The southern borders were porous enough for them to get in, but operating inside the United States was a risk they'd never take.

"I didn't realize our president was in Russia," she said, truthfully.

"It's his first foreign trip. He made Russia a priority. As you know, relations have been strained since they sort of blame us for the deaths of their previous two presidents."

A-Rad and Kaley had assassinated the president of Russia eighteen months ago. He was a despot who deserved it. He was replaced by someone even worse. A-Rad and Kaley returned to Russia and took him out as well.

In response, the Russians surprisingly installed a more moderate leader, someone friendly with the West. Both men were highly popular in their countries. The President of the United States campaigned on improving relations with Russia. He had won his election in America by a landslide and had only been in office less than two months.

Brad was named CIA director shortly thereafter and easily confirmed by the Senate since he had already been the assistant director for a number of years.

"Why would they kill the president?" Jamie asked.

"You tell me."

"How would I know?"

"I have a theory. The president made it a priority to capture them. One purpose of the Russian trip was to assure the Russian president of that fact."

“They wouldn’t kill him over something so trivial as him vowing to capture them.”

“Well, they did. The reason doesn’t matter. And there’s going to be fallout. People are going to blame Russia for this. I’m trying to keep World War III from breaking out."

“I won’t believe it until I see it or hear it from their own mouths.”

“Watch the video I sent you.”

Jamie walked to her office, her heart pounding as she fired up her computer. She opened her email, and her breath caught in her throat as she watched the shocking video. The president was gunned down while standing next to the Russian president at a parade welcoming him to Russia.

The satellite image clearly showed the two assassins. It captured their forms as they fled the scene. One shot briefly captured Kaley’s face. No doubt about it. It was them.

“There must be some explanation,” Jamie said, her voice trembling, though she couldn’t think of one.

“The explanation is that they let their powers go to their heads. Having the ability to end someone’s life comes with a great deal of responsibility. They began to think of themselves as gods, deciding when killing was justified. This time, they took it too far.”

Jamie didn’t answer. She had no way to defend their actions without it looking like she might’ve been complicit.

“It doesn’t matter now,” Brad said, with a bitter tone. “It’ll be over for them soon.”

“What do you mean?” she asked, dread creeping into her voice.

“Turn on your television. The Russian army has them trapped in a warehouse about a mile from the scene. I watched them on satellite run into the building, and I didn’t see them come out.”

“Are you sure it’s them?”

“Positive. I saw their faces there as well. Clear as day. It’s them. The Russians know it too.”

Jamie turned on her television and was met with footage from Russia playing on all the major networks. The warehouse was surrounded by a small army, including tanks and hundreds of soldiers with machine guns.

The press was even showing pictures of A-Rad and Kaley as the suspects. Accusing them of the killing of the President of the United States and the two Russian presidents. Brad obviously wasn’t the only one who had images of their new look.

If they were inside that warehouse, their lives were in grave danger.

“I can send you the pictures of them running into the warehouse if you want,” Brad said. “You can see for yourself.”

“No, that’s okay. I believe you.”

“I can only hope A-Rad and Kaley are killed quickly. Otherwise, the torture will be unimaginable.”

This was the first time Brad had used A-Rad and Kaley’s names since the Norway incident. He had avoided being associated with them in any way. It must truly be over if he was willing to speak their names so freely.

Jamie decided to end the call.

After she hung up the phone, she turned off the television. She couldn't bear to watch two of her closest friends being killed by the Russian army or dragged out of the warehouse like animals.

The pain in her heart was unbearable.

She collapsed into a chair, buried her head in her hands, and sobbed uncontrollably.

ORDER FUGITIVES ON AMAZON

The heart pounding, page turning thriller is available now at the link below:

https://www.amazon.com/Fugitives-Kaley-Presley-Thrillers-Book-ebook/dp/B0CKFLNBKP

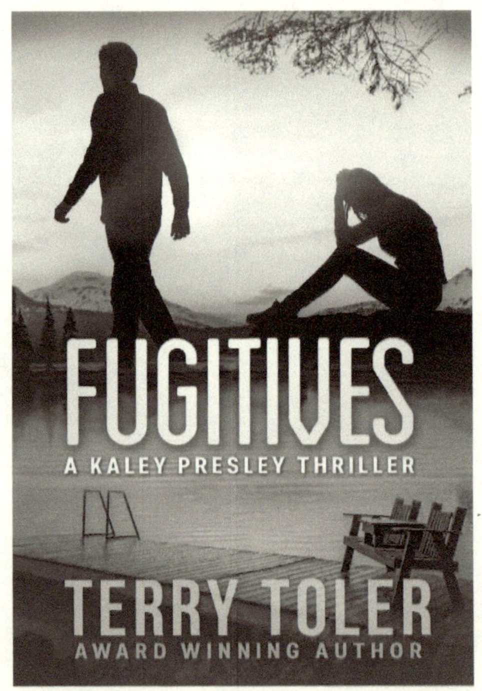

Thank you for purchasing this novel from best-selling author, Terry Toler. As an additional thank you, Terry wants to give you a free gift.

Sign up for:

Updates
New Releases
Announcements

At terrytoler.com

We'll send you an eBook, *The Book Club*, a Cliff Hangers novella, free of charge.

READ MORE BOOKS FROM TERRY TOLER

Jamie Austen Thrillers

Read all the Jamie Austen Thrillers. They must be good. They've been number one on Amazon in ten different countries. Click on the link below.

THE JAMIE AUSTEN THRILLERS (12 book series) Kindle Edition (amazon.com)

https://amzn.to/3vmPUy7

Cliff Hangers Mystery Series

Who wants to read a good mystery? We've got you covered! Read the Cliff Hangers where homicide detective, Cliff Ford, solves crimes in Chicago, with help from his wife Julia. These books have everything Terry Toler is known for. Page turning suspense, a hint of romance, and an ending you won't see coming.

The Cliff Hangers Mystery Series (4 book series)
Kindle Edition (amazon.com)

https://amzn.to/36WX3go

About Terry

Terry Toler is an Amazon international # 1 best-selling and award-winning author. He writes clean fiction with a message and life-changing nonfiction. He's a public speaker, entrepreneur, and has authored more than forty books.

Sign up for his newsletter where you'll get free stuff, exclusive content, and news of releases and promotions. He can be followed at terry-toler.com.

If you like his books, please take a few minutes to leave a review on Amazon. We really appreciate it. It helps draw more readers to his books. Thanks!

www.ingramcontent.com/pod-product-compliance
Lightning Source LLC
LaVergne TN
LVHW091036080826
845145LV00002B/512

* 9 7 8 1 9 5 4 7 1 0 2 5 2 *